THE KARMA RETREAT

GRANT FINNEGAN

ALSO BY GRANT FINNEGAN

For Sharon

THE KARMA RETREAT

Every action has a consequence.
So always try to be good.
—Richard Eyre, British film director

Don't

Stop

Me

PROLOGUE

HOW DID THIS HAPPEN? HE WONDERED. HE WAS intelligent enough to understand most things, but this made no sense whatsoever. Seconds ago, he had been lying on a mat in a meditation class. He hadn't even wanted to go to Bali, goddamn it. St Barts, in the Caribbean was his first choice, but his nagging wife had other ideas.

He remembered the pleasant earthy smell of incense, the guttural moans interspersed with words coming from the meditation teacher. It was all quite relaxing.

Seconds later, he opened his eyes.

Where the fuck am I?

He looked around. For some reason, he was in a dilapidated hut. The smell of incense been replaced by sewerage, rotting garbage and stale body odour. Movement in the corner of the hut made him sit up in fright.

He locked eyes with a rat, before the rodent scurried out of a well-worn hole in the wall. By day's end, he had realised that he was thousands of miles away from Bali and had woken up in the middle of the slums of Dhaka, Bangladesh, coincidently, where the factories who manufacture much of his company's apparel were located.

But that was just the start.

He was a 55-year-old man. And yet not anymore, at least on the outside. Instead, he bore the resemblance to a skinny, teenage boy, dressed in filthy clothing.

The humidity in the hut was so intense that he started to feel woozy.

This could not be happening.

He never believed in karma. It was complete bull-shit. Only those hippie, yoga type weirdos sipping on their purple potato lattes gave it any credence, followed by jilted ex-lovers that hope a bus will come along to run over their cheating ex-partners.

But he was starting to question his beliefs, as the reality of his current situation became clearer.

It had come for him.

And he knew why.

CHAPTER ONE

Chad

Boston, Massachusetts, USA. February 2025.

'YOU KNOW HOW MUCH I'VE BEEN LOOKING forward to this, right?'

Standing at the bathroom sink, Chad Miller glanced at his wife of fifteen years, who was waiting for a response.

'Yes, you've been telling me every day for the last two weeks.'

'But you don't want to go, do you?'

She stood in the doorway with stony eyes.

It was 11.05 pm and the CEO of DOSTME Sportswear International had just arrived home. Conversation after a seventeen-hour workday never came easy; it was rare for him to come home before 9.00 pm these days. He turned to the mirror and took a long, deep breath. His blue eyes were lifeless, the lines below more pronounced by the day. A head of thick blonde hair was doing that middle-aged thing, receding into the netherworld, much to his chagrin. A strong square jaw, almost robot-like and thin lips below a nondescript pointy nose. Back in university, he had been the strapping, good-looking athletic type, but it had all slipped away due to neglect by the time he hit forty. His once lean and muscular body was no longer a priority to Chad. The company share price had taken its place.

It began about fifteen years ago, when his fortune broke through the $500-million mark. It was at this point that he started to believe the misguided notion that the money and status that he now had would make up for the lack of sex appeal. But what was he thinking? His wife was very attractive and far too intelligent to fall for that.

He shifted his eyes to his wife in the reflection, but Crystal's eyes had glossed over. He knew she was miles away, and Chad begun to wonder how much longer she would have a hyphen and the word Miller stapled to the end of her name. He returned his gaze to his ageing face. Had the last fifteen years of her life really been a complete waste of time? And yet, deep down, he knew that money wouldn't be enough to make her stay. Even with a long-winded prenup, she would walk away with more than enough money to live happily ever-after on her own. And anyway, no amount of money could give her back the last decade and a half of her life.

He pictured her with a microphone in her hand. She had recently retired from her job as a CNN sports reporter, and Chad reminisced about how stunning she was on camera. A long mane of blonde hair pulled into a shoulder-length ponytail bobbed from side to side, revealing a small set of almost elfish ears. Chad sighed.

About a month before, he'd come across one of her women's magazines that Crystal had left open and had given the article a cursory glance. Something about a cheater's guide to avoid being caught, from a woman's perspective. Apparently if you were a man planning to have an affair, it said, then you should make sure your lover uses the same perfume as your wife's favourite. He'd blanched when he read it. He'd made that mistake more than once. He'd wondered at the time if she knew, but then shook his head. Of course, she knew. It's why she'd left the page open to begin with. Real subtle.

Chad watched as Crystal's lips twisted into a smirk and for a moment, he believed that she was smiling at him. He smiled back, but his thoughts drifted to the amazing sex he'd had less than ninety minutes ago with a 23-year-old hooker. Okay, so her perfume was a bit overpowering, but wow, what she did with her legs was beyond impossible. He blinked, and his mind returned to the bathroom and recalled what he had agreed to do with Crystal and sighed again. Despite everything, he needed this vacation, even if it involved all this new age mumbo-jumbo she was into these days. Personally, he thought meditation was for idiots, nonetheless a tropical holiday did mean he would escape the dreary grey skies of Boston for a short time. And seeing her hips move beneath her silk dressing gown, had made him remember how magnificent she was, wearing next to nothing.

'You got me,' he said. 'I would happily spend twenty-four hours in a plane, darling, if only to see you in a bikini.'

CHAPTER TWO

Angela
Bray, Berkshire, United Kingdom.

'I MET HIM ONCE,' ANGELA SAID, SIPPING ON HER white wine. 'Heston.'

Suddenly, her face contorted with disgust.

'This wine—,' she met eyes with the man sitting across the table from her, 'is lukewarm. For heaven's sake, you'd think for the price of a set of diamond earrings at Harrods, they could serve it at the correct temperature. Waiter!'

Her son had already threatened that if she mentioned one more time that she'd met one of UK's most revered chefs, Heston Blumenthal, that it would be the last time he ever brought her to the Fat Duck. But, since it was her birthday, it meant he had to swallow his annoyance at her perpetual, pompous behaviour, and she knew it. As she set the glass down and began waving her arms as though she were drowning, he caught sight of a woman at the main counter, who smiled at Jack, and Angela sensed his mood improve in a heartbeat. His girlfriend of five years had been the maître d' at this restaurant for close to nine months now. She shook her head from side to side and smiled at him, before the woman locked eyes with her.

Angela Jones was one of England's most well-known oncologists. Her reputation in the field was legendary. So were two other things, the latter known to only but a few: the size of her ego and her unbridled, explosive temper. Thankfully, a waiter appeared, apologising, and swiftly swapped out her glass of wine for a new one. Angela sipped on the new glass of wine and sighed deeply. Crisis averted. *Fifty-seven years of age.* She sighed.

A solid woman, standing tall at about five foot eight, she had the sort of build more aligned to a rugby player. Angela's hair was dark brown and always worn in a tight bun. She couldn't recall ever wearing it any other way. A skincare regime had never been on her radar, and although she had been quite pretty in her youth, the process of ageing had not been kind to her. That morning, as she looked into the mirror, she saw thin, almost invisible lips and small grey eyes. But, she knew her stuff and had new patients lining up to be seen by her, so surely that was worth a few cosmetic sacrifices.

Jack, on the other hand, looked nothing like his mother, rather, he was the spitting image of his father.

Six feet one, with a decent build, dark brown hair and big gentle brown eyes. The guy was a good-looking English lad.

Angela knew Jack had been making eye contact with Sophie from across the room. A smile crept across her face and Jack looked at her with curiosity, as if his girl-friend had spiked her wine with some sort of untrace-able liquid amphetamine.

Sophie made an unannounced visit to the table after seeing the look of desperation on Jack's face that he thought he had hidden from his mother.

'Everything alright here?' she smiled, standing closer to Jack than Angela.

'The first wine was room-temperature-warm, but now it's been rectified, my dear,' Angela spoke in a condescending tone.

Sophie smiled.

'How many hours until we get on the plane?' she whispered to Jack with a tight jaw.

Angela pretended that she hadn't heard her.

'Darling,' Angela handed the glass to Sophie with a nod, indicating that she'd like another.

Before Sophie could even register the look of disdain that Angela knew she reserved just for her, Angela cleared her throat.

'I know I've not spent any time with you lately,' she said to Jack. 'So, I've made a decision which will change that.'

Sophie's face dropped.

'What would that be, mother?' Jack said, his words tainted with fear.

Angela grinned at them both this time.

'I'm going to come on the tropical holiday with you. We can finally spend some quality time together!'

Sophie made eye contact with Jack, in a look that Angela knew could only mean, *kill me now*. She wondered if Jack was thinking the same thing.

CHAPTER THREE

Amelia
Holmby Hills, California, USA.

IT WAS A PICTURE-PERFECT HOLLYWOOD DAY IN the City of Angels for Amelia Langston. No hint of any clouds, or for once, smog, and she breathed in deeply, and smiled. Pierre, her personal assistant, had just texted her, and it had her grinning. She couldn't resist snapping a selfie and looked at it for a moment. Not bad at all. After a bit of tweaking, she would upload it to her social media accounts.

Amelia was in a playful mood. She asked Pierre for the 'code-word,' a word only the two of them knew, after being hacked a few times in the past.

She didn't have to wait long.

Another pinging sound from her phone and there it was in front of her. She smiled.

Sitting on the lounge chair next to her pool, she felt a tingle of excitement pass through her with the news. Her ranking on Twitter had just broken into the top twenty-five. Pierre decided not to tell her NASA was still one spot in front of her. Ouch.

Amelia scrolled down the Twitter rankings until she spotted the woman currently ranked number eleven. She pursed her lips. Personally, she had nothing against Kim Kardashian, but the twist in her gut as she studied the woman's smile in the photo was driven purely by jealousy.

Amelia just wanted everything the Kardashian had. The family, the fame, the sisters, her looks and her body. Not happy with the hundred-or-so million that she'd amassed, or the fact that for many years she was one of the America's most recognisable actresses, she knew that most people would give anything to have her life. But as Amelia sipped on her Bloody Mary, the only thought in her mind at that moment was what was on the screen of her smartphone. A ping and pop up box told Amelia she'd received another message. She assumed it was one of her girlfriends congratulating her about her change in Twitter rankings.

It was Pierre again.

She cursed his name as she swung her legs off the lounge chair.

'Pierre, stop bothering me on your day off,' she said.

Amelia was due to fly out tomorrow and her assistant was reminding her to pack.

Her destination – Australia and a four-week shoot in Far North Queensland. Fit and lean, she'd trained in Karate since she was a young child, but although Amelia didn't train as hard as she used to these days, she had made sure she stepped it up for the last three months. Having her own state-of-the-art gym and Dojo, she wanted to look as good as she could for this film, and making a movie with an Aussie heartthrob was surely worth the long flight and the extra training. But before she arrived in Australia to drool over Chris Hemsworth in person, Amelia would be making another stopover and if it hadn't been a stone's throw away from Australia, she would have found an excuse to opt out.

Amelia was in no mood to go to Bali with her friend Gemma before the shoot, but even she had come to realise that her list of legitimate friends was getting shorter by the day.

'Bali, here I come,' she said to the glistening pool as she reclined in the sunshine.

CHAPTER FOUR

Logan
Vaughan, Toronto, Canada.

LOGAN JACKMAN TOOK ONE FINAL DEEP DRAW OF his e-cigarette. He'd spotted someone who resembled his wife from across the car park and wanted to get one more puff in before she walked any closer. As the large plume of vapour came billowing out of his mouth, he turned and made his best attempt at a smile.

As Bethany, his wife of ten years, came closer, he could see the snarl on her face. She thought the e-cigarette thing was a joke. It was his latest attempt at giving up smoking. He may have given away the Belmont King Sizes a couple of years ago, but these things were just as bad in her opinion. To her, it was still smoking. Albeit without the yellow stains on his fingers and the wretched odour on his breath.

Being a Friday in the shortest month of the calendar year, it was still winter and both Logan and Bethany wore typical winter jackets, measured in the thickness of inches, like anyone who'd lived in Toronto all their lives.

'Beth,' the car salesman said.

'Logan,' his wife replied.

The ensuing few seconds of silence was awkward – a typical exchange for most couples standing in front of this nondescript building, in Jane St, Vaughan.

'Ready?' his wife said with the same enthusiasm as an inmate on death row.

'As I'll ever be,' Logan said.

'Thank you,' the woman said, 'for coming in today.'

Her smile was far too enthusiastic for a winter's day, Logan scowled. They sat down on the couch across from the woman, unmoved, as per the big smile set on her face.

At $240 an hour, Logan thought, no wonder this was the very first thing she always said when they first sat down in her office. If he had his time over, he would not have followed his old man into the car sales business. He would have become a marriage counsellor. All he'd have to do was sit there and say a few words, pretend to give a shit about the couple sitting in front of him, and let them work it out for themselves.

'Thank you, Court-ten-ay,' Beth smiled.

Logan tried his best not to wince every time he heard his wife say the marriage counsellor's name, arguing that it should be pronounced Court-nee.

Fifty-five minutes later, Logan had wished he'd spent the last fifty-four minutes headbutting a wall. Surely that would have been less painful. He would have got more out of it, he mused. But as the session began to draw to a close, he reminded himself why he'd been coming here and paying off Courtney's condo in some far-off tropical paradise. Probably in Florida. A small part of him wanted to try to make it work with his wife, but he didn't see how sitting in this room once a week was going to help. Beth grabbed his hand and squeezed it tight, bringing his thoughts back to the room in a flash.

'No way!' she gushed.

The marriage counsellor nodded, before her huge smile appeared.

'You can't be serious, tell me you're not serious, Court-ten-ay!'

Beth was almost squealing.

'What's happening?' Logan said.

The marriage counsellor lent forward and said to Beth, 'the offer stands, you are more than welcome to take it if you wish.'

'You have no idea how much I'd love to!' Beth gushed.

'What did I miss?' Logan said, dryly, blinking back to reality.

'Two of Court-ten-ay's other clients had signed up for a holiday through her travel company. A retreat where you can work on your marriage. And they had to cancel at the very last minute,' Beth said.

'This morning,' Courtney chimed in.

'So, she has offered you and me the opportunity to take their place, at a discounted rate of course, and I think we should do it. It could be the best decision we ever make.'

'Somewhere warm, I hope,' Logan attempted a smile.

The marriage counsellor nodded with her annoying level of enthusiasm.

'You bet, Logan. Ever heard of Indonesia? There's a beautiful, island there. They call it Baa-lee.'

CHAPTER FIVE

LOGAN LEFT COURTNEY'S OFFICE AND WONDERED what the hell he'd agreed to.

It was more about what Beth wanted, really. He was just getting dragged along for the ride, kicking and screaming.

Beth was out with girlfriends tonight. Logan ate takeout whilst surfing the internet so he could find out more about this 'amazing retreat!' *Courtney's words.*

The Samsarana Wellness Retreat.

He found the website after a short search, but then decided to do to some checking. Lately, Logan had become fixated on people's reviews on just about everything. From hand blenders and car salesmen *(surprise surprise)* to hotel rooms, to name but just a few.

'The flashiest websites in the world can often be just that. Reviews often cut through all the hype and give it to you straight,' Logan often said to friends at work.

Shit, some people have the knack of writing creative reviews, Logan thought, as he started reading the newest review for the Samsarana Wellness Retreat:

Nestled in lush tropical rainforest overlooking the clear waters of the Ayung River, one of Bali's original wellness retreats straddles the side of the hill, meeting Mother Nature with a long embrace. Since the birth of the millennium, the hills of Ubud had become the epicentre of these hotels on the Indonesian island. The browser-savvy holidaymaker has a plethora of choices, from the cutting edge, where infinity pools seemed to float above the canopy of the rainforest, to the cheap and rather nasty, where air-conditioning is an open window and dessert an unpeeled orange on your plate.

As with pubs in London, gelati kiosks in Positano and steakhouses in Texas, competition for the wellness tourist dollar in Ubud was fierce.

In a Zen kind of way, of course.

Although it lacked the architectural 'wow' of some nearby retreats, this one was well rated and has a legion of fans the world over. I insist you go there and experience it for yourself.

The Samsarana Wellness Retreat.

Really? Logan laughed. 'Who does this guy think he is, Dan fucking Brown?' he said incredulously.

Logan rolled his eyes and took a sip of his beer.

He wanted to send the guy a message and ask him the following questions:

'What's the Wi-Fi like, huh?'

'They serve alcohol there, right?

'Did you see any bikini clad girls around the pool, or are they too busy immersing themselves in the "well-nesses" of the retreat?'

Logan stared at his bottle of Moosehead Lager and stifled a gasp. If this was one of those hard-core retreats that was alcohol free, he would die a slow death.

'Alright, alright,' Logan said to himself.

He clicked his mouse and closed the pages on the browser, suddenly losing all motivation. He would check out the Samsarana Wellness Retreat's own website during his lunch break tomorrow.

Now, he thought, smiling, *speaking of women in bikinis,* he started to type other words into his search engine.

CHAPTER SIX

Chad
Denpasar, Bali, Indonesia

THE PACIFIC INTERNATIONAL AIRWAYS FLIGHT touched down on the runway of the Denpasar Airport with the ease of a pilot who had done it a thousand times before.

'I hope you enjoy your stay here in Bali, ladies and gentlemen. On behalf of the Captain, we'd like to thank you for flying with us,' a voice crackled over the speaker.

'He sounds too young to be in the cockpit,' Chad said to Crystal as they both rose from their first-class seats.

'It was one of the smoothest flights across the Pacific I've ever been on,' Crystal fired back.

When Chad's sleep was deprived, his lack of respect for anyone around him intensified, unless they had more money than him. Even stretched out in a comfortable first-class seat, Chad still struggled to sleep for extended periods. Though he'd never admit it to anyone, Crystal knew what the problem was: her macho husband was shit scared of flying.

'How was your flight, sir?' The chauffeur said as he cast his smiling eyes into the rear of the car.

Chad stared at the Balinese driver as if he'd told him that he wouldn't wash his car with a DOSTME t-shirt in a month of Sundays. Crystal gave him a nudge with her elbow, jarring him out of his sleepy stupor. Chad turned and gave her a dirty look.

'Our flight was fine, a little long, you'll have to excuse my husband, he's a little deaf thanks to a childhood car accident,' she said.

It seemed to take the driver a few seconds to absorb what the pretty American lady had said, Chad thought. He daresay found their accents a little hard to decipher at the best of times.

'Oh. No worries, Missus Miller, thank you,' he said.

It would be the last thing he said to the couple for the duration of the 28-mile journey to their destination. Chad felt Crystal glance at him as he stared out the window in silence. Traffic at most times of the day in Denpasar was manic. Unlike roads in the United States, those around Bali's capital were often overrun with moped Motorcycles, the first and most affordable choice of the Balinese locals and tourists. As their town car fought its way through the bustling main thoroughfare in Pesanggaran, the mopeds momentarily swamped their car, like a protective escort. Crystal reached over and took Chad's hand.

'You're thinking of her, aren't you?'

It took the millionaire a few moments to turn his attention away from the window and back to his wife. He stared at her for a few seconds with a stoic expression. He knew she hated when he did it but he couldn't help it. He knew who Crystal was referring to: Serena, Chad's younger sister. He avoided talking about her.

Of course, he was thinking about Serena. How could he not, given where they had just landed, he thought, with a mixture of guilt and shame. He was the famous asshole brother who should have been ashamed of the way he treated her. Not long after her twenty-fourth birthday, Serena set off on the holiday of a lifetime, backpacking with four of her girlfriends. During the family dinner the night before she departed, Serena surprised her family with something. She announced to them all that she had forgiven him.

He flatly told Serena there was nothing to forgive, and she could go to hell. Twelve hours later, Serena flew out of Boston with her friends, and would never talk to him again.

It was October 12th, 2002 and their first destination was Indonesia. After throwing their bags in through the door of their hotel room, the girls excitedly set out to explore the nightlife. Paddy's Bar in Kuta had been the driver's suggestion as they piled into the taxi at their hotel.

'Chad?'

He'd been staring out the window in a trance-like state and had not responded to Crystal's question.

'No,' he said, and Crystal turned away, rebuked.

Serena never left Kuta.

The terrorist bombings that night, ensured that Serena, along with two hundred or so other innocent people, never saw their loved ones ever again.

The Bali Bombings.

CHAPTER SEVEN

Chad

CHAD REMAINED SILENT FOR A WHILE, EVEN though he knew it made Crystal uncomfortable. As always, the conversation about his little sister had ended right there, Chad style. They travelled on for another twenty-five miles with no further discussion, his head lolling from side to side, as the car navigated the winding roads of Ubud, only waking up with a start now and then. Moped after moped sped past their car, their riders ranging from the elderly, to young adults with one or more child strategically placed somewhere on the bike. He watched Crystal's astounded face and chuckled to himself. Only a few wore helmets or protective clothing around these parts and yet, they all seemed relaxed with this precarious form of transport, and it was something that clearly disturbed her. But none-theless, he could see that she found the hills of the Ubud landscape intoxicating. It was as if someone had turned up the colour in her eyes, and even Chad had to admit how beautiful it was. She looked relaxed and in another world. Chad had argued that there were far more luxurious (and expensive) places they could have gone, some much closer to Boston. But Crystal said that she was sick of the Bahamas, the Dominican Republic and the Virgin Islands. She'd wanted to go to Asia for a long time, wanting to experience more depth and culture. Maybe even a spiritual awakening. She would never be able to explain to anyone the strange driving force that had compelled her to travel to Bali, and to this retreat in particular.

As they were now the only car travelling on the narrow and deserted road, Chad could see that they were coming to a dead end.

The BMW pulled up at the traffic cones that had been placed across the road by a couple of road construction workers. As the driver pressed the button for his window and it began to open, one of the workers wandered over, and the two exchanged quick fired words in Balinese.

Satisfied, the driver nodded.

He closed his window and peered into the rear vision mirror. He turned to Crystal.

'Missus Miller, we are here, although I do need to

apologise to you and Mister Miller. I will not be able to drive you right up to the entrance of the retreat.'

'Why the hell not?' snapped Chad.

Crystal jumped.

'Sorry,' the driver said, nervous, 'the road up ahead is broken. They are fixing now, but the car cannot cross over,' he said.

'Chad, would you mind your manners?' she whispered.

She turned to the driver and said, 'it's okay, my husband is exhausted from the trip. How far is the walk up to the entrance of the resort?'

The driver looked uncomfortable.

'Only a hundred feet Missus Garcia-Miller, sorry, so sorry,' he said.

Chad scoffed. Clearly the long journey had jogged his memory of his wife's married name, and threw the door open to get out of the car.

'It's okay,' Crystal handed him a crisp hundred-dollar bill, and the driver's eyes lit up when he realised it was an American bill. Chad went to say something about the generous tip but for once, kept his mouth shut. Smart move. With the bags out of the car, Crystal walked up the narrow driveway in front of her husband and Chad could see a checkpoint closer to the entrance of the retreat manned by two fit and grinning young men. As they walked towards the security guards and their hand operated boom gate, Chad lagged behind a few steps, before cursing, his eyes fixed on a figure a little further up the road. Crystal took a deep breath.

'Chad, don't.'

A beggar.

As the figure approached, Chad realised it was a woman. Her clothes had seen much better days. Her face was aged and sun-worn, and was partially hidden by a flimsy shawl.

Crystal was flinching, waiting for his inevitable reaction and he knew it.

'Get a damn job, lady,' he barked, standing about six feet away from the beggar.

She appeared not to understand him.

As he walked within a few feet of her, she held out her hand and offered him a bracelet.

'One dollar,' she stuttered in English.

Crystal reached into her handbag.

'No!' Chad spat, 'if you encourage them, they will never get it together. Don't.'

Crystal looked at him, helplessly, but he doubled down. The beggar's eyes were pleading, but she eventually withdrew her hand and cast her eyes downwards.

He watched Crystal attempt eye contact with the beggar in order to reassure her with a kind smile. But the woman held her gaze firmly at the ground.

As he turned away, Chad heard a sound, before spinning around and casting his dark eyes on his wife.

'Did you hear her?' he barked.

'No,' Crystal shrugged. 'What are you talking about?'

'I swore she called me something.'

Crystal rolled her eyes at him.

'Tightass asshole?' Crystal said, as she walked past him.

CHAPTER EIGHT

Chad

CRYSTAL HAD WOKEN AFTER A SOUND AND refreshing night's sleep. She'd always been a heavy sleeper and although Chad seldom complained about it these days, she often gifted him with the odd sounds of snoring from time to time. By the time she'd showered and dressed and made herself look presentable, Chad was only rising from what he hoped was a mood enhancing night's sleep.

'Morning, sleepyhead,' she said. Her face suggested that she had hoped for the same thing.

'Morning to you,' Chad said as he rubbed his eyes and found himself taking a second look at his wife. She stood at the end of the bed. Her lime green summer dress revealed much of her flawless skin, and he found himself reflecting on his less-than-ideal mood yesterday after the long flight.

'I could eat a horse. I'd kill for some Bircher Muesli and a decent coffee,' Crystal said to him as she cast her eyes out their room's window and into the lush canopy of the rainforest.

'Why don't you head off to breakfast and I will be there after I have a shower?' Chad said.

Crystal nodded, her stomach growling.

'Alright,' Crystal said.

As soon as the door was closed, he ran his hands down under the covers.

Chad reached for his phone, wondering if he still had that very inappropriate photo of the 23-year-old hooker. As he unlocked his device and laid back in bed, he heard the door of their room open. He froze.

'Sunglasses would be han—' Crystal said before she came around the corner.

'Checking, err, sales figures,' he said.

'Uh huh,' she said. 'I can see that.'

She grabbed her glasses and without saying another word, exited the room, ensuring that the door closed with a little more emphasis.

Chad had a secret app on his phone where he hid his extensive collection of lewd photos. After the magazine incident, he wondered if Crystal had figured out how to get into it. He remembered that annoying IT friend she had from work. It would have taken him five minutes to crack it, if not less. He wondered if she'd gotten into it last night. The latest pics were date-stamped the same night he'd come home late before they'd talked about this holiday they were now on. *Shit.*

Chad dressed quickly and met his wife at the restaurant door. As they entered, Crystal let out an impressed whistle. The room itself had a wall on one side covered with beautiful tapestries from local Balinese artists. A high-pitched thatched roof dotted with ceiling fans that provided gentle movement to the humid air added to the tropical ambience. She looked across the room and gasped at the ornate, rounded arches that revealed views of the incredible Balinese morning, as well as the large ravine filled with a lush green rainforest forming its own tapestry of nature. Chad could hear the calming sound of the water flowing down the Ayung river not far below. The morning light reflected off the river as if passing through a large, crystal chandelier. Crystal took a deep breath and smiled.

'Good morning, Mr Miller and Missus Garcia-Miller and welcome to our dining area,' a happy looking young woman said to her. 'My name is Ni Luh, would you like to enjoy some breakfast?'

Crystal nodded and they were led to a small table on the far side of the room.

'Latte, extra hot if you don't mind,' Chad said as he sat down before Crystal ordered her coffee.

Crystal sipped on her water and glanced around the dining area.

They had been booked into some meditation session

in the early afternoon, according to the retreat program a few weeks ago. Crystal had been immediately excited, but Chad had baulked at the idea – sitting on some mat with his legs crossed wasn't high on his priority list. But he knew that it would offer him some leverage later on, so he had said nothing.

Chad wondered who out of all of the diners would be there.

'We won't have to actually hang out with any of these guests after, will we?' His eyes perused the menu. 'I deal enough with annoying people every day.'

He glanced up at Crystal. Her eyes were doing that thing again.

'You're very quiet Missus Garcia-Miller,' Chad said.

Crystal continued to stare into the rainforest, and sighed.

'I thought breakfast was your favourite meal of the day,' Chad said, beckoning the waiter.

'It normally is,' she murmured.

CHAPTER NINE

Chad

'Do we have to go?'

Crystal relished in the horrified look on her husband's face. 'It's a meditation class, darling. Not a death sentence.'

'I'm not going.'

'Now, now,' Crystal patted him on the shoulder, 'I know you'd rather stay here in the room with one hand on your smartphone.'

'I was checking sales figures—'

Crystal held her hand up and cut him off.

'Look Chad. If I can be honest, I actually thought this holiday would be our last chance at reconnecting. So, how about you consider doing something I would like to do for once? And anyway, it's part of the program.'

He cursed himself for not pushing harder to go to St Barts.

After seeing the photos of Pixie, the hooker, earlier that morning, he considered telling Crystal to shove the Samsarana Resort and its meditation class up her ass. He could be landing on the runway at Gustav Three Airport in a day and a half. Hell, he could fly in Pixie too and have her waiting for him in his favourite suite: The Villa Diane, at the Le Carl Gustaf Hotel. He could be lazing in the infinity pool overlooking picturesque St Barts, sipping on a glass of an expensive champagne, maybe a Louis Roederer Limited Edition Brut. Hell, Pixie's flights would cost less than a bottle of that bubbly, but it would be worthy compensation for being dragged all the way here.

Chad turned to look at Crystal's face and sighed again. If he didn't want her to leave, he had to meet her half way. He would go to this class, but at some point later today or tomorrow, Chad would ensure the next time he laid down to sleep, it would be somewhere far, far away. Without his wife lying next to him.

Chad told Crystal that he at least wanted to stretch his legs and explore the resort a little, assuring her he would meet her back at their room five minutes before 1.00 pm. When 12.55 pm came and went, Crystal found her husband at the poolside bar. 'Get lost on the way back to our room?' she said, icily.

'Alright, alright, don't get your knickers in a knot,' Chad said as he downed his bourbon.

'I needed a little sip of something to calm down all the excitement for this meditation class.'

Crystal shook her head.

'Let's go,' Crystal smiled as she ushered him down the pathway towards the meditation room.

CHAPTER TEN

Chad

CRYSTAL LOATHED TARDINESS, SO WHEN THEY HAD both arrived late at the entrance to the room, Chad knew she was swallowing her embarrassment as best she could. It wasn't the first time that she'd had to apologise for him, and he knew it wouldn't be the last. There were at least a dozen people already seated in front of a meditation teacher. He turned his head and made eye contact with them.

'I'm sorry we're late,' she said.

'Come, come, it is fine.'

As Chad walked in behind Crystal, he checked his watch. He then looked down to see a man studying him. He presumed it was the teacher. They found a space to sit.

'Now before I introduce myself,' the meditation teacher said, 'I will ask everyone to pick up a mat and form a large circle starting here,' he gestured.

Chad sat down on a mat next to his wife, his elbows resting on his knees. He couldn't wait to get the hell out of there, but smiled to himself, knowing once he got through this class, he'd be home free.

'My name is Henry and I welcome you all to this meditation class today here at the Samsarana Resort,' he said.

Chad took a moment to check him out. He couldn't put a finger on his accent. The guy looked American, maybe part European. Dressed in white yoga pants and a sleeveless jade-green shirt, the guy must spend half his life in some secret gym hidden beneath the resort. Chad felt a stab of jealousy, noticing Henry's lean toned arms, thick mop of dark hair and tanned face, and wondered if Crystal was checking him out as well. With penetrating blue eyes above a relaxed smile, the guy must have had women lining up for this class. Chad found himself once again wishing that he was in better shape.

'Alright,' Henry said to the group, 'before we commence, I'd like to go around the room and have you all introduce yourself. So, why don't we start with you?' he pointed to the woman on the other side of the circle to his far right.

Chad rolled his eyes. *Fuck me*, he thought, he would be the last person to have to introduce himself to the rest of these idiots and now would have to sit there and listen to their banal self-introductions. *Great.*

CHAPTER ELEVEN

Chad

'Hi, my name is Beth,' the woman said nervously. 'I'm here with my husband,' she gestured to the man next to her, 'and we are here to take a break and rejuvenate ourselves.'

Tanned Henry smiled.

Light-brown hair nestled around her shoulders, her brown eyes beamed positivity.

Try-hard, Chad thought.

Henry nodded before he cast his eyes over to her husband, and the man cleared his throat.

'I'm Logan, Beth's husband,' he said, 'and I'm here because my wife wanted to come to a retreat in Bali.'

Chad sniggered loudly and Crystal shot him a look.

Chad thought Logan looked a little out of shape.

He could already see a sheen of sweat covering the man's exposed skin. It made him feel a little less self-conscious.

'Thank you, Logan,' Henry said, turning to the next woman.

'Gemma,' she smiled, 'I'm here with my friend Amelia,' she nodded to the woman next to her, 'to soak in this wonderful island and,' her eyes twinkled at the teacher, 'the people.'

Gemma was petite, Chad thought. She couldn't have been more than five and a half feet in height. Short, pink hair, with attractive features. She was cute. Not really his type, though.

Her friend seemed to look expectantly at the teacher, almost as if she were waiting for him to introduce her to the class.

'Hi Henry, I'm Amelia.'

A couple of gasps in the room got his attention and he looked at her closely.

'Amelia Langston,' she flicked her head as if it made her name sound better.

Ah. Chad thought he recognised her. He wondered if her ego could exude any more bandwidth. She was better looking than her friend, he thought. Tall and slender with muscular definition in her tanned arms and shoulders. Her skin was smooth and blemish free, with big brown eyes and a confident smile. More his type, for sure.

'Oh, and I am here because my friend,' she patted

Gemma on the shoulder, 'needed a holiday wing-woman.'

Tanned-Henry gave her a fleeting nod, before he turned his attention to the next person.

'Angela Smith—" the woman said, appearing agitated, sweaty and uncomfortable sitting on the floor.

'—and I'm on holiday here with my son and his girlfriend.'

Boring. Next.

The two people sitting next to her shifted on the floor before introducing themselves as the 'son' and the 'girlfriend.' Henry worked his way through the rest of the attendees, before he turned to the latecomers.

Crystal's introduction was flawless. Enthusiasm reflects interest, Henry thought, and she had it in spades. Her husband, not so much.

'Chad Miller,' he said with a cocky grin, 'I'm here to find out the meaning of true happiness—,' he said, meeting Henry's eyes '—without my millions of dollars.'

Henry stared at him for a time. The ensuing silence was heading towards awkward.

'I can guarantee you will find it today, Mr Miller,' Henry eventually said.

The meditation teacher took a deep breath before turning his attention to everyone in the class.

'Shall we begin?'

CHAPTER TWELVE

Chad

'I WOULD LIKE EVERYONE TO SIT IN A COMFORTABLE cross-legged position,' said the instructor. 'Good. Place your hands on your knees,' he showed everyone what he meant, 'and now take a long and deep breath in through your nose expanding the chest and the belly, stretching up the spine as you take a breath in, and relaxing as you breathe out. I would like you to do this several times. 'Now,' the instructor glanced out into the afternoon sun through one of the open archways before turning his attention back to the room, 'I want you all to close your eyes.'

Chad watched as everyone sitting around the circle did as he had asked. Some, of course, much quicker than others. He wondered how many classes Tanned-Henry had conducted, and whether he ever lost his patience. He wondered if anyone else was as distracted as he was right now. He opened his eyes a peek and saw a few others do the same. A few whispered to each other. He watched Amelia Langston give a slight huff as she relaxed her body and he chuckled.

Forty-five minutes later, the teacher was telling the class, 'Good—I ask you all to lay on your back on your mat. Get nice and comfortable. This is the last exercise in our session today. I am very confident most of you will find it quite profound and life changing.'

Chad scoffed, but Henry didn't seem to react.

Crystal peeked with one eye over to her husband and let out a tut sound.

'Seriously?' she said in an annoyed tone.

Chad gave her a fleeting glance before he took a deep breath and, in his own time, closed his damned eyes.

'Steady your breathing.' Henry commanded, softly, before proceeding with some kind of prayer. His words sounded like an ancient incantation and even Chad had to admit that the resonance of his voice was mesmerising.

As Chad daydreamed of the spa, Pixie and the bottle of bubbly in the Villa Diana, he felt a strange calmness wash over him as the ambience of the room fell away. Like a passing breeze over the balcony of his suite in his daydream, the words swirled around him before falling into the spa and tingling every inch of his skin below the waterline. The warm water of the spa bubbled away as Chad stared out over the remarkable view of the Villa down to Shell Beach, its water a light turquoise blue. He was in heaven. He held a champagne flute filled with something cold and bubbling. Chad picked up the tall glass and brought the rim to his lips, before taking a slow sip. At that moment, he wondered if things could get any better.

Feeling a sudden movement in the spa next to him, he realised it could indeed get better.

Pixie.

If she wasn't naked now, Chad grinned, she would be in a matter of moments.

Without even turning in her direction, he reached for her neck, ready to run his hands over her smooth, delightful skin, but felt something odd.

Pixie was wearing a T-shirt in the spa.

As he went to stroke her neck, he stopped.

Her neck felt hairy.

A moment before he turned to investigate this, Chad swore for a split second someone was sitting not ten feet away in one of the luxurious deck chairs of his suite.

Henry. The meditation teacher.

Dressed in a white suite, Safari style.

Jesus. This dream is turning weird, Chad thought.

The glass of Brut dropped out of his hand in

surprise, smashing on the spa deck as he turned toward Pixie. But it was not Pixie.

Staring at him was a scruffy, dirty, dark-haired teenager. He was fully clothed, wearing torn pants. No shoes. When Chad noticed his t-shirt – he did a double take. The kid was wearing a light blue DOSTME t-shirt and Chad felt a sense of déjà vu. His face was burned into Chad's memory.

Firstly, he wanted to ask who the kid was and what he was doing in his spa.

Then, where the hell was Pixie?

Without speaking, the teenager lent over and slapped him hard in the face.

Chad tried to fight back. But the teenager was strong for his size. He grabbed Chad by the neck and lifted him out of the spa.

'Dip,' spoke the boy.

Chad wanted to ask what he meant, but didn't get the chance.

The teenager grabbed him under the arms and tossed him effortlessly over the rim of the spa. Chad landed with an almighty thud on the deck of the plush suite.

As the back of his head hit the polished wooden planks, his vision went black.

CHAPTER THIRTEEN

Logan

WHAT THE HELL IS THIS, THOUGHT LOGAN. HE WAS dreaming a few moments ago, he was sure of it. There was no other explanation. But he didn't feel as if he had been dreaming, he felt perfectly awake now.

I am a man, he thought. *A 49-year-old car salesman. I am married to Beth...*

Something about his surroundings gave him a terrible sense of déjà vu.

As the seconds ticked by and this bizarre sense of reality started to kick in, Logan began to feel out of sorts. This desk. This office. He knew it. He felt like throwing up.

He looked down and saw that he was wearing women's clothing. A dress, a blouse, with breasts big enough to need a bra to support them. He reached up and ran his hands through long hair, feeling dangling earrings as he brought them down. Stifling a sob, his mind began to spiral into a tailspin, making him feel as if at any moment he was going to faint. As he stood up from the desk, he saw a couch. He felt it calling to him.

Maybe I need to lie down for a few minutes. When I wake from a power-nap, everything will return to normal and this powerful dream will be a distant memory.

As Logan approached the couch in front of him, he attempted to run possible logical explanations through his mind.

He must have died in Bali, he decided. On the mat of the meditation class. There was no other explanation for it.

But as the dizziness took hold, he glanced through the glass partition of the office and out into the waiting room, where there is one person sitting there, staring back at him. Henry, the meditation teacher, dressed in a sharp blue business suit. As Logan's body hit the sofa, he knew exactly where he was and it all clicked into place.

Somehow, he was now Courtney.

His marriage counsellor.

Amelia

Amelia could feel the excitement emanating from Gemma and to be honest, it was somewhat annoying.

Gemma had been gushing over the meditation teacher from the moment they entered the room, and when Henry talked to the class, there was no doubt in Amelia's mind he had on several occasions held his gaze in their direction.

Poor Gemma, Amelia thought, as they went through the motions of the class which were now drawing to a close. Gemma was attractive, somewhat, but she knew he hadn't been staring at Gemma, but her. She was used to men lusting after her and Henry was only human after all. Her mind drifted to Australia, and she pictured herself on location in Far North Queensland. She had seen photos of the house they were renting for her whilst she was filming there and it was stunning: a large Hamptons style home, with an infinity pool that over-looked the ocean. She'd not been to Port Douglas before, but it sure as hell appeared idyllic. In her daydream, her feet dangled in the water of the pool, whilst she sipped on a Margarita.

'Don't drink it all at once,' the unmistakable Australian accent made Amelia smile. Chris Hemsworth. Amelia turned to watch the actor walk across the tiled area of the pool from the bar and she wondered if she'd ever seen a more magnificent sight. She laid back on her towel and stared into the clear sky, hearing the voice of the meditation teacher, in the distance.

It was then that Amelia heard footsteps from the other side of the pool. When she looked up, she spotted a man walking towards her, dressed in dark blue khaki pants and a white t-shirt, with an armful of pool cleaning items. She thought there was something familiar about him.

He took off his sunglasses, before nodding to her. The pool cleaner was a spitting image of the meditation teacher.

'How strange,' she said, laying back down and closing her eyes.

CHAPTER FOURTEEN

Amelia

WHEN AMELIA OPENED HER EYES, SHE SENSED SHE was still lying on a towel near the pool, but something was different. This was a public swimming pool. There were people everywhere and it was noisy.

'Give it back!' she heard a girl scream nearby.

She felt jostling behind her. A teenage boy and girl were fighting.

'It's mine!' shouted a boy.

'You bought it with my money, give it to me!' the girl squealed.

Amelia turned to tell the annoying kids to cut it out. When she met their eyes, they both looked at her in amusement.

'What are you looking at, Porky Pig?' the boy said.

'Give it!' said the girl as she wrestled the large cup of overflowing soft drink from her brother, before it suddenly came cascading down over Amelia. Ice and all.

'Asshole!' Amelia screeched.

'Hey fatty,' the girl said, looking down at her, 'mind your own business and don't call my brother names!'

She threw the empty drink cup at Amelia, before turning to her brother.

'Let's get out of here before chubs tells on us.'

Amelia had never been called any of those names before. Dozens of people were now staring at her. When her eyes ventured to her wet towel, she found herself frozen in horror.

Her body was now entirely different. Her black one-piece bathing suit struggled to keep her fuller body from popping out. It was all too much.

Amelia felt overwhelming dizziness and her vision narrowed. She fainted.

Angela

Angela couldn't wait for the darned class to be over, but she went through the motions alongside Jack and Sophie regardless. She didn't like the tropics, she found the heat oppressive. The ceiling fans were creating some movement, but not enough. She hoped if there were any more activities to be undertaken with her son and his annoying girlfriend, that they would be done in the comfort of an air-conditioned room. Lying on her back now, staring up at the swirling ceiling fan above, she admitted that gate-crashing Jack and Sophie's holiday was a bad idea. The idiotic notion of reconnecting with her son on a holiday now felt ill-conceived. Jack and Sophie were following the teacher's every instruction, like two little lapdogs. With their eyes glued shut, she was able to stew in her own frustration in private.

She had never been there for Jack. It was one of the many reasons why her marriage with Benedict had ended. He would have been right at home at this meditation class. The guy's middle name could have been Zen. In the end, Benedict had conducted himself throughout the divorce in the most infuriating way. With dignity. She had felt a slight pang of regret then, but fate robbed Angela of any chance of redemption with her ex-husband. Cancer. The irony had never left her. One of the United Kingdom's top oncologists and she was unable to do a damn thing for him. She still thought about it to this day.

Angela cursed herself, once again, her mind returning to the stuffy room. If they had gone somewhere like Spain, or Portugal, she could have at least high-tailed it back home. But they hadn't, they'd chosen Bali, and she'd chosen to come, so Angela resigned herself to the fact she was stuck here for the next two weeks.

Briefly, she wondered if she could create a situation

involving an urgent need to be back at the hospital in London. Angela knew Jack and Sophie would probably not believe her, but it didn't matter. All three of them would be up happier this way and she knew it. She would even treat herself to a first class ticket on the way home. Angela smirked at the decision.

Angela closed her eyes and thought about her recent purchase of an apartment situated on top of the Battersea Power Station. She had spent little time settling in to the expensive abode, and her mind drifted over its indulgent floor space. With the potential extra week now up her sleeve, she could take some time out to enjoy the view from her balcony and relish in the location. Apparently Sting lived in one of the Penthouse apartments nearby.

Although she'd zoned out for pretty much the entire class, the teacher's words were now drifting deep into her mind. As the seconds ticked over, Angela felt as if someone had placed a light duvet over her body. She found herself being pulled into a daydream, where the sensation of drifting off to sleep was coming towards her as if on a wave and she didn't mind at all. She found herself in her new apartment, lying comfortably on her bed. Spread-out under the cover, her arms, hands, neck and upper body felt the luxurious duvet and cushy mattress and she wondered if there was ever a time that she felt more relaxed.

A sound from outside caught her attention; it

sounded close enough that it could have come from her own private balcony.

Strange, Angela thought. Access to the balcony was only from her apartment.

There it was again.

Now she heard it a bit clearer.

Angela swore it sounded like a pair of secateurs, trimming one of her large potted plants, which could only mean that someone had to be out there doing it. She sat up on her bed, shifted forward and placed her feet on the thick rug sitting on the floor, affording her a proper view of her balcony.

She'd not called a gardener, but there was one standing with his back turned to her, clipping away at her plant with the expertise of a surgeon. He wore a pair of green overalls, with 'Power Station Gardening Service' emblazoned in large letters on its back.

Hold on a second, she thought. *Benedict?* He always loved his garden.

She knew she must have been dreaming.

As if the gardener sensed her staring at him through the window, he turned in a slow arc and Angela swallowed at the pleasing sight.

'Oh my,' she said to herself, putting her hand to her mouth.

It wasn't Benedict. It was the meditation teacher, Henry.

Angela had no idea what was going on, but as if on

autopilot, she pulled herself back onto her bed and laid down once again.

When Angela opened her eyes, she felt a wave of nausea, quickly followed by gut-wrenching vomiting. As her focus sharpened, she wondered why in God's name was she seeing what she was seeing. She was in a hospital ward – in her hospital. When she caught sight of her arms, she felt a stab of fear. They were pasty white and bone thin. For whatever reason, she felt the sudden urge to run her hands through her hair. Except, there was no hair.

She was bald.

From the corner of her eye, Angela spotted a kidney dish and reached for it, pulling it into her lap just in time. As she threw up, she wondered how it was possible for a dream to be so realistic.

'This is not happening,' she announced, 'stupid fucking dream.' She shook her head and hoped at any moment she would wake up back on the mat at the meditation class.

Angela never slept well, even in hotel rooms. She had found the bed at the retreat stiff and unforgiving and had told anyone who would listen that an ironing board would have been more comfortable. She had obviously fallen asleep in the class and was now dreaming heavily.

'What did you say?' a voice asked from close by.

Angela turned to her right and came face to face with someone in the bed in the next cubical, staring at her with curiosity.

Angela stared at her for long enough for the woman to repeat the question.

'What did you say, darl? Did I hear you say something about a stupid effing dream?'

'Shut up and mind your own business, darl,' Angela snapped, emphasising the word *darl* with a sarcastic drawl, sending the other woman back into the middle pages of her tabloid magazine.

'Suit yourself,' muttered the woman under her breath, 'but you know as well as I do, bitch, this ain't no dream.'

Angela swung her head back and shot the woman a filthy look. She was about to give her another mouthful, but felt movement to her left. She turned and made eye contact with the person standing in front of her bed, and she froze, unable to speak. Her chest tightened, as her teeth clenched together, her jaw feeling as if it was having some sort of spasm. The nausea reappeared in her gut and this time she was unable to get to the kidney dish in time. She threw up in her lap. The woman stared down at her, not amused.

'The nurses have better things to do than clean up your mess.'

Angela met eyes with the woman and found herself staring at a woman who could have been her twin and quickly uttered a prayer that this nightmare would end quickly. The woman was wearing one of her workday outfits, with the same name badge, even the same hair pulled back within an inch of its life and the sour, unhappy face.

It's me, Angela recoiled. *But it can't be.*

CHAPTER FIFTEEN

Chad

WHEN CHAD OPENED HIS EYES, HIS HEART BEGAN to race. This all felt too real. He remembered being in the spa at Villa Diana and as his mind flicked through the slide-show of the event, he remembered the teenager who was in the spa next to him. The one who picked him up like he was a rag doll and threw him out of the spa with next to no effort. His vision came into focus. He was in a ramshackle hut. Rusty corrugated iron formed a roof that was held together by rope and twine, the walls patched together by wood off cuts and cardboard boxes. The small space was crammed with junk. All sorts of odds and sods. Everything was pushed up against the walls as if the most important thing to whoever lived here was to free up as much space as possible on the dirt floor. Why, he had no idea. Everything looked as if it had come from a junk heap. Nothing of value. All dusty, broken, second, third and fourth hand.

Chad was hit by an overpowering stench. It was as if an open sewer was right outside. When he lifted his arms in an effort to sit up, he had the horrible realisation that an overpowering smell of body odour was coming from his own armpits. Coupled with the odour from outside, Chad felt slightly ill. When he eventually sat upright, he stared down at himself and gasped. Scrappy long pants, dirty t-shirt, bare feet the colour of ash. His toenails were hideous. He felt himself begin to cough a long, deep, and painful cough and realised that not only did he feel ill, but also hungry, and thirstier than he had ever felt before. He closed his eyes and willed himself back to reality.

'Wake up, wake up, you moron.' He slapped his face a few times.

Chad felt movement in the corner of the hut, and his eyes met those belonging to a huge rat, dark and beady, before the varmint turned and scurried out through a hole in the wall.

'Shit!'

He scrambled back through a flimsy door and when he landed, found the source of the stench: a steady stream of dark putrid water flowing right down the middle of the path.

Chad glanced at the reflection from the puddle he

had just landed in, and realised in shock that he was staring directly at face of the teenager from the spa.

'Dip!'

Chad heard someone shout a name, but was too engrossed in his own confusion.

'Dipankar, what are you doing?'

A boy about the same height, wearing dirty, dishevelled clothing similar to his, was standing over him. His grin was buried underneath grit and grime, but Chad could see it all the same. He stared at him, confused.

'Who are you talking to?' Chad wanted to say. 'My name is Chad. Chad Miller. I am the CEO of DOSTME International! I don't belong here!' But before those words even began to form in his mouth, the boy stepped closer and patted him hard on the back.

'Dipankar, we are late for work. Come on. We will try to find another defective T-shirt for you when we get to the factory,' he said, ushering me to move down the dirt track with him.

'Work? Where is work. I work?'

He stared at me, dumbfounded.

'You feeling okay Dipankar?' he stepped closer and looked into my eyes.

'To be honest, I can't say I am, err—'

His expression changed, a curious look on his face.

'Did you knock your head, Dipankar? Have you forgotten my name?'

Chad couldn't help it. He stared and shook his head.

'Dipankar, we can't miss another shift. You know the boss. He will punish us if we miss another one. And after all these years you have forgotten your best friend's name. Come on, let's get going or we will be late.'

As the kid shuffled him along the dirt path, Chad couldn't help but have a bit of a chuckle to himself. He was clearly losing his mind. This was not happening.

'We need to get you something more comfortable to sleep on, Dipankar. We have lived across from each other all our lives. If after all this time, you've forgotten my name, Abhoy, you mustn't be sleeping.'

Abhoy walked ahead of Chad with the intent of a someone who under no circumstances wanted to lose his job. After about ten minutes of hard slogging through dirt tracks and a shanty town as far as the eye could see, with its crowded and narrow streets, Chad wondered where he was taking him. He struggled to keep up with 'Abhoy' who had been jabbering on as if Chad was supposed to hear him from three feet behind with all these people, cars, trucks, mopeds and bicycles swarming around them making it all but impossible to make out his words.

Still, he nodded and hoped that at some point the urge to throw up would cease.

'Come on,' Abhoy shouted.

They walked around a crowded corner and Chad found himself millimetres away from colliding with a guy on a bicycle with bales of what appeared to be rags strapped so high on his back it begged belief as to how he could be riding with so much strapped to his back.

He shouted something, but Chad could not make it out. He was sure it was not of a warm and fuzzy nature.

When the building across the road came into full view, he found himself stopping dead in his tracks, halfway across the road. An old clunker of a truck blurted out its horn, missing him by inches, making no effort to slow down.

The sense of déjà vu was overwhelming. Chad had been there once before, but at the time, refused to go inside. At the time, he didn't see the need. He stared at the sign on top of the factory, as Abhoy told him one final time to hurry.

DOSTME INT.

CHAPTER SIXTEEN

Logan

'MR AND MRS JACKMAN ARE HERE FOR THEIR 2.00 pm appointment, Ms Lushgrove.'

Logan woke, but kept his eyes closed, praying to anyone who cared that the dream was over and he was back somewhere familiar. He didn't care where—the meditation room at the resort in Bali, or home, anywhere. As long as he didn't have breasts, long hair and was wearing women's clothes. But when he sat up, it dawned on him that whatever the hell was going on, was still going on, and not only that, but his former self and his wife were about to walk through the doors. Logan panicked. *What am I supposed to do? Spend the next 60 minutes talking to them as if I'm Courtney Lushgrove, Marriage Counsellor?* he thought. His mind was spinning full tilt, but instinctively, he knew he had to hold it together until he figured out how the hell to get out of the bind that he'd found himself in. Or to wake the hell up. He lifted himself off the couch and stood up. Feeling woozy, he turned to peer into the waiting room. There was no one sitting there. Logan knew he was sitting there a little while ago. He was sure of it.

He started to think, fast.

Henry, the meditation teacher. He did this. He must have. But first, Logan had something else he needed to do, and that was somehow get through the next sixty minutes talking to Beth and her husband.

'Hello,' Logan had no idea what else to say.

Beth and the other Logan looked at him as if something was off.

'Come in,' he strained to speak as he realised that his doppelgänger had an e-cigarette in his jacket pocket. His heart yearned for a drag. Logan pointed to the couch and they sat down.

'You seem a bit off, Court-ten-ay,' Beth said with concern. The man next to her looked at him as if there was nothing wrong at all.

Logan decided to compartmentalise. He told himself this was the most realistic dream he had ever experienced. All he needed to do was fudge his way through it. He just had to pretend to be Courtney until he woke up and then it would all be over. Easy.

'I am feeling a bit off Beth, but let's press on,' Logan felt his cheeks flush as he spoke to his wife but, none-theless, got himself comfortable in Courtney's chair.

'How was your holiday?' It came out of Logan's mouth as if on autopilot. *Maybe this is how it works.*

The couple met each other's puzzled expressions before Logan turned to the counsellor and shrugged.

'Not sure what you are referring to Courtney,' a little smirk appearing on his lips, 'maybe you are getting us mixed up with another couple?'

Logan felt his cheeks reddening and his core temperature rising.

'We haven't been on a holiday for some time,' Beth's tone was more sympathetic.

Logan took his eyes off him for a beat before he turned to Beth.

'Maybe you'll have to come on the next work-junket to Vegas, baby. Now there's a holiday,' he said. Beth rolled her eyes before Logan turned to him, shooting a 'see what I mean?' look in his direction.

It's the damnedest thing, Logan thought, sympa-thising with his other self. He knew the reason he had acted like this was because he had found coming here a waste of time. All they were doing was giving Courtney their hard-earned money, just to sit there and listen to her condescending diatribe. A part of Logan felt the instinct to stick up for him.

'Vegas, huh,' Beth said with a heavy dose of sarcasm. 'I wouldn't want to disturb your little late night, I-have-to-leave-my-phone-in-the-hotel-room-and-be-out-god-knows-where- till-dawn, activities.'

He shifted on the couch, his spine straightening as if he was fielding off a personal attack. 'I've never done that,' he spat. 'You're being paranoid again. I've always kept my phone on me and I've never gone out late at night in Vegas either!'

Things were getting weird. Logan knew full well what Beth was referring to, and thought back to the very night. He had gone out and got up to things that would make Beth call the divorce lawyer in a heartbeat if she knew. Something inside him shifted as he sat there looking at Beth and her defiant husband, and the words were out of his mouth before he could stop them.

'Bullshit, Logan. We both know you are fucking lying through your cheating little teeth.'

Fuck. Logan thought. *What did I just say?*

CHAPTER SEVENTEEN

Amelia

AMELIA OPENED HER EYES. FOR A BRIEF MOMENT, all she could see was the blue sky above. She was back at the pool in Port Douglas. Hunky Hemsworth must have gone inside. He had mentioned he was hungry after all. But all of a sudden, a boy's face appeared directly above her. A complete stranger.

'Are you okay, Margarita?' he said. Amelia stared at him and completely misunderstood what he said.

'Margarita, yes, please. I am very thirsty,' she said. The boy stared at her with a mixture of concern and amusement.

'Margarita, are you feeling okay?' he said. Amelia's brain registered the noise around her, again. Strange noises. People. Lots of people. Amelia was still at the public pool. The Hollywood Pool, according to the sign on a nearby building. Her eyes darted down to her body again and were utterly repulsed by what she saw. 'This is not fucking happening,' she screamed inside her mind. She was still the overweight teenager.

'Margarita, you are starting to freak me out. You are making a scene. I think I need to get you home, so you can get Mum and Dad to help you out. Something has happened to you,' he said. Amelia sat up and shot the guy a look.

'Why do you keep on calling me Margarita! I want a Margarita! Is it why you keep on calling me one? And who the hell are you anyway?'

Some people went back to whatever was preoccupying them before Amelia made a scene. A few continued to watch, bored with their magazines and smartphones. The guy lent closer and this time spoke with a more serious tone.

'I am your brother, you dimwit. Now get your things together, I am taking you home.'

Amelia took a closer look into his eyes. In another life and at another age, she would have found him kind of cute. Dark eyes, with a thick mat of short, jet-black hair, matching eyebrows, and a confident, attractive face, structured for maybe a Hugo Boss advert. He possessed a tan her friends would swoon over and a bona fide six-pack. Perhaps he was of South American descent. Or maybe Mexican.

Growing up with a wealthy father, Amelia never had anything to fear. She'd grown up more pampered than Paris Hilton's Chihuahua and more protected than Beyoncé and Jay-Z. The guy handed her some clothing and a small bag, ushering her to her feet, and Amelia could feel countless eyes staring at her. This would normally give her bottomless ego a fix, but today she felt like it was doing the opposite. She felt so exposed, and alone. As he waited for Amelia to get her stuff together, a couple of girls walked past and smiled.

'Hey Antonio, looking good today huh,' one of them said, winking at him from above her sunglasses.

As he smiled and nodded, Amelia found herself making eye contact with them. Their expressions fell away in an instant before they turned and walked on. The last time Amelia Langston had cried was at the Golden Globes a couple of years ago. Natalie Portman had inched her out for the Gong for best supporting actress. Amelia found it quite upsetting, but this was next level.

As she followed this Antonio guy across the pool grounds, she sobbed.

Angela

Angela felt a rage building inside.

'I wish I'd never attended the stupid meditation class,' she screamed to herself. It was Sophie's idea. And she had been naïve enough to think she should go as well. So much for trying to bond with Jack. Now this.

'Well?'

She was staring at – herself.

She had just spoken – to herself.

The woman who looked like her on a normal day was giving her one hell of a filthy look and for the first time in her life Angela had found herself staring at her face, wondering if she did actually look like this when she was at work. The woman looked as angry as she felt at that moment.

'Well what?' she snarled back.

The woman in the bed next to me started to laugh, making no attempt to keep it down.

'Jesus Christ, Doctor Smith,' she dropped her magazine on her lap and took a deep breath, turning to Angela. 'Woke up on the wrong side of bed this morning?'

Angela boiled, ready to give her an earful, but as she heard the footsteps belting on the tiled floor getting further and further away, she noticed that the other version of her had already done a 180-degree turn and was storming off in a huff.

'Don't worry about her, Mary,' the woman coughing as soon as her words left her mouth. Angela looked at her and the woman's face let her know that she could tell that her expression was as vague as the beige coloured walls around them.

'Mary?' Angela heard herself say the words and

realised how unusual it must have sounded. The woman gave her a quizzical look and Angela found herself staring at her. Why, she didn't know. The woman winked, as if somewhere inside her head she must have known that Angela was having the world's worst day.

'Chemo does it to us all darl,' her eyes softened and for the first time today Angela felt a strange warmth towards her. Quite unusual.

'It's okay Mary. Rachel. Rachel Winterbottom,' she said in mock solemnness, holding her hand out with a grin.

Angela realised what she was saying. This Rachel woman must have thought that she was someone called Mary. The woman smiled at before taking a sip of water.

'But you can call me by my high school nickname, alright?'

Angela nodded, still trying to figure out how to get out of this nightmare. When she said nothing, Rachel's face lit up with a grin.

'Cold-arse!!'

She and another patient started to laugh and Angela could not help but wonder how she could be experiencing these feelings in an actual dream. They were so real that she could feel a panic starting to rise. When the laughter subsided between Rachel, AKA 'Cold-arse,' and the other patient, Angela knew the woman must have felt her staring at her again. As she swallowed, a dark cloud passed over her consciousness and without even thinking about what she was about to say, the words croaked out.

'How long?'

Rachel's jovial mood slipped away and as it did, she gestured to Angela and then to herself.

'Darl, you and me, we're like Thelma and Louise,' Angela saw her eyes glaze over. 'When the car goes over the edge, we'll both be in it.'

For a moment Angela was confused by the metaphor, but as she processed what Rachel meant, she felt herself preparing to vomit. Seconds before it came out, Rachel held up four fingers.

'Months.'

CHAPTER EIGHTEEN

Logan

LOGAN SAT THERE STARING AT THE EMPTY COUCH, losing his frigging mind. His memories took him back to the junket in Las Vegas, two years ago— one of the events that sent his marriage into a tailspin. He was stupid and careless and was caught up in the hype. If there was ever going to be a fourth instalment to the Hangover movies, that trip would have been it. Logan was one of the top five salespeople in his company – out of the fifteen car dealerships they owned, with over 250 sales people, and he was in the top echelon. The top 2.5 per cent. A framed, gilded certificate adorned his office wall, and they had given him a bonus so big that he didn't know where to start spending it. The kudos on his resume would open more doors in his industry than he could have even kept track of, should he have ever wanted to leave.

Being in the top five, he also got to meet the man. The Musketeer. The 'techno king' himself. Elon Musk.

It had made them all feel invincible. And before he could wipe the grin off his face, the five of them were doing shots in some bar, at 11.30 am. When he had called Beth at 6.00 pm that day, she knew. Logan could hear it in her voice. But, riding high on the day's events and full of Dutch courage, he told her to stop being a stick-in-the-mud and that he'd call her in the morning.

'Excuse me, Courtney.'

The voice disturbed Logan from the visions of Las Vegas, and he blinked himself back to reality. It was him.

Well, it was Logan. The other Logan.

'Logan,' he struggled to get the words out, 'can I help you?'

The other Logan walked a step closer, studying the counsellor, and Logan was sure he noticed him bristle. Staring past him for a moment, Logan could see him working his jaw as if he was finding it hard to speak.

'Can I ask you a question?' he said, turning his head, and Logan found his eyes hard to read.

Logan took a deep breath and nodded. He didn't know what else to do. He was in free fall.

'How did you know I was lying about Vegas?'

Logan wasn't sure what he was going to say, but

before he could think of anything, the other Logan added, 'has Beth being coming to see you alone?'

Logan shook his head and realised quickly that he had made a mistake. A big one. He should have lied. This was going to raise another, obvious question.

'No?' He stepped closer and Logan could feel the electricity in the air changing and not for the better.

'Our session is over. We'll have to take this up another time.' Logan started to feel angry, both with himself, and the guy standing too close to him.

'I don't know what the hell is going on here, *Court-e-nay*, but I suggest you stick to the script and mind your own damn business when it comes to the specifics.'

Even though Logan still could not fathom how this is all was happening, he knew that the person standing in his space was trying to intimidate him. And he didn't like it.

Logan stood up, ensuring that he made eye contact with the man in front of him.

'You'd better watch your tone. I know you better than you can imagine.'

He backed off. Logan trapped inside Courtney, awkwardly moved until he reached the office door.

'And when I get back,' Logan hissed over his shoulder, 'you will not be here.'

He heard a distant groan of acceptance, before heading straight for the toilets, planning to douse his face in some cold water and try to figure out what he was going to do. As he passed through the door to enter the men's bathroom, he bumped into a man who gave him an odd look.

'Lost your way?' he asked.

Chad

If Chad thought it was hot outside, the inside of the factory was even worse. The place was jam-packed with people. There were sewing machines – loads of them – in rows, the space in between them barely wide enough for anyone to fit through. Hanging overhead, black cables ventured down to each sewing machine, part of what appeared to be an unsafe network of cabling.

Behind every sewing machine, were workers all of different ages, all with their heads down, sewing what he knew was DOSTME clothing. The ubiquitous logo was everywhere.

The workers appeared as if they'd run the Boston Marathon in a winter jacket. Sweat poured off them, some wore next to nothing, trying to stay as cool as they could.

A haze of smoke blanketed the factory floor, with many of them smoking without taking their hands off their sewing machines and the smoke ash fell to wherever it landed, on the clothing, the machine, or the floor. Chad was aghast. Thank the lord above for the industrial sized washing machines that these would be thrown into, before they were shipped to America.

As Chad found himself taking another glance at the floor, he spotted unorganised piles of DOSTME clothing next to many of the machines. The floor of the factory was filthy, with workers moving up and down the aisles, stepping over the piles of attire as best they could, but mostly standing on them without giving it a second thought. Like him and Abhoy, most wore no footwear. A bell clanged somewhere on the other side of the factory floor.

'Sit next to me?' Abhoy smiled.

Without waiting for an answer, he ushered them down one of the aisles, where he sat down at one of the machines.

'Let's go,' he tilted his head in the direction of the machine next to him.

Chad sat down and as the reality of the moment dawned on him, he could feel the heat starting to make him feel ill. Body odour had never smelt this strong. It permeated everything.

Abhoy reached behind his machine and pulled out some material from a tray sitting on the floor. He smiled again, which was starting to annoy Chad. *How could he be happy at this moment?*

'First one to a hundred?' Abhoy rolled his shoulders before wiping the sweat off his brow.

'First one to what?' Chad said, but then noticing the

pile of material sitting in the tray, he put two and two together.

As he swallowed, feeling the dryness of his throat, he longed for a big glass of water, the sweat was pouring off him, making his hands clammy. When he wiped his brow, he wondered what was wetter, his hands or his forehead. Chad closed his eyes and wondered what version of hell this was.

Abhoy seemed to notice his lack of activity, so he leant over and in hushed tones said, 'get on with it Dip, the Supervisor is coming.'

Chad turned to him before following his gaze to the entrance to the factory floor.

A tall man scanned the room, his clipboard held across his chest by his left forearm. Even from a distance, he appeared menacing. He seemed to spot the two boys and, after a beat, glanced at them harshly.

Chad turned to Abhoy. 'Where can I get a drink of water?' he asked.

Abhoy took his eyes off his sewing machine, bursting into laughter, before turning back and fixing his gaze on the seam of the shirt.

'I don't know what's wrong with you today, Dip, but you know as well as I do, we don't get a cup of water until we finish our shift,' he said.

'How long is our shift?' Chad found himself asking, knowing full well it would have Abhoy wondering who the hell he was.

'Shit,' said Abhoy and Chad noticed the Supervisor

heading in their direction. 'Get on with it or else you'll get into serious trouble. Hurry.'

With his head down, he realised he'd not answered Chad.

'Twelve hours,' he hissed under his breath, 'fifteen if we don't finish.'

CHAPTER NINETEEN

Amelia

AMELIA FOLLOWED ANTONIO DOWN SANTA MONICA Boulevard. They had walked in silence for a while, and he strode in front of her as if he didn't care if she lagged behind, and she was struggling to keep up.

'Where are we going and what's your hurry?' she asked.

Antonio walked for another few moments before he paused and turned around almost colliding head on with her.

'What has got into you today?' he said.

She could see the look of frustration etched on his face, before adding, 'you made a scene back there, it was pretty embarrassing, Rita.'

Amelia didn't know where to begin.

She knew that if she told him her real name was

Amelia Langston and that she had been transported from a meditation retreat in Bali, into his sister's body in downtown Hollywood, he would think she'd lost her mind. Which, to Amelia, felt like she had.

'I think something's wrong with me,' was all she could get out of her mouth before he turned away and kept walking.

'Mum and Dad can deal with you,' Amelia heard him say over his shoulder, as he walked on.

The thirty minute walk ended abruptly when Antonio, now a clear fifty feet ahead of Amelia, turned without notice into the entrance of a house. Amelia ran forward, her legs hurting and her lungs burning. She stopped at the front of the house he had entered, putting her hands on her knees, trying to catch her breath. When she stood up straight, she took in the full view of the house, and noticed an older woman standing on the front porch, staring back at her. Amelia could guess this person was Margarita and Antonio's mother. She could see the resemblance. Dark hair, olive skin and similar features, with a floral apron that screamed housewife and mother to teenage children.

The house was old, dated and working class. Dark brown, two storey brick with a few ill-matched outdoor chairs on the small porch. The small front garden was overgrown with unruly grass and bushes, a large tree right on the edge of the footpath cast the entire front half of the house in a shadow. In the distance, Amelia could hear the hive of traffic.

Amelia stared at the woman for a few moments.

'Are you going to stand out there all day Margarita?' the woman said to her from the porch, her eyebrows raised as she asked the question.

Amelia took one step forward, before another, wondering when this nightmare was going to end. As she followed the woman inside, Amelia found herself surprised at how nice the house was compared to outside. It was small, but well-decorated and neat as a pin.

She followed the woman into the kitchen. Whatever she was cooking, it smelt delicious, and made Amelia's stomach groan.

'Talk to me young lady,' the woman said with her back turned to Amelia, 'Antonio said some kids at the pool were picking on you.' As the woman turned around, she stared at Amelia and shook her head. A heartfelt smile crept across her face, before she nodded for Amelia to sit on one of the seats.

'Baby,' she walked over to the other side of the island bench, 'come and sit and tell your mother all about it,' she said. Amelia had been an actress for a long, long time. Something about Margarita's mothers' words, or more so tone, sounded – put on. She parked the thought for now.

Amelia, as if on autopilot, side stepped to the stool

and found herself sitting on it. Margarita's mother paused in reflection before speaking.

'Antonio told me it was kids from your school,' she said.

When the woman met her gaze, she leant over and placed her hand on Amelia's shoulder.

'It's alright Margarita, it won't matter for much longer, those awful children at school picking on you,' the woman said, a frown creeping across her face as the words left her lips. Amelia wondered what the woman was talking about.

'What do you mean?' as she added 'Mom,' Amelia realised she hadn't meant to even say the word. Margarita's mother closed her eyes. When she opened them again, Amelia could tell she was fighting back tears. Wiping her left eye, she shook her head.

'Because your father lost his job today, Margarita. He said he is sick of LA and wants to move. You know this is his reaction to every problem. Pack up and move.'

Amelia still had no idea what the hell was happening. She hoped that at any second this damn dream would stop, and she would open her eyes and be back in her own body.

'What about you, Mom? Do you want to move again?' Amelia couldn't believe the actual words that were coming out of her mouth. *Mom?*

'It doesn't matter what I think Margarita, if your

father wants to move, who am I to have an opinion about it?' she said.

Amelia was about to say something when they heard the slam of a door, and Margarita's mother flinched.

Amelia heard footsteps approaching before a man appeared from the hallway.

'Great day to be fired, Elena,' he said to Margarita's mother, as he dropped his bag on the floor.

Elena turned to him, smiling, before taking a couple of steps towards him with outstretched arms. As the man took a step forward, coming into the kitchen under the fluorescent lights, Amelia now had a good look at him.

It was at this moment something inside her mind flipped a switch.

She knew this guy.

Oh, shit.

Angela

'I have four months to live?' Angela stared at Cold-arse. Rachel looked at her curiously.

'What's got into you all of a sudden, Mary?' she said.

Angela could feel the queasiness subside, but in its place an annoyance which made her feel almost normal. Someone had to be fucking with her. She had no idea how, or why, but she knew this was some sort of big messed up joke. *And who in their right mind who had a surname Winterbottom, would happily call herself Cold-arse?* How had she gone from the meditation class in that godawful retreat in Bali, back to the hospital where she worked and was, where she believed she was admired and respected, was anyone's guess. Well, maybe not admired, but surely respected. It wasn't her fault that most of the nurses who worked in the Oncology department lasted no more than twelve months.

She'd once told the Medical Director of a well-respected London hospital never to question her knowledge, ethics, or procedures during a heated boardroom meeting. Suffice to say, her employment in that particular hospital ceased at the conclusion of the same business day.

Angela could feel her anger rising from deep within. She realised there was something she could do. Throwing the sheet and blanket to one side, she swung her feet out of bed. Her head spun and the pain in her skull thumped.

'What are you doing!' Rachel exclaimed.

'Leave me alone!' Angela spat at her, as she swung her head in the direction of the doorway at the end of the ward. As she took a few steps forward, she could feel the weakness in her bones rattle her. Still, she pushed on, letting her feet lead her through the ward.

By the time she reached the doorway, she was exhausted. As she hobbled her way to one of the doors in the hallway, one of the nurses at the station asked what she was doing. Ignoring the voice, she pushed through the door. Angela reached the inside of the bathroom, relieved that it would all be over shortly. All five cubicles were empty, much to her relief, and she headed in the direction of one of the five vanities sitting on the opposite wall.

As Angela reached the first sink, she ran some water and rinsed her face. Wiping her face with a paper towel, she knew as soon as she met her own eyes in the mirror that this ridiculous moment would end and everything would return to normal. She would be back in the meditation room and in a few days' time she would fly home.

First class, glass of champagne. Maybe a few.

Happy days.

When she lifted her head, a desperate, guttural cry came from the back of her throat.

Staring back at her was one of her patients.

Mary Wilson.

Stage 4 Lung Cancer.

Four months to live.

CHAPTER TWENTY

Chad

CHAD HAD NO IDEA WHAT HE WAS DOING.

He'd never sat at a sewing machine before.

The millionaire felt a churning in his stomach. As the seconds ticked by, he could sense that something bad was coming. Chad could not remember the last time he felt fear. It had been so long, that it felt foreign to him. As foreign as this body he was now inside and this awful, crowded factory.

'What are you doing!' the voice cut through the thick air and Chad jumped in fright. With all the noise and all the movement going on around him, Chad had not realised he was standing centimetres away.

The Supervisor.

Chad turned and met the man's eyes.

'Stitch!' the guy said.

Before Chad could do anything, Abhoy said 'It's okay, Supervisor. Dip is not well today. I will help him.'

The guy stepped over to Abhoy.

'What did you say?' he said.

He stood there looking at him with menacing eyes.

He raised his hand as if he was about to hit Abhoy, but at the last second turned his hand into a pointed finger.

'Stitch! he said.

The man turned to Dipankar. Chad couldn't figure out why the guy was being such an asshole. The Supervisor pushed Dipankar's sewing machine which resulted in him suddenly falling backwards. Whether this was intentional or not, the result was unexpected.

Chad fell backwards. His head hit the concrete floor with a thud.

When Chad woke, the pain in his head ached. He was back in the ramshackle hut, with no idea how he got there.

Abhoy's face appeared in his field of vision.

'Are you okay, Dipankar?' he said.

Chad was about to ask him for some Tylenol, although he knew that this would be like asking for a cold beer. Not going to happen.

'He's one serious son of a bitch,' Chad blurted out.

Abhoy nodded.

'Why did he do that?' he said.

Abhoy shrugged his shoulders.

'I don't understand why you ask this, Dipankar. Have you somehow lost your memory?' he stared at Chad in confusion.

Chad stared at the wall and wondered what his reaction would be if he told Abhoy who he was.

'I don't know what's happened to me,' he said. Abhoy's eyes seemed to take in his words and when it came down to it – it was the absolute truth.

Abhoy lent over and patted him on the shoulder.

'You have been working in the factory for as long as I have. Six years, Dipankar. How did you forget to sew?'

'Can I ask you what is going to sound like a strange question, Abhoy?' Chad said.

He nodded.

'Are we the same age?'

'Yes,' he said.

Chad knew this was going to sound like he had lost his mind and memory, but he knew he had to push on.

'Abhoy. How old are you?' he asked.

A noise outside caught his attention, but he turned back to Chad.

'I am fifteen, Dipankar. As are you.'

Jesus Christ, Chad thought. *This kid has been working since he was nine years old?*

Without any forewarning, the front door suddenly flung open.

Within seconds, there we no less than six strangers inside the hut, all of them crammed in together.

'Dipankar had a fall at the factory. He has hit his head,' Abhoy said. Chad was grateful that Abhoy chose not to said anything about his memory loss that morning.

His attention was drawn to a man and woman. The others were children. They were all of varying ages, two of them quite young, a boy and girl and the other two, a pigeon pair, slightly older. All of them dressed in dirty clothes and in the need of a shower. Chad put two and two together, even with a splitting headache. The older couple were the children's parents.

From the grave expression on the man's face, Chad believed he was Dipankar's father.

The woman standing next to him, must have been his mother. Chad saw tears welling through the grit and the grime around her eyes and on her face.

She lent down and placed her hand on the side of his face, rubbing it gently, and Chad was surprised how good it felt.

'Don't touch him,' the father barked at her, pushing her arm away.

Chad felt a chill pass over the back of his neck, despite the air inside the hut being thick with humidity. The man bent down and thrust his dirty finger inches away from Chad's nose.

'You stupid boy—' he sneered, his breath putrid '—
how we feed your brothers and sisters,' he bent down
and now had his face in mine, '—if you not work!'

He slapped Chad's face, hard.

Welcome home.

CHAPTER TWENTY-ONE

Logan

LOGAN VENTURED BACK TO THE OFFICE. HIS TRIP
to the bathroom had been an experience. When he sat
behind the desk, he could see by the clock on the wall
that it had just hit 5.00 pm.

As if on cue, he saw movement in the office
windows before the receptionist appeared at the doorway. Her grin was similar to the one Courtney wore
when they were last there as clients. Cheerful and downright annoying.

It was not possible people could be this happy at
work.

'You have yourself the world's best evening, boss!'
she gushed.

Shit. He swallowed. Hard. Even though Logan had
met her many times, he never learned her name – and

Logan was good with names, having learned years ago, that if you want to sell a stack of cars, that it was an important relationship-building detail. Husbands, wives, children, pets, he was the master. But he needed to know what it was first. He had to fudge it.

'And you make sure you have one yourself—' he froze in the middle of an awkward and long pause, '—too!'

The young girl gave him a quizzical look.

'Will do!' she said, and in a flash of an expensive looking camel coloured overcoat – she was gone. Logan waited at least 30 seconds. When he was sure she had left the office, he headed to the door and took a peek around the corner.

The receptionist was gone.

Logan walked to the front door and locked himself in before ducking around to the reception desk to try to find something that told him what her name was. Running his finger down the directory listing, he found what he was looking for, and couldn't help smirk.

No way, he thought. *That can't be your name.*

Her name was Tindwer.

Logan sank into Courtney's office chair. The Mac sitting on her desk was sleek and huge, a complete contrast to the thin and petite keyboard. He tapped the keyboard to wake the screen, and it came to life. After finding

Courtney's driver's license in her handbag, Logan looked up the address on Google Maps. Sorted.

After getting his bearings, it hit him that he knew nothing of her personal life. Was she married? Single? Seeing someone?

Would he need to deal with her partner when he arrived at her apartment? The thought made his heart drop. Chad wasn't homophobic, by any stretch, but he wasn't in the mood to get cosy with a man, even if he did possess a female's body. *No thanks.*

Chad searched for and found Courtney's Facebook profile. No relationship status, and the profile photo was just of her. *What a relief,* he thought, until he realised that it was no indication of a relationship status, casual or otherwise. After all, he didn't have a couple's photo on his. Beth had accused him of being unromantic. He guessed that having a car in his photo didn't help. A Tesla, of course.

Chad checked through her photos, holding his breath as he scrolled through the first few dozen images. There didn't seem to be any significant men in her life. He was in the clear.

Scrolling on, he stopped at a photo of Courtney with about four other women in a bar, champagne glasses raised with a sign being held up by one to the far right.

"Happy Divorce Day, Courtney," it read. Chad felt his apprehension finally evaporate. One less thing to worry about.

Something then came to mind. Chad brought up Google in the browser and typed in the words "Samsarana Retreat Bali." Just as the result of the search appeared, Courtney's phone pinged and Chad glanced at the screen. He read the message, bile rising in his throat.

He read it again, hoping that he had it wrong.

'We still on tonight, sexy? XXX P.S. I got that new lube that you wanted.' The message was punctuated with eggplant emojis and Logan didn't know what made him shudder more.

If this wasn't bad enough, Chad glanced at the screen and realised that there were absolutely no results for Samsarana Retreat.

CHAPTER TWENTY-TWO

Amelia

'MARGARITA,' HE SAID IN AMELIA'S DIRECTION, 'DO you mind going upstairs so your mother and I can talk?'

Amelia mirrored the man's faint smile and slipped off the bar stool. She remembered seeing the staircase when she walked into the house. Trying to avoid saying something out of character, she sauntered off and by the time she took the first step on the staircase, could hear strained words coming from the kitchen. Part of her wanted to stay where she was and listen to what was being said. Whatever the discussion, it was getting heated and she decided that it would be wise to go upstairs rather than be busted for eavesdropping.

Finding herself on the top floor landing of the house, she could see an open door leading to a bathroom and another two doors on opposite sides of the hallway.

Both were shut.

Ambling her way down the hallway, she could hear the dull thud of music coming from behind one of the doors, along with a muffled voice. Antonio's room. She turned her attention to the other door, opened it, and froze.

Staring back at her, was not one, but four of them. Courtney and Kim Kardashian and Kylie and Kendall Jenner, larger than life on Margarita's wall. Amelia clenched her fists, fighting the urge to curse out loud, and she felt her breath growing short.

Turning her attention to the dresser, Amelia saw a reflection of herself in the mirror and took a step closer. Staring back at her was Margarita.

The teenager was short, slightly pudgy with a head of thick curly hair. Brown eyes, a little acne, but nothing that couldn't be taken care of with some treatment. She couldn't have looked more different from Amelia Langston.

'WHY, WHY, WHY!' She burst into tears, falling onto the bed. 'I want out, I want out, make it stop, NOW!' she sobbed to herself, as she curled into the fetal position. She heard distance footsteps on the stairs.

Her life as Margarita, had just begun.

CHAPTER TWENTY-THREE

Angela

SEEING MARY'S FACE STARING BACK AT HER, ANGELA shivered. She recalled the first time she'd met her patient. She was about five foot seven, in peak physical shape and had a healthy head of mousey-blonde hair. A perfect, symmetrical face with a tiny nose and huge, blue eyes. To Angela, women like Mary triggered a warped part of her deep sub-conscious. She had grown up knowing she was average looking. Being bullied at school, more so from other girls than boys, had left a permanent imprint in her mind. It was something she'd never dealt with, even as an adult. But now, she could see Mary's good looks were slipping away. Her eyes seemed smaller and the brightness of the blue faded. Her weight had dropped and she was now thin, her skin bone white, as if dusted with talcum powder.

Angela stared into Mary's eyes for a moment. *'Not looking so gorgeous now, are you?'* Angela let the thought do a couple of laps around her head, before a sudden noise from the doorway startled her.

'What are you doing?'

Angela turned her frightened expression away from the mirror. The voice had come from the open doorway, where a nurse stood with a quizzical look on her face. Angela looked at her nametag and saw that her name was Bec.

'Can I wash my fucking face?' Angela spat back.

The nurse's originally friendly expression darkened for a moment.

'Now, Mary,' the nurse stepped through the open doorway, 'what's with the eff word, I don't think I've ever heard you swear before. Are you okay?'

'I am fine,' Angela growled back at her.

'Help you back to your bed?' the nurse asked.

'NO!' Angela spat, 'I need to use the toilet,' she turned to the cubicle, 'unless you want to wipe my arse too?'

The understanding veneer slipped away from Bec's face. Copping this sort of abuse was clearly not part of her job-description.

'I'll see you back at your bed. Potty mouth,' and before Angela could fire another round of attitude, the nurse was gone, the door shutting with a soft click behind her.

Angela made it back to her bed, but not after almost

falling over in the toilet from another bout of dizziness. She had sat on the toilet for another ten minutes before building up enough strength to try to get back to her bed without assistance.

'Abusing Bec, in the toilet?' Cold-arse admonished Angela after she fell onto her bed, 'What's got into you today?'

'For Pete's sake,' Angela said through gritted teeth, 'these bloody nurses need to stop being so damn sensitive.'

In silence, Rachel moved her legs out from underneath the sheets, gasping as her feet touched the cold floor. She took the three steps over to Angela's bed and sat down on the side of her bed.

'What do you think you're do—'

Cold-arse ignored her and moved even closer.

'Listen here,' she whispered, 'I don't know what's got into you today Mary—"

Before Angela could tell the woman her name wasn't even Mary, the woman raised her right arm and stuck a bony index finger right in Angela's face, and grabbed her shoulder to shake her.

'—but you have no bloody right to talk down to the very people who are trying to help us, right?'

No one ever threatened Doctor Angela Smith.

'Shit, Mary, why'd you make me do that?' she peered to her left and to her right, 'I'm sorry darl, I didn't mean to grab you like that.'

Angela felt herself struggling to respond, she felt as

if she had no strength in her arms to give the woman a slap back in retaliation, which she badly wanted to do.

Rachel stared down at her lap, 'the nurses are overworked as it is. They work long shifts and they have to deal with the doctors too.'

Angela felt the nausea rising. She felt weak and deep inside felt as if she were standing at the top of a long, slippery slide. If she fell into the slide, there was no way of making it back.

'I thought the doctors here were the best in their field?' Angela responded.

Rachel eyed the ward to ensure there were no staff anywhere in sight.

'Rumour has it,' Rachel said, leaning in closer to confer with Angela, 'I've heard a few nurses talk about one doctor in particular. They call her Vinegar Tits behind her back.'

Angela sat up and found herself curious as to who out of her colleagues these nurses were referring to. 'Who are they talking about?' she said, her mind flicking through images of each of her fellow doctors.

Rachel grinned back at Angela, as if this was a trick question, and Angela gave her a quizzical look, before it dawned on her.

'The nurses say her very own husband had cancer, but Vinegar Tits let him die.'

CHAPTER TWENTY-FOUR

Chad

CHAD STARED UP AT DIPANKAR'S FATHER. IF HE'D known what he was thinking, he thought, he'd go berserk. As the heat from the left side of his cheek subsided, Abhoy spoke in hushed tones and before Chad knew it, he was out the door.

And if he thought this shit couldn't get any weirder, in the tiny confined space, everyone else sat down and proceeded to stare straight at him. For a moment, Chad wondered if they knew he was someone else, before he was ushered out of the entrance of the hut by Dipankar's mother, dragging him by the scuff of his sweaty shirt. She stared back into the hut for a beat, as if making sure that her next words could not be heard. She pulled Chad a few feet down the muddy pathway, and he attempted to sidestep the steady stream of putrid water trickling down the middle.

She lent in close and shook her head.

'Dipankar. I know you are the oldest of our children. But your father. You cannot speak to him like that in front of your brothers and sisters. You know what will happen if he gets mad,' she said.

'That piece of fucking shit, I am going to rip his head off and piss down his throat,' Chad thought, words that thankfully did not pass through Dipankar's lips.

'Okay mother,' Chad said. It seemed like a safe response.

When she stepped closer and stared long into his eyes, he had the strangest feeling. He had never been close to his biological mother, he always felt as if she favoured his little sister. Serena's death wasn't his fault but his mother never let him forget the rift between them, and it had strained their relationship somewhat. But standing here, in this filthy place, he felt a kind of warmth he didn't realise that he needed.

Chad smiled.

'I'm sorry, tell me how to make this up to you,' he said.

As they stood and smiled at each other, Dipankar's father watched from the entrance of the hut, the expression painted on his face anything but warm and fuzzy.

Logan stood at the front door to the apartment, feeling like an intruder. But as he peered into the door's reflection, he caught sight of Courtney's shoes and her clothes. Never had he ever felt so out of sorts. The drive from Courtney's office to her apartment had been a surreal experience, and one taken in silence. He kept thinking about how he'd typed the words 'Samsarana Retreat' into the Google search bar.

'No results found.' Three words he was unable to escape during the entire 30-minute drive, almost as if they were everywhere. On every street sign, every billboard. Every number plate.

No results found.

He wanted to call Beth. Hearing her voice would have been enough. How would he begin to explain all of this to her? Logan knew he would come across as being out of his gourd, and she would think Courtney had lost her mind.

Not only that, there was 'another' Logan parading as her husband.

'Jesus Christ,' he said to himself, standing at the door.

He fished Courtney's keys from her handbag and after three failed attempts at finding the right key, the fourth key slipped into the hole and turned with little effort.

He knew, as he pulled into the underground garage

of the East Bayfront Apartments that Courtney's place was likely to have magnificent views of Lake Ontario. He was not disappointed. It was stunning. As he walked toward the ceiling-to-floor windows, the view out and across the lake from the tenth floor had Logan experiencing a touch of envy. She was obviously doing well for herself, he thought with annoyance. The exorbitant fees he and Beth paid at every session, had paid for this expensive pad. The holiday to Bali was booked through Courtney too. He wondered how much profit she'd made on that trip. As he contemplated this, Courtney's phone pinged. The message on the screen made him grit his teeth.

It was the same guy from a short time ago.

Only now he was standing at the door.

Logan panicked. What the fuck was he supposed to do now?

CHAPTER TWENTY-FIVE

Amelia

AMELIA HEARD A FAMILIAR SOUND. SHE SAT DEAD still on the bed and listened.

Zzzz. Zzzz. Zzzz.

Amelia scanned Margarita's bed, checking the dresser drawers. Zzzz.

There it was again.

She turned her attention back to Margarita's bed, slipped her hand underneath the pillow, and pulled out Margarita's phone, groaning when the screen came to life. The Kardashians and Jenners again, their smiles beaming back at her. What the hell was it with her obsession with this family?

Margarita had received a message. Swiping the screen, Amelia accessed it and the attached video. Someone had been filming earlier at the pool, when the cup of soft drink was thrown over her, and her heart sank as she could hear people in the video laughing at Margarita as if it were the funniest thing they'd ever seen. It sounded like a group of girls.

When the clip ended, Amelia realised whoever sent the video had also sent a message too: 'lookin' good at pool today fatty lol time to trim those brows too thanks for the show ugly rita'

Amelia read it twice before bursting into tears. Could this damn day get any worse?

It had been decades since she'd been bullied. Except back then there were no smartphones. Now the bullies could get to you anywhere, anytime.

Spotting Margarita's school bag slumped against her desk, Amelia shuddered. If she was getting bullied at home on the weekend, what would it be like for her at school?

Amelia had not slept, following a visit from Margarita's mother, who had by that stage heard the full story from Antonio. She spent most of the evening staring at the ceiling, occasionally checking her own social media profiles, hoping for a clue about what this was all about, or, more importantly, how she could snap her fingers and return to being herself.

There was nothing.

Amelia was then struck by a thought.

Pierre.

The issue was – she couldn't remember his number. She cursed herself – it was in her phone, she'd never had to memorise it. Flicking to Instagram, she found his account and began to type him a message.

Halfway through, she stopped.

Pierre received dozens of messages a year, people trying to get to her through him. Some sounded as if they should be locked up in a padded room, with the key Fed-Ex'd to Mars.

'Shit,' she whispered into the darkness, staring at his smug face on the screen.

There had to be a way.

Her mind drifted to Australia, and her heart panged when she thought about the upcoming movie she was due to shoot. Amelia felt as if she'd been robbed. By now, she should have been in Far North Queensland, rubbing shoulders with a Hemsworth.

'The retreat!' she exclaimed.

Amelia began to type the words into the search bar, but felt her desperation rising.

'FUCK!' she said, loud enough for her brother to respond through two closed doors.

'Go to sleep, Rita!' he said with an authoritative tone.

It dawned on Amelia in a flash. Gemma had booked the holiday and all the other arrangements had gone through Pierre. Amelia cursed again, quietly this time, and knew she would have to search through retreat listings in Bali to find it. For hours she searched TripAdvisor, Booking dot com, Expedia, Best Retreats in Bali dot com, Retreats in Bali dot com, where-in-god's-name-is-the-name-of-the-retreat-she-visited dot com.

Amelia felt something inside of her twist, as her mind tried to reconcile her nagging thoughts. She could not find the Samsarana Retreat. Either it wasn't listed in any shape or form, anywhere online, or there was another reason – and this one hurt her head – it didn't exist. For the second time in a day, Amelia began to cry and this time, couldn't stop.

As the morning light broke through the curtains, she felt sick with the prospect of having to go to school, trapped in Margarita's body. Hearing movement downstairs, she made the decision to not go. She would say she was sick. But at 7.15am, someone else had other ideas. Antonio didn't even bother knocking.

'Hurry up Rita, we can't miss the bus, come on!' he said.

He was gone before she'd had the chance to say no, and five minutes later, Amelia's plea's fell on deaf ears.

'No Margarita. Those awful girls at school are not going to ruin your life. The only way out is to be brave,' Margarita's mother said.

'Easy for you to say,' thought Amelia.

Amelia slipped into a pair of jeans and found a windcheater draped over the end of the bed. When she turned and saw herself in the mirror, she could not help but want to crawl back underneath the bedsheets.

Somehow, she made it downstairs. A solitary piece of toast sat on a plate on the kitchen bench, covered with what appeared to be some sort of chocolate spread like Nutella. Amelia sniffed it and made a face.

'Eat up Rita, we are out of here in a couple of minutes,' her brother said, not even looking up from his phone.

Amelia couldn't recall the last time she had a piece of toast, let alone with Nutella spread all over it, and ate it with reluctance, longing for an egg-white omelette, accompanied by an Espresso, or a Bloody Mary. Or today, maybe both.

Amelia picked up the school bag and after an awkward hug from Margarita's mother, followed Antonio out the front door, who, after placing earphones in his ears and slipping sunglasses on over his eyes, headed off down the street. All Amelia could do was follow and hope this time she could keep up.

The Los Angeles morning sky gave Amelia a sense of comfort, at last something familiar, and something that they could not take away from her. She loved the clear blue sky of cloudless mornings, albeit often shrouded in a layer of smog by the end of rush hour most weekdays. As she trailed her brother, keeping up with his rapid pace was made difficult by the jeans pulling tightly around her thighs.

Antonio, was apparently in no mood to talk to her.

Ten minutes later, to her relief, he stopped at a bus stop, glancing back in her direction.

Before she could catch her breath, the bus pulled up with a squeal of brakes and exhaust fumes. Amelia couldn't recall ever travelling on public transport before, but watched Antonio closely, as he walked down the aisle without her, flopping into a seat next to another boy.

They nodded, neither bothered to take either their earphones out, or sunglasses off. Amelia could only assume they knew each other.

The back of the bus was filled with other students. Feeling unsure what to do or where to sit, Amelia slipped down into an empty seat halfway down from the front.

As the bus pulled out, she wondered what would happen if she were to ask the bus driver to take her to an address in Holmby Hills. After a few moments, Amelia could hear the sound of sneering and laughter coming from the other students at the back of the bus. Margarita's phone pinged in her hand. Another message from a random number.

'Mornin miss piggy,' was all it said.

After more sneers and laughter, a group of girls sitting at the back of the bus made Amelia wish she'd followed her gut instinct and not come to school today.

'Oink, Oink. Oink Oink,' they said at the same time, in between laughter.

CHAPTER TWENTY-SIX

Logan

LOGAN FUMBLED FOR THE VOLUME SWITCH, BUT before he could turn the darn sound off, it went off again. In the silent apartment, the noise amplified. Stifling a breath, Logan checked the message.

'I presume that you're still getting ready for me?'

Logan felt his stomach lurch at the knock on the door, more insistent this time. His first reaction was to ignore it and hide. He turned to make a run for it, but Courtney's heeled shoes betrayed him on the tiled floor of her apartment.

'Mother Fu—' he went to say, but the guy was already onto him.

'I can hear you, you know. How long are you going to make me wait, Hot Buns?'

Logan stopped dead in his tracks. Hot Buns? He

needed to deal with this guy, and fast. He clip-clopped to the door, yanked it open, ready to tell this sucker to beat it. He did it with such force the guy stepped back in alarm.

But not as alarmed as Logan, as soon as he recognised the man standing before him.

Chad

When Chad returned to the hut, he saw Dipankar's brothers and sisters sitting on the floor, a look of fear etched on their faces. None of them attempted to make eye contact with him, except the youngest girl, who met his eyes. He could see she was fighting back tears. Her bottom lip quivered, but she sat there in complete silence.

Dipankar's mother spoke, 'we need to prepare for sleep soon. It may be best if we do this before Father comes back.'

'Where has he gone?' Chad asked without giving the question any thought whatsoever.

The other kids bristled, especially the youngest girl.

Dipankar's mother gave him an astonished look, before taking a deep breath and shaking her head.

Jesus, Chad thought, *who is this frigging guy?*

'To work,' Dipankar's mother said, although the

expression on her face did not reflect any truth in her answer.

Chad stood there for a few awkward moments as the other children began shuffling around on the dirt floor. He couldn't believe what he was witnessing. Half of the floor was bare ground and the other half was covered with worn, thin cardboard in different shapes and sizes.

None of them had a pillow.

As they shuffled close to each other, he realised why there was a gap between the youngest girl and the wall of the hut on the opposite side. The look on the little girl's face, beckoning Chad to lie down next to her, made him realise that Dipankar made her feel safe.

The last thing he wanted to do was lie down on the floor of this hut. But with everything that had gone on today, he could feel mental and physical exhaustion catching up with him. As the others shuffled about before lying still, Chad knew the time was up. If he did anything other than lie down on the thin piece of cardboard, he'd be asking for trouble.

He laid on his back and stared up at the ramshackle ceiling.

His Kluft mattress at home in Boston cost him $39,950 two years ago. It was worth every cent. It was insanely comfortable and he couldn't recall the last time he'd had an average night's sleep. Now, he was lying on wafer thin cardboard. He could feel the dirt on his legs, his bare feet touching the earth, weaving its way into the gaps of his toes.

Chad wasn't a fan of sleeping without a pillow either, but right now, he'd even take a $7 Walmart one over this. But as the back of his head began to register how hard the ground was, he knew the chances of any pillow tonight were as slim as the slither of cardboard he was lying on.

'Dipankar,' she whispered.

Chad felt a tiny little tap on the side of his arm, from Dipankar's little sister, lying right next to him. Before Chad could think of what to do or say, she came closer and whispered in his ear.

'Can you hold my hand, Dipankar? I'm scared I won't be able to sleep unless you do.'

It wasn't the sound of her voice that persuaded Chad to open his hand and let hers rest in his, it was the fear he could hear in her words.

As he lay there, eyes open, staring at the piece of tin fixed to the roof with rope, he found himself thinking of the only sister he'd ever had, and for the first time in his life, Chad thought about how badly he had treated her.

Chad had never laid a hand on his sister Serena, but he had tormented her verbally and emotionally, forever making fun of her, demeaning and teasing her both at home and at school. His parents had threatened to ship him off to boarding school if he didn't stop. His good behaviour lasted a few weeks before his old habits returned. A year before her trip to Asia, it had all come to a head. After months of his relentless, childish behaviour, Serena had had enough. A rumour had been circulating around school for some weeks about Chad's 'performance' one night at a recent weekend party. The word in the locker rooms, was that Chad had stage fright during a private interlude with a female student and Chad's 'little Chad' had failed to rise to the occasion. He'd tried to blame it on the Budweiser's but the girl couldn't help but share the incident with her friends. It didn't take his fellow students long to come up with a nickname. Droopy, the Basset Hound. For weeks he had endured students barking every time they walked past.

Woof. Woof.

And finally, Serena Miller had something epic over her older brother.

Chad arrived home this particular night, licking his wounds, his pride in tatters. When he came into the kitchen, Serena was at the stove, with her back to him. He didn't bother to say hello, grunting as he opened the fridge, concealing her momentarily from his view. Serena cleared her throat.

'Woof. Woof,' she said, and as Chad closed the door, she turned her back to him and tended to the pot and pan on the stove.

'What the fuck did you say?' Chad snarled.

She turned to him and grinned.

'You heard me, Droopy.'

The beer bottle was already travelling at high speed from Chad's thrown arm at Serena, before it hitting her fair and square in the jaw. Ten stitches to Serena's chin later, the doctors said that she was lucky that the projectile didn't collide with her skull a few inches higher.

Chad was grounded for 3 months.

He stopped taunting her, but didn't speak to her unless he had to. Not once did he apologise.

As he lay with Dipankar's sister's little hand in his, Chad pictured Serena's face and for the first time in his life felt something he'd never felt before.

Regret.

CHAPTER TWENTY-SEVEN

Angela

Angela felt her cheeks flush. Either it was Mary's declining physical condition, or the radiation therapy, or both.

'That's bullshit!' she said, not caring how her comment was received.

Her fellow cancer patient gave her a quizzical look.

'What?' Rachel said.

Angela shook her head.

'I don't believe it,' she said, trying in vain to come across as someone who had no vested interest in the conversation.

Problem was, it wasn't working.

'Did you hit your head in the little girl's room?' Cold-arse smirked.

'No!' Angela spat back.

Rachel took a sip of water from her cup.

'Okay,' Rachel sat upright as best she could, 'so you think what I am telling you is bollocks?'

When was this bloody nightmare going to end?

As if on cue, Dr Angela Smith walked past the two women moments later, in her usual brusque manner.

Angela turned back to Rachel and shook her head.

'I'm feeling a bit off today,' she said. 'Remind me what the nurses told you about her?'

Rachel scanned each side of the ward, carefully.

'Vinegar is the most loathed Doctor on this floor. She's most likely the most disliked Doctor in this entire hospital,' Cold-arse said in hushed tones.

'The entire hospital?' Angela knew she wouldn't be high on the Hospital's Christmas card list, but being quoted as the most hated was a bit of a stretch. Surely.

'Do you wonder why this ward has such a high turnover of nurses, my dear Mary?' Rachel said. Before Angela could retort, Cold-arse continued, 'they only hang in there for a year so that it will look good on their resume. Rachel took a long and deep breath, although she was enjoying holding court and dishing the dirt. 'So, one of the nurses was talking to another patient, who gave me all the gossip. Even her only child thinks she's the devil incarnate! I don't know how this nurse found out, I think someone who knows someone, is friends with his girlfriend. What's the thing they say, "ten degrees of separation?"' Rachel burst into unannounced laughter before she clutched her chest.

Angela was reeling. Jack hated her? He thought she was the Devil? She felt blindsided, wounded.

'Six degrees, Cold-arse,' she said under her breath.

Rachel nodded, not at all concerned she was four points off.

'So, does the girlfriend share her son's views?' Angela asked.

Rachel shrugged her shoulders, inverting her lips before turning it into a grin.

'What do you think, Mary? If your very own son thought you were the evilest creature on planet earth, what do you think his girlfriend thinks?'

Angela would never speak to Sophie ever again. The self-righteous little bitch. For that matter, she wondered how she would ever find it in herself to speak to Jack again.

'So, she's a little on the non-fluffy side,' Angela said, 'but she sure as hell knows what she is doing.'

Rachel gave Mary another quizzical look.

'You got a soft spot for the Vinegar?' she mused, glancing around the room, wondering if anyone else was cottoning on to this little nugget of information.

Angela was about to defend herself, but hesitated. It was enough for Cold-arse to break into a wide grin.

'What in the lord's name happened to you in the toilet, Mary?' she shook her head but never lost the grin. 'You hated her yesterday,' she added.

Angela was now getting pissed off. She was losing control of her anger, as she often did.

She felt the overall predicament she was trapped in closing in on her, as other patients seemed to be now watching her and Rachel deep in conversation.

'It's not just the nurses who call her Vinegar Tits, Mary. The other doctors on this floor and many others throughout the hospital, all call her this behind her back. They even take it one step further and use a code word whenever they're around her. If I didn't loathe her myself, I would find it a little awful to be honest.'

Now Angela was fully invested in this conversation.

'What's the code word?' Angela said.

Rachel once again checked both ends of the ward, looking out for Dr Smith. If she overheard what she was about to tell Mary, Cold-arse may find herself in deep shit with the very nurses she was defending.

'They use the code word T.V.,' Rachel grinned.

'I don't get—' replied Angela, and it then dawned on her.

Vinegar.

Tits.

V.T.

T.V. was the initial in reverse. How original.

'But here's the kicker,' Rachel lent in closer. 'When Dr Smith is on duty, the nurses and even some doctors play this game. What they do, is see how many times they can use the term T.V. around her. They even have a secret sweep, every week. The one who can say the term T.V. or even Television, around Vinegar Tits the most, gets the pot at the end of the week.'

Angela was ready to stand up and start laying into every nurse who worked on the floor, but something jogged her memory. She swallowed, her throat dry from all this talking.

'And I guess they get a bonus if they mention T.V. or Television to Vinegar Tits herself?'

Cold-arse broke into a fit of laughter.

'So, you do remember!'

Angela felt as if she'd been sucker-punched. Every week the nurses and to her annoyance, many of the doctors, asked her the same question. She never understood why they ever bloody well did.

'What are you watching on T.V. tonight,' or if it were a Friday, 'What are you watching on television this weekend, Dr Smith?'

Angela's hands curled into balls of rage and Rachel rose from the bed.

'I guess I will fill you in about all the gossip surrounding V.T.'s dead husband another time,' she said, as she lifted herself off Mary's bed.

As she did, Angela opened one eye and stared long at the back of the woman's head.

The first thing she would do, when she returned to her own body, was find Rachel and sort her out.

The nurses and Doctors too.

God help them all.

CHAPTER TWENTY-EIGHT

Logan

'Shit!' Logan said. 'What the fuck are you doing here?' he blurted.

Of all the men to be standing at the door, it had to be this middle-aged fucker on the prowl, he thought.

The man certainly wasn't looking for this type of greeting tonight. Not with a three ounce bottle of lubricant in one hand and a bottle of Dom Pérignon Brut Champagne in the other.

'Courtney?' the man said, regaining his composure.

Logan was flummoxed. The shock of recognizing the man standing at Courtney's door sent a shock wave throughout his entire body. *Well err, Courtney's body.* He felt as if he were about to faint.

Logan stared at him for one further second before slamming the door, pulling off Courtney's shoes and running towards her bedroom, dumping her phone on the counter on the way through and slamming her bedroom door shut behind him, ignoring the sound of the persistent knocking on the front door.

When he saw the bathroom, Logan repeated the process, until there were no more doors to slam behind him. He stood against the vanity, staring at the bathtub, and shuddered when he realised just why he may have ended up with that creep at the front door.

When was this nightmare going to end?

Amelia

Amelia wondered if she slouched far enough down in her seat, then perhaps she would be out of view and the girls making fun of her would stop. The jibes, snickers, laughter and pig sounds continued for another five torturous minutes.

'Oink. Oink.'

When the bus finally pulled up on Sunset Boulevard, the school kids rose from their seats and shuffled their way towards the rear door. Amelia remained seated until she knew she would be the last one to get off.

When she finally did, she turned and stopped.

A school girl was standing in middle of the aisle staring her down, and the movie star felt a sense of dread. The girl stood there with a grin on her face. She was tall, with blonde hair. pulled taut into a high ponytail.

'Come on Rita,' she said, 'no time to waste,' she added, gesturing for Amelia to exit in front of her.

There was something in the glint of the girl's eyes and how she worked her jaw trying to suppress a smirk, but Amelia had no choice but to swallow the dread and do as she was told.

Amelia took the first step down, and the girl grabbed her schoolbag, pinning Amelia's shoulders back. She leaned in close and Amelia could feel her breath in her ear. Her voice was calm, which made it all the more unnerving.

'Kermit was not here to protect you today, Miss Piggy,' she whispered. The girl released Amelia's school bag, sending her sprawling down the steps towards the pavement and Amelia stumbled forward, struggling to remain upright, but the other girls who'd been making fun of her were waiting right outside for their ring-leader, and they'd cushioned Amelia's fall as she came flying out of the bus.

Amelia snapped.

For the first time since she'd become this poor, bullied school girl, her ego kicked in.

'Fucking enough,' she spat as she collided with the other girls, who pushed her away as she grappled for her balance.

'Watch it, fatty,' said one of the girls.

She felt a tap on her shoulder, Amelia turned

around and realised it was the blonde girl, looking down at her. The bus had gone. Blonde saw the grins on the faces of other girls standing behind Amelia, before she glared at her.

'No one man handles my girls, little porky,' she said and without any hesitation, her left foot sprang out and tripped her up. But if the blonde had ever checked out the biography of Amelia Langston on Wikipedia, there'd be one little detail which may have been of interest to her. Amelia was a black belt in Chun Kuk Do, known these days as the Chuck Norris System. Her father had known Carlo Ray (Chuck) Norris since their time in US Air Force in Korea. She was one of his youngest students in his emerging Karate discipline.

In a total of about 1.6 seconds, Amelia shifted her feet into a solid stance and shot out her right hand. As her open palmed hand deflected Blonde's foot with centrifugal force, the girl lost her balance, her right foot twisting as her body began to stumble and in the same motion fell backwards.

Although Amelia had no intention of doing anything other than deflecting, her second move was so swift she followed through and before she could pull back, the damage was done. She'd hit the other girl in the stomach. Blonde fell, groaning in pain, and the stunned school girls parted to watch Margarita Serrano adjust the school bag on her back, before rolling her shoulders and walking away.

She didn't look back.

CHAPTER TWENTY-NINE

Chad

MOVEMENT TO HIS LEFT ROUSED CHAD FROM SLEEP and he sighed as the sickening reality slapped him hard in the face. He was still Dipankar. He was still in the slums of Dhaka.

'Dip?' although there were hushed conversations in the hut from the brothers and sisters, Chad searched for the origin of the voice and found it in the doorway.

Abhoy.

Chad surprised himself by feeling relief seeing the guy standing there, poking his head through the door.

'Abhoy,' Chad said, 'what is it?'

Abhoy gave him a quizzical look and flicked his head outward and Chad rose to his feet and stepped over the others. The two oldest siblings were sitting up, whispering to each other, whilst the two younger ones remained asleep.

Chad's muscles were tight and aching from sleeping on the ground and he wondered where he could find a pillow for the next night. If there was a next night.

Abhoy shook his head before a small grin appeared on his face. Chad would recall a thought about this moment much later on – Abhoy always seemed to be in a good mood.

'How's the head, Dip?' he grinned.

Chad shrugged his shoulders, in an instant realising he may be making a rod for his own back by insinuating he was fine. He needed Abhoy to believe he wasn't okay and his memory, as Dipankar, was playing up.

'Oh my head's still sore,' Chad fashioned a frown on his face and added, 'I didn't sleep last night,' for good measure.

Abhoy studied him.

'Well, let's get going,' Abhoy said finally.

'Are we going to work?'

Abhoy bristled, before shaking his head, 'not yet, Dip, first we need to get something to eat. You did hit your head hard yesterday, huh?' he said.

Chad followed Abhoy as he shuffled off down the path.

To where, he had no idea.

Abhoy took him through the heart of the slums, the paths so narrow in some places they had to jostle through people moving in the other direction. Most were reasonable and everyone seemed to be going about their own business. But from time to time, Chad would make eye contact with strangers who would make his skin crawl.

Most appeared as if they'd not bathed in months, which he guessed they hadn't. Everyone wore a layer of filth as if it was a spray-tan available at some nearby booth.

Clothing was the same. Dirty, old and in tatters. But from time to time, he would spot someone wearing a long sleeved shirt, or a sports jersey which appeared unusually clean – carrying an air about them too, as if they were proud to be wearing a piece of clothing fit for a wealthy man. Footwear was a low priority, it seemed, found at the bottom of the list following food, water and shelter.

Abhoy moved on through the narrow walkways at a brisk pace, and Chad worked hard to stay on his tail. Through the haze of people and low-hanging smog, Chad could see the pathway growing wider. The two boys came to the end of the shanty town and at this point Chad realised why the smell of rotting waste was suddenly so overwhelming. It was a stench he would not easily forget. An enormous garbage dump stretched out before him and he found it hard to believe a tip could be of this magnitude. It stretched out in all directions for what must have been miles. Dozens of birds squawked among themselves in the air above, all evidently searching for their next meal. As Abhoy lead Dipankar further into the foul smelling wasteland, it dawned on Chad why they had come.

They were here – to do the same.

'What's wrong, Dip?' he said. The millionaire stood there, horrified. He would have thrown up, had there been anything in his stomach to begin with.

Not waiting for an answer, Abhoy continued on his way and Chad snapped out of his shock and followed behind as Abhoy waved to a stranger in the distance. He was of similar age, build and looked busy.

When they reached him, he checked Dipankar over, warily.

'What's with him?'

'The Supervisor made him fall,' Abhoy said, 'he hit his head.'

The guy shrugged his shoulders.

'Whatever,' he muttered, pulling something from the flimsy bag he was carrying.

He handed a smaller bag to Chad and said, 'don't eat it all at once.'

Chad took the bag and wondered what the hell it was. Upon closer inspection, he could see that it was the plastic packaging for a loaf of bread. But it was virtually empty.

'Money,' he said.

'What for?' Chad said.

The kid, not much bigger in physical size to Dipankar, all of a sudden snatched the bag out of Chad's hand. Abhoy raised his hands.

'Easy, Dip, give him the money.'

Chad turned to him and said, 'I don't have any money.'

Abhoy rolled his eyes and pulled some coins from his own pocket. He handed the money over and was given the bread bag without a word.

'This is breakfast?' Chad asked.

He opened the bag and couldn't believe what was in there. No bread, only a handful of crusts. *What. The. Fuck,* he thought. Chad wanted to run after the kid. They'd been ripped off.

'Your brothers and sisters will be getting hungry,' Abhoy said.

Chad was gobsmacked.

Abhoy stepped closer to Chad.

'Remember, we need to keep them healthy. Don't forget our plans. It will be happening soon.'

Chad stared into Abhoy's eyes, trying to avert suspicion. He knew he'd have to try to figure it out later. He quickly changed the subject.

'But the money I earn at the factory. Can't we afford to buy something better than this to eat?' he asked.

Abhoy shook his head in disbelief.

'Don't tell me you have forgotten where your money goes.'

Chad's gut told him the answer would not please him. His gut was spot on.

'To your father,' Abhoy finished.

CHAPTER THIRTY

Angela

ANGELA SPENT THE FIRST FULL NIGHT TRAPPED IN Mary's body staring at the ceiling. Although the ward was in darkness, sleep was eluding her. Try as she may, she still could not figure out why this was happening to her. After all, there was an answer for everything.

But not this.

She loathed anyone who believed in the supernatural. All anyone had to do to get her hot and bothered was to ask Dr Smith if she believed in UFO's, ghosts, or the goddamned Loch Ness Monster. Don't even dare mention Bigfoot, or as one of her patients once humorously misnamed 'the abdominal snowman.' She would fight to the death arguing the famous 1967 American footage claiming to film a real life bigfoot was nothing more than an actor in an ape suit taking the piss out of anyone silly enough to think otherwise.

As the hours drifted by, Angela still believed this was all a dream and at any moment she would wake up, back in her own body. She wondered if the trip to Bali was all part of the dream and found herself cursing under her breath in the silent ward.

Cold-arse, bugger me, Angela fumed. Rachel snored as if she'd had a change of body experience too. Maybe the real person inside her was a truck driver who'd been to the local pub and had downed nine pints of Guinness. It sure as hell sounded like it.

The sea of thoughts in her head ceased as she finally drifted off into a deep sleep.

Angela opened her eyes and sat up, startled that it was daylight. Rays of morning sunshine beamed through the windows, with the false promise that today was going to be a better day.

Nurses and patients mingled in other parts of the ward. Rachel was done snoring, her bed was empty. Her attention turned to the foot of her bed. Standing there was Doctor Angela Smith FRCPE.

'What?' Angela snapped from her bed.

Doctor Smith stared at her.

Angela felt trapped in a kind of surreal alternative

reality whilst she was staring at herself. This was five ways weird and when things got weird, Angela always got angry.

'Why are you standing there, staring at me?' Mary said.

The corners of Dr Smith's lips seemed to curl into a snarl. She turned to a nearby nurse.

'Wilson, radiation,' she barked.

Angela laid there for a moment before she realised that it was her that was supposed to be going to radiation therapy.

'NO!' she barked.

Doctor Smith gave her a withered look.

'Excuse me?' she said.

Angela sat up in her bed. She was going to give the nursing staff something to talk about over lunch, that was for certain.

'Don't speak to me like that,' she spat. 'And I'm not going to any radiation therapy.'

Dr Smith walked a couple of steps towards the patient, seemingly surprised at her fiery words. Mary had woken up on the wrong side of bed, that was for sure, she thought. Not that she cared.

'Suit yourself,' the Doctor said, turning and walking off.

'You want it to win, sooner rather than later, your choice,' she huffed as she walked away.

Angela heard the words and in a flash of confused

anger, found herself angry – with herself, the other Dr Angela Smith.

'No wonder your husband's dead,' she sneered.

Her doppelgänger stopped, appearing to bristle at Angela's words, before walking away, her clipped heels echoing from the other side of the ward.

CHAPTER THIRTY-ONE

Logan

FULLY CLOTHED, LOGAN FELL ONTO COURTNEY'S bed and was asleep in seconds. He woke to the sound of a fire truck roaring down Queens Quay, and Logan could see from the light outside that it was morning. He sat up in bed before quickly realising that he was still trapped in Courtney's body. He felt as if he were Robin Williams, dressed as Mrs Doubtfire, in full make up. But unlike the actor, no matter how closely he looked at his image in the mirror, Logan was nowhere to be seen because the eyes staring back at him in the mirror adjacent to the bed were Courtney's. He studied her face, hoping that by some weird act of cosmic magic, the woman staring back at him in the mirror would provide some credible explanation.

As he waited for an answer he knew would never

come, a chill ran over his body as he recalled the events of the night before.

Jerry Springhare was here.

His boss, and Courtney Lushgrove…together?

What.

The.

Fuck.

The manager at Woodbridge Tesla was nicknamed – not unsurprisingly – Jerry Springer, not helped by the fact that he wore similar glasses to the nineties television host. If he shed a few pounds, he would be the spitting image of him. But there was one little detail scraping the insides of Logan's mind now. Jerry Springer was the most married man Logan had ever met. A veteran of the profession, two and a half decades in.

Logan pulled himself out of bed. When he found where he'd thrown Courtney's phone the night before, Logan hesitated. Jerry had sent scores of messages, signed with what had obviously been Courtney's nick-name for him.

Big Boy.

Sweet mother of Jesus, Logan thought. He felt a queasiness rise in his empty stomach.

Big Boy had been busy, judging by his high-octane enthusiasm.

A calendar notification popped up, and he scrolled through to see what sort of day lay ahead for her, wondering if he was obligated to carry it out. For the second time in a matter of seconds, he found himself cursing out loud, using words his mother would not have appreciated. Courtney had a full day of appointments. The first one was at nine.

Logan placed the phone on the counter and wandered over to the apartment windows. As the sun rose over Lake Ontario and Toronto Islands in the foreground, he took a deep, painful breath.

'Why?' he said to the world outside.

The total silence of the apartment offered no response.

Logan stood back and thought about the day he was about to have. He would have to shower, dress and find something for breakfast. And at some point try to make himself look presentable. Courtney always appeared well-dressed, Logan considered. In her earlier years, Courtney would have been a pretty good-looking woman. She still was, he thought, although not his type.

His mind ticked off what he needed to do before he left. The showering, dressing and breakfast sections of the morning seemed doable. But there was one thing which sent shivers down his spine.

The makeup part.

Three hours after waking to the wailing sound of the sirens of the city fire trucks, Logan pulled into the carpark of Courtney's office suite.

Show time.

The three hours in between had been challenging. Taking a shower in Courtney's body for starters, then trying to figure out what to wear. Breakfast was a non-event. The only thing resembling a breakfast dish was a huge bag of organic bran flakes. Bran was the breakfast for four legged creatures you bet on at the racetrack. And 'organic' to Logan meant eco-tastes-like-shit because all the fun stuff (mostly sugar) had been left out.

Fortunately for Logan, Courtney enjoyed a decent coffee at home. The Juro Giga 6 Coffee Machine screamed big dollars and came with a myriad of knobs and buttons but once Logan figured out how to get it working, it produced a latte good enough to take in a travel mug for the drive to work.

He stepped out of the car and wondered how he was going to get through each of the appointments unscathed. Six one hour long appointments. All couples who were handing over wads of cash to have a woman, who was sleeping with a married man, tell them how to make their marriage work. What a bloody hypocrite, Logan thought. When the day came, if it came, the first thing he would do when he was himself again would be to pay Courtney Lushgrove a visit and tell that to her face.

When he arrived at the office suites, handbag awkwardly slung over one arm, his mind parked the issue with Courtney. It was time to bullshit his way through a day's work. Surely, counselling couldn't be too different to sales, he thought. He had done it hundreds of times before – convincing people that a car would be perfect for them regardless if it was the truth or not, but even Logan knew that his bullshit-o-meter would be red-lining all day.

When he reached the top of the stairs, he took a deep breath as the glass doors of Courtney's office came into view. Her receptionist was at the front desk, typing away on her keyboard.

Here goes.

'Don't say Tinder. Don't say Tinder. Don't call her Tinder.' Logan took a deep breath as he pulled the door open, and the receptionist took her gaze off the screen and smiled as her boss entered.

'Morning Courtney!' she beamed. 'Top of the morning!'

Logan noticed a sudden change in the young girl's expression, as he took a couple of steps towards her.

'Morning Tinder!'

Shit! 'Tind-wer, Tind-wer, Tindwer.

'How was your evening?' Logan felt relief at the fact that the receptionist was keen to move on. But as her eyes met his, he could tell there was something about him, or rather, Courtney, that was off to her.

'Not bad,' was all he said in response, before he dumped the handbag in Courtney's office and slipped into the bathroom.

Although he'd done his best attempt with her

makeup before he left Courtney's apartment, knowing it was subpar, Logan was relatively sure he didn't look like a hooker doing tricks at 3am. Now, he looked at the bathroom mirror and gasped. Courtney's red lipstick was smeared over the lower half of his face.

The coffee cup. Shit.

For the first time during this hellish ordeal, Logan saw the humour in his situation.

As he went about making himself look presentable, Logan overheard Tindwer greeting someone with the same intoxicating enthusiasm as she had done when he first entered the office.

His first appointment for the day.

Seven hours later, exhausted, Logan wondered how he was supposed to do this five days a week. Every couple, except for the last appointment, had issues way beyond two people who'd fallen out of love for each other. He would have to work hard tomorrow to even appear to know what the hell he was doing.

Not to mention, still trying to figure out how to get back.

'Courtney—,' Tindwer's voice came through the intercom, having long forgotten his misstep with her name, '—your 4.00 pm appointment is here.'

Logan was so spent, he couldn't be bothered

checking the appointment sheet to see the names of the couple about to enter.

'Send them in,' he said, staring out of the office window for a moment.

He wondered where his wife was and what she was doing. He felt a pang somewhere deep. It surprised him to realise that he missed her.

A sound at his door snapped him out of his momentary daydream. When he saw the woman walk into the room, he was taken aback at her familiar face. But when the woman's husband entered the room directly behind her, Logan's lungs turned to stone.

You can't be serious.

Jerry Springhare.

Logan's Boss.

Middle-aged-fucker-on-the-prowl.

Big-Boy.

Shit.

CHAPTER THIRTY-TWO

Amelia

AMELIA'S FIRST DAY AT SCHOOL AS MARGARITA WAS arduous, to say the least. Returning to the classroom after all these years was one thing, doing it trapped in someone else's body was another. The line between a bit of innocent, schoolyard fun – and the edge of the abyss where all too often, vulnerable kids pummelled by constant bullying decide there was only one way out was a thin one. Amelia had no idea how Margarita had survived the taunts, the name-calling and being pushed around the busy hallways between classes.

When the bell rang at 3.10 pm, the first thing Amelia wanted to do was flee. She couldn't wait to get back to the safety of Margarita's room at her house, where she would barricade the door and begin to attempt to unravel the mystery of how she got there.

She searched for Antonio in the halls, but couldn't find him. Recalling the bus route from this morning, she retraced her steps from the bus stop at Western Ave near Lemon Grove Ave and up to the left turn at Sunset Boulevard. As she found her way down Orange Drive and rounded the corner on Sunset Boulevard, she suddenly froze. The only saving grace was the bullies on the bus from this morning were all busy face down on their smartphones. Amelia took one step forward, for a moment thinking she could handle it. But when she saw the blonde girl from that morning's altercation, she hesitated. Without knowing how long it would take, Amelia made a snap decision. She would walk home. And so, she headed off down Sunset Boulevard, ducking into an alley when the Bus drove past. Twenty-five minutes later, Amelia felt exhausted from her walk. Hot and sweaty, she stopped for a few seconds in the shade. Out of the corner of her eye, she spotted a building up ahead.

5808 Sunset Boulevard. Netflix.

Amelia walked as if in a trance, towards the building.

Gemma worked there. Her best friend who had talked her into going to Bali with her, the one who for all intents and purposes, could still be lying next to her in the meditation room at the resort, or, could be sitting in her office on the eleventh floor.

The security guard at the front entrance area didn't let her get within twenty feet of the front door, even when Amelia dropped Gemma's full name, job title and direct phone number.

'No appointment, no entry, young lady,' the bored security guard said. He indicated the conversation was now over, turning his attention to someone else approaching the front door.

When she finally arrived home, Margarita's mother told her she was off to the supermarket to fetch some groceries.

'And don't forget your homework' she said as she opened the front door.

The hell with homework, Amelia thought. What was the point?

Her mind flicked back to the Netflix building and the one employee she was desperate to speak to. Her best friend. As she sat at the kitchen table, feeling relieved that she was home alone, Amelia wondered what she would say to her if she were able to even get through to her.

After searching the kitchen cupboards, she found a glass and poured some water into it and as she drank, something on the bench caught her eye. A pile of letters and bills sat to one side of the kitchen bench, but it was the third document down and the logo in the top-left corner that caused her to do a double take.

She moved closer to the bench and setting her glass

down, she pulled out the document and stared at the familiar logo in disbelief.

Stonelang Productions. Her own production company. As she pulled the letter out and read a few lines, her heart sank. It was a letter of termination addressed to Francisco Serrano, a contractor for a movie she'd recently worked on. It was supposed to be her debut as a producer. However, the project had run out of funding a few months in. Many had accused her of mismanagement.

Amelia dropped the letter back on the pile, suddenly feeling sick. The signature that had authorised the termination was hers.

CHAPTER THIRTY-THREE

Chad

CHAD HANDED OVER THE BAG OF CRUSTS TO ONE of Dipankar's sisters. The other three siblings hovered around her as if they'd not eaten in weeks.

Chad couldn't watch.

He stepped through the front door and welcomed the ephemeral breeze on his face, but not the stench. He stepped back closer to the wall and watched the world around him. The slums were like nothing he'd ever seen before. Smoke billowed from makeshift chimneys dotted throughout the mass of rusty corrugated sheets of iron. They stretched out in all directions as far as his eyes could see. Two mutts meandered down the path right in front of him, thin and emaciated. They walked as if in a daze, with nowhere to go. Chad cringed at the thought of what would happen if the dogs died, but he pushed it out of his mind as kids ran past him, in a swarm of swinging arms amidst giggles and banter, chasing after each other until they disappeared into the haze of smog and smoke. He rested his back against the wall and for the hundredth time in the last twenty-four hours tried to figure out why this had happened to him.

But as an old man shuffled past, dragging some sort of two wheeled contraption behind him and spraying the filthy muddy water onto the path near Chad's feet, the millionaire reflected on who he was as a person for the first time in his life.

Chad knew that he was a ruthless businessman with a win-at-all-costs attitude, caring about making as much money as possible, and if others working for him were underpaid, he didn't really care. He'd always had an over-inflated ego, even as a child. He'd shared too many beds with too many women, treating those closest to him with contempt. A song entered Chad's mind. As he heard Denis Leary's voice, singing the chorus of his 1993 cult hit, Chad nodded to himself.

Right on.

I am an asshole, he thought.

Chad wiped dust from his left eye and as the song stopped playing in his head, two faces came to mind. His wife Crystal and Serena, his long dead little sister.

He could have treated them better. He knew this now.

Chad spotted Abhoy in the distance through the smoky haze, moving towards him, and watched as he approached. Chad noticed that Abhoy always seemed to be walking with intent, a young man with responsibilities. And considering the life he was leading and all this around him, the other admirable quality about Abhoy was that he never behaved like someone who was defeated. In fact, quite the opposite.

'What are you doing, Dipankar?' Abhoy asked him, as if Dipankar standing there was an unusual sight.

'Just shooting the breeze,' Chad said.

Abhoy stopped moving and stared into his friend's eyes.

'You're saying things I've never heard you say before.'

Abhoy frowned before his lips turned into a grin.

'The knock on the head,' he added, more of a statement than a question.

'I guess so,' Chad said with a shrug of the shoulders.

Abhoy stepped closer.

'Will you be able to work today, Dip?' he said.

Chad found the question surprising, considering what had taken place at the factory the day before.

'I still have a job?' Chad said, surprised.

Abhoy shook his head and this time the smile was spread from one side of his face to the other.

'Why wouldn't you?' Abhoy said.

'The Supervisor?'

Abhoy shrugged his shoulders, this time the nodding of his head was much more pronounced.

'You've lost your memory Dipankar, haven't you?' Abhoy asked.

Chad started to reply but Abhoy cut in.

'That is what he's like all the time,' Abhoy said.

The millionaire was lost for words.

Some hours later, Chad met with Abhoy and thanked his lucky stars he didn't need to find his own way to the factory. Chad would have no idea which way to go. The slums were an intricate maze of narrow paths, stretching on for miles in all directions. After a laborious thirty minutes of walking, with infrequent conversation, the slums ended and the busy streets of Dhaka began. The zebra crossing painted across the busy street was as useless as road rules in Dhaka. Chad watched in a sort of morbid fascination at the scene before him.

Beat up, ancient buses, cars, trucks and what had to be the world's largest gathering of rickshaws, sped down the busy street ignoring all pedestrians trying to cross the road.

Some buses and cars slowed when waved at by pedestrians, as if this was the sum of their cooperation, giving the people on foot half a fighting chance to make it across the road and on their way. When it came to Abhoy and Chad's turn, Abhoy crossed the road in a flash. His feet barely touched the ground. Chad's relief at making it halfway across the road, avoiding the crowded bus who passed him in a blur of rust, was short-lived. The motorised rickshaw hidden from view of the bus came so close to running him over, Chad feeling its side mirror skim the side of his right arm. Lucky for him, the driver turned his steering just in the nick of time, but made no qualms about telling Chad what he thought of having to do so. Eventually, the two of them rounded the corner to the factory. Chad felt a heaviness in his chest when he saw the sign.

DOSTME Int.

He stared at the logo, recalling how he'd first come up with the name all those years ago.

DOSTME.

Don't

Stop

Me.

The night he had come up with the name, he thought he was king of the world and had always big-noted the name as an idiom like the well-known brand, Nike.

Just do it.

He often wished he had come up with their slogan, often feeling a pang of jealousy because his brand would never be quite as strong and Chad knew it. But the name DOSTME was not just some marketing spin to attract the savvy sportswear consumer. It was about Chad and his ego. And now as he entered the stifling hot clothing factory, full of sewing machines and sweaty, overworked and underpaid people, he had a sudden thought.

What a stupid name.

The bell clanging on the stroke of the hour informed the workers it was time for the change of shift. As if watching a re-run of the scene from the day before, Chad watched on as the interchange between the people working at the sewing machines and those taking over from them, occurring in a mosh-pit type of movement.

Abhoy was off, pulling Chad by the arm, who moved his feet as best he could through the aisles of people heading in the opposite direction. As was the case yesterday, people mumbled greetings to each other as they made way for the replacement shift-workers.

When Abhoy sat down at the same sewing machine as he did the day before, he motioned for Chad to slip into the machine right next to him.

'We are going to get our quota done today Dip,' he

said, giving him a serious look for a moment, before his thin lips gave Chad a reassuring smile.

'Okay?' he added after Chad didn't respond.

Chad scanned the enormous factory floor.

He turned to Abhoy and said, 'Yes.'

He couldn't think of what else to say, considering he still didn't know how to sew a damned thing. As he watched Abhoy set up his machine, readying himself for his first garment, Chad had the sense of being watched. His thoughts were confirmed when he caught a glimpse of the man staring at him with cold eyes. The Supervisor.

Chad flinched when he saw who was standing next to the tyrant. Dipankar's father.

'Does my father know the Supervisor, Abhoy?' he blurted out without thinking how stupid the question may be.

Abhoy turned to Dipankar, who had the same incredulous look etched on his face.

'I sure as hope whatever happened to your head heals itself soon,' Abhoy said.

He turned his attention back to his sewing machine, getting the garment into position and spoke without bothering to look back over to Chad.

'The Supervisor,' he said, 'is your dad's brother, Dip.'

After a few seconds of buzzing the garment through the machine, he shook his head in wonderment.

'How do you think we work here?' Abhoy added.

Chad watched Abhoy sewing as if it was second nature. He knew that if he didn't start sewing immediately, he'd be in deep shit. He picked up a piece of an open garment behind him and recalling how Abhoy had done it, took a deep breath and gave it his best shot.

Although he was much slower, Chad was surprised at how well he'd had sewn his first garment. It looked more or less the same as the one Abhoy had thrown in a box behind him, so Chad did the same. Thirty minutes later, Chad could feel the rhythm of the process starting to take hold and he could feel his confidence rising. He was getting better, and it felt good.

'Here I am…sitting in a tin can…far above the world,' Whenever he felt good like this, he would sing to himself, and today it was a line from one of his favourite David Bowie songs. He hadn't realised he'd sung it out aloud until Abhoy gave him an odd look.

'What did you say?' Abhoy said.

'It's from a David Bowie song.'

Abhoy's face creased. 'Who is David Bowie?'

Chad wouldn't know how to explain his way out of it, so he shrugged his shoulders and went on sewing and singing, until he looked up to see the Supervisor come into view. He flinched.

'Dipankar,' he said, 'come to my office.'

Chad stopped mid-stitch and rose from his machine. As he followed the guy into his office, he spotted what was surely the biggest ashtray he'd ever seen in his life.

Bugger me dead, Chad thought. The object was, he soon realised, an old hubcap, brimming with what had to be hundreds of cigarette butts. He suddenly understood why the windows of the office were so filthy with a thick yellow nicotine smudge.

As if reading the millionaire's mind, the Supervisor pulled out a pack of Benson & Hedges from a drawer and slipped one of the cigarettes into his mouth and lighting it, before blowing smoke straight into Chad's face. His expression changed from ugly to pissed-off.

The Supervisor's dark skinned, weathered face, almost always looked angry. He had deep set eyes, almost a little too close together, and his long, thin nose sat atop a thick, Tom-Selleck-esque moustache, as black as his matching eyebrows and thin, dirty, balding hair.

When he smiled, his teeth reminded Chad why long-term smoking wasn't good for the choppers. His teeth were as yellow as the office windows.

'Your father tells me you hurt your head yesterday,' he said.

Yeah because of you, Chad thought. The Supervisor raised an eyebrow. 'I'm fine,' Chad lied, not knowing what else to say.

'You see Dipankar,' his uncle sat forward, 'you may be my nephew, but it means nothing to—'

The Supervisor's words were interrupted by a man who arrived unannounced at the open doorway and bellowed in the Supervisor's direction, 'we have big problem in loading bay boss!'

If Chad thought he was copping it, this guy was about to experience something next level.

'Don't interrupt me!' the Supervisor shrieked, still staring at Chad, before he cast his angry eyes on the guy standing at the door.

'Sorry, Boss,' the guy sounded in fear of his life, 'but you need to come.'

The Supervisor butted out his cigarette.

'You. Wait here,' he said.

Chad sat there for a few moments, deep in thought.

He had no idea where this was going.

Suddenly, he spotted something familiar on the desk, buried under a pile of files.

'You can't be serious,' he gasped.

It looked so old. He'd forgotten that laptops once looked like this. It had to be over twenty years old at least.

Chad's instincts told him this idea would not end well, but he ignored them.

He stepped around to the Supervisor's side of the desk and pushed the folders off the NEC laptop. Its keyboard was dirty and the letters so worn that Chad could barely read them.

'Email,' he murmured, as his eyes darted between the screen and the entrance to the Supervisor's office. All Chad could see were dozens of people sitting behind their machines, hard at work. The humming sounds filtered through to the Supervisor's office.

Chad found himself trying to navigate the stupid

cursor controller in the middle of the keyboard. All he had to do was find the Google browser and he'd be on his way. Easy. To his astonishment, he was able to somehow fudge his way around the dinosaur of device to the Google home page, but soon realised he'd not been checking the entrance to the office.

The Supervisor was standing in the doorway.

CHAPTER THIRTY-FOUR

Angela

DR SMITH'S FACE WAS THUNDEROUS AS SHE LEFT the room. Even the nurse standing nearby was backing away from her, and she was at least ten feet away already. The young woman had worked in Dr Smith's ward for nine excruciating months. Cold-arse told Angela that she'd been applying for other nursing positions for weeks, to no avail.

As the nurse went to leave, she found herself bumping into a colleague.

'Sorry,' she mumbled.

'What's the problem?' her colleague asked, but the strained expression on her face said it all. They shared a look.

Dr Angela Smith, FRCPE.

Angela watched on, angry for reasons she couldn't

decipher. She felt as if she was the victim of some sort of deception. She had been cheated. This anger however, which was her default response to any given situation, was now so red-hot, that she realised she'd never experienced anything like it before.

How was she in her patient's body with this person, who looked like her, giving her a filthy look? She closed her eyes for a moment before her mind went into meltdown mode.

Breathing became difficult. Her chest tightened. She felt the room spin.

She glanced again at the two nurses standing outside the doorway to the ward.

This would all get out now. She knew that the rumour mill would go into overdrive. The nurses, like any workplace, loved nothing more than a good gossip, and this would be front page news in the cafeteria, for days, maybe even weeks to come.

Angela, trapped in Mary's body could see Dr Angela Smith standing in some sort of suspended animation to the other entrance to the ward from the nurses, as the seconds turned into minutes. But strangely, it was someone else's face that appeared in her consciousness. Benedict Battinson, her late husband.

By the time Benedict was diagnosed with lung cancer, their marriage was in a terrible state. They'd been sleeping in separate rooms for years, sex was a distant memory. More like flatmates, they had somehow existed in the same space while not being a part of one another's lives. Jack was an added layer of complexity in the household. More so to Angela than Benedict. She knew. She could feel it. Jack was on her husband's side. Fortunately for him, he was rarely home to see his parents ignore each other. Then one day he simply moved out.

Working as an executive in one of the UK's largest steel fabricating businesses, Benedict was often away for weeks, sometimes months at a time. It suited Angela just fine. She knew her husband had a good heart and at one time in her life she appreciated the fact that he loved her, but as she grew older and work consumed her, Angela began to care less and less about her husband's love, and although Benedict tried to keep their marriage alive, he gave up in the end, and like many in his shoes, he turned his attention to other things that brought him happiness. She regularly wondered about Benedict and his female colleagues, more so when he was away on business for long stretches of time. But if she was ever able to find out the truth, her thoughts on the matter would prove irrelevant, given her casual disdain for their partnership. Angela knew he was better off finding someone who could reciprocate the love he had to give, but she was selfish. And had refused to let him go. It's not that she didn't want him, she didn't want anyone else to have him either.

Despite this treatment, much to Angela's surprise, Benedict would always find the time to do something nice for her. She recalled that one time that he had bought her an exquisite bouquet of flowers. Benedict had long gone to bed, but a little white card sat upright by the vase, illuminated by a nearby streetlight as she opened the front door.

Angela picked it up, reading, as she walked towards the rubbish bin.

'Happy Anniversary. xo,' it had read. Angela did not feel a skerrick of warmth towards Benedict, or his memory of dates, and the flowers remained in the vase until the water had turned to a murky brown and the flowers sat dead and lifeless.

The next day, Benedict was fighting for his life.

The tumour in his right calf was the size of a large walnut.

Benedict thought he'd just pulled a muscle. All he'd done was drag his golf buggy around eighteen holes at the golf course, and once it was removed, Benedict thanked his lucky stars they'd found it. He'd made a full recovery, albeit with a worthy scar. Even his golf swing improved.

Eighteen months later, the day after he'd bought Angela flowers, Benedict arrived home after his morning walk, light-headed, and feeling out of breath.

He called Angela, who was too busy to answer. She ignored his call and returned to her rounds, and Benedict had bitten the bullet and called himself an ambulance. The doctors ran a myriad of tests. A day later, they knew the cause of his breathing problems. Being married to one of Britain's leading oncologists, his doctor assured him that he would be in good hands.

'She's the best of the best,' the doctor told Benedict, after the diagnosis was confirmed. 'She will knock this on the head in no time. You are a lucky man,' the doctor patted Benedict on the shoulder. But Angela had lied to Benedict, convincing him that radiation and chemotherapy were unnecessary.

Lie.

'They can just cut it out,' she had said. 'The margins will be clear, honey.'

Lie.

She had told him that this was a unique situation, something other doctors would not understand, nor agree with.

Lie.

So, they needed to keep it to themselves.

Lie.

She promised to help him get through this.

Lie.

As Doctor Smith brusquely walked back through the ward, trying to regain some dignity, Angela tried again.

'You lied to Benedict,' Angela hissed, raising her

voice as the doctor passed. 'You wanted him to die. How does it feel to know that you killed your husband, you fucking cow?'

The doctor stopped, but this time turned around to face her. The two shared a look of pure vitriol.

CHAPTER THIRTY-FIVE

Logan

'COURTNEY,' JERRY SPRINGHARE'S WIFE FILOMENA greeted her with warmth and sincerity.

'Thank you for coming today,' Logan's mind was spinning. He had no idea how he was going to get through this.

'Why don't we do a recap,' Logan found himself addressing Filomena. He couldn't look at him. From the corner of his eye, he swore he could see a tiny grin on one side of Jerry's face.

'Filomena, why don't you start us off?' Logan asked. He found himself wanting to cross his legs and do everything he could to shield his body from Jerry's beady, sleazy eyes.

Filomena Springhare lent forward, resting her hands in her lap, seemingly keen to start the discussion.

Middle age had been kind to her, Logan thought. Her dark brown hair was short and held back from her face by a gold hairband. Big hazel eyes gazed out at him and her perfectly applied lipstick revealed a lovely smile.

Logan had to wonder why her husband was knocking on Courtney's door with his hands full of things Logan wished he could delete from his memory.

Lube and bubbles.

Bubbles and lube.

'Well as we have discussed in the last two sessions Courtney,' the woman's face turned serious, 'I believe my husband no longer loves me. But he insists he does.'

Logan reached for his glass of water and nodded.

Before he took a drink, Logan said, 'and why do you believe your husband no longer loves you, Filomena?'

Logan's timing for rejuvenating his dry throat could not have been worse.

'Because Jerry here is fucking someone else, Courtney,' she said.

Logan almost choked.

It took Logan a moment to recover from his coughing fit.

Jerry had not moved a muscle, though Filomena had stood up the moment the coughing started. Logan gestured that he was fine. Between splutters he asked Filomena to continue.

But he couldn't help wondering, was Filomena's comment directed at Courtney? Did Filomena know about Jerry coming to her apartment the night before? He took one more deep breath through his nostrils before turning his full attention to his boss.

'What is your response to your wife's comment, Jerry?' Logan spoke with as much authority as he could muster.

Jerry studied Courtney for a moment and Logan fought the urge to squirm in his seat.

Filomena had always been pleasant to Logan whenever their paths crossed at work functions and now, she sat there staring at Courtney as well, her expression neutral.

'I'm not perfect, Courtney—'

Here we go. The bullshit-o-meter in Logan's brain began to red-line.

'—but my wife's comments are unfounded,' Jerry said in an even tone.

Filomena shook her head, although her face remained passive.

'Like the time in Vegas with your work buddies huh,' she said, turning her eyes to Jerry after she'd completed the sentence.

Shit, Logan thought, he remembered this junket. This was another junket altogether from the one where he'd personally met Elon Musk and later turned into a raging-party animal. On this other junket, they'd partied all night but hey, what happens in Vegas, stayed in Vegas, right? The word on the plane trip home was a particular Sales Manager was spotted leaving a certain establishment at 3.00 am. He'd never admitted it to any of his work colleagues, but Logan knew it was true. Because he was the one who had spotted him.

'I don't know how many times I am going to hear about Vegas,' Jerry said, shaking his head.

Filomena watched him for a few minutes, before she slowly turned her attention back to Courtney. The woman was a picture of calm and Logan had to admit he was in awe of her, sitting right next to her husband who thought he could lie his way out of anything.

'Can I make an unusual request, Courtney, if you wouldn't mind?' Filomena said, sitting up straighter as if she meant business.

'Of course, Filomena, what do you have in mind?' Logan responded with a curious expression.

'Would it be possible to speak individually?'

The expression on Jerry's face changed immediately.

'I don't think this is normal procedure with a marriage counsellor,' Jerry said in a panicked tone. Filomena continued to look at Courtney, awaiting an answer and it was at that moment Logan felt a light-bulb switch on inside of his head. It was as risky as hell, but it might just pay off.

'Sure,' Logan lent forward, 'why not. Now who—' Logan's words were cut off, his question no longer needed answering. Filomena had decided who Courtney would be talking to first.

Logan had to admit he wondered if this was going to end up being an ambush. But it was too late. Jerry's wife was already rising from the couch.

'Jerry can go first and I will go second.' Before Logan could respond, she was already on her way to the office door.

'What the hell has got into you?' Jerry's jaw set, his words whispered, but heavy with anger.

'I should be asking you the same fucking question,' Logan was pleased with his quick fired response.

'We had arranged to see each other last night.' Jerry was working his jaw, his head darting to the office door to ensure his wife was out of earshot.

'—but you acted as if I were a complete stranger when you opened the door,' he added.

Logan could not think of where to go, so he began with putting his boss back in his place, before he tried to figure out what do with him for the next few minutes.

'I had a difficult day yesterday,' Logan replied, avoiding Jerry's eyes.

'Well, that's just great, Courtney,' Jerry spat. 'But did you not think about how this would inconvenience me?

The room fell into silence as they stared at each other and Logan knew he wanted to get things moving towards his goal. He checked the clock on the wall. He didn't have long before he would have to deal with Filomena. On her own. Jesus.

Did Jerry's wife know Courtney was having a sexual affair with him?

He was not looking forward to finding out.

'Look, Jerry,' Logan said, 'is this a good idea?'

'What do you mean?' Jerry said.

'Remind me Jerry, how long have we been doing… err…what we've been doing?' Logan fumbled.

'You've never played games before Courtney,' Jerry said, his words now back in whisper mode, 'so why start now?'

'How long has it been, Jerry?' Logan lent forward, his tone was sharper.

But before he could answer, Logan knew he had just a few precious moments left with Jerry, and he needed to get on with it.

'Before you answer my question, Jerry, I need to ask you a few questions about someone else. Oh, and I know this will remain between you and me, huh?' Logan threw in a wink.

He was getting the hang of this.

'Who?' Jerry said, Logan could see he was annoyed but he pressed on.

'Logan Jackman,'

Jerry frowned.

'What about him?'

'What is he like? Good guy? Good at his job? Is he good at his marriage?'

Jerry sat forward, 'why you all of a sudden interested in Logan, huh?' his grin turned sleazy, 'what, you want to fuck him too?'

Logan shook his head, checking the clock. He was almost out of time.

'Don't be ridiculous,' he said to Jerry, 'just answer the question.'

'He's okay, I guess. Don't like him, he's full of himself. Thinks he's better than everyone else, including me.'

Logan was shocked. He always thought that he and Jerry were tight.

'Is he a good husband, does he treat his wife okay, you know?' Logan stumbled over his words.

Jerry shrugged his shoulders, he smiled at Courtney as if what he was about to say would bring him some sort of pleasure.

'Is he a good husband? Well, everyone at work remembers the junket in Vegas where he shagged a couple of whores. So, there's your answer as far as that is concerned.'

Logan was about to speak. He could see Filomena pacing up and down in the waiting room, but Jerry Springhare had more dirt to dish up.

'—he comes here, right?' He didn't let Logan even answer, 'not sure why. Someone at work told me just the other day that his wife is having an affair—'

Jerry seemed to relish in the gossip and his eyes went bright, 'and not with some well-hung guy either' seconds before the office door opened, Jerry's grin was childish.

'—with another woman.'

CHAPTER THIRTY-SIX

Amelia

AMELIA WAS IN SUCH A STATE OF FLUX, THAT SHE didn't hear the back door open. She also didn't hear the person come up the hallway, until he was standing in the doorway.

'What are you doing?' Margarita's father said.

The Cisco Kid, is what they called him.

Why would I, of all people, sack the Cisco Kid? she wondered. Cisco, to those close to him, was a pro. He was one of the best set builders around, with a reputation of being hardworking and easy to please.

Margarita's father was average height, with a happy-go-lucky roundish face. With Mexican parents, his dark hair was an abundance of tight curls, with smears of silver working their way from the sides. Big cheeks and a great smile.

But today, his eyes focused on Margarita, and darkened.

'Are you okay—,'

She realised something was missing. '—'Dad?' She threw it in for good measure.

The Cisco Kid stood there motionless for a moment, before he walked towards the island bench until he was now within a few feet of her. He dropped his wallet and keys near the pile of letters. The severance letter sat visible at the top.

'Well,' he said, staring out into the afternoon through the kitchen window, 'you've read the letter, Margarita.'

He let his words hang in the air, before he turned and this time stared into Amelia's eyes.

'—so why don't you tell me, how I am,' Francisco added.

Amelia sat back down on the kitchen stool. At that moment, Amelia was reeling from the letter as much as Margarita's father was.

She turned her attention to Margarita's father and said, 'but it's just one job? You can get another, right?'

The Cisco Kid turned and in a flash, pushed all the letters and documents onto the floor.

'It doesn't matter!' He stood against the kitchen bench as his words became strained.

'The only thing you need to worry about Margarita, is packing your bags, you hear me?' he said.

Amelia could feel something deep in her chest, but

she'd not had anything akin to an anxiety attack for years, so she had no idea why she was having one now, yet her body was doing it regardless.

'Pack? What do you mean? I don't know what is going on here,' Amelia said the words in all honesty.

The Cisco kid lent forward, now his face was a little too close to Amelia's.

'Because we have to move, Rita,' he said, Amelia felt his warm beer breath on her face. She blanched. He walked to the kitchen sink and fixed his gaze out through the kitchen window.

'Where are we moving to?' she said.

He bowed his head, before turning around and facing her.

'Well, you said you always liked spending time with your Aunt Sofia, Margarita. Now you will be getting your wish,' Francisco said.

Aunt Sofia? Amelia had no idea who this person was. Or where in hell she lived.

'Remind me where she lives these days?' Amelia asked, regretting the question the moment it was out of her mouth. She should have found out another way, she thought.

Too late.

'What the fuck has got into you, Margarita? You were there two weeks ago, is this your idea of trying to be funny?' he said. Before Amelia could say anything, Margarita's father cursed in Spanish before storming out of the kitchen.

Aunt Sofia, she thought. *Who is Aunt Sofia?* She reached for Margarita's phone, accessed her contacts and found 'Aunt Sofia' in the address book. When Amelia read her address, she gasped.

'No, no, no,' Amelia cried.

Pierre's family lived there. And Pierre's family had died there, his parents and two little sisters, the victims of a home invasion. Drug addicts were to blame apparently, although this was never confirmed. Pierre, heartbroken and devastated, had sworn he'd never set foot in the Zip Code ever again. To this day, a decade on, he hadn't, and Amelia had no desire to go there either.

Oakland, on the east side of San Francisco Bay.

One of the most dangerous places in California.

CHAPTER THIRTY-SEVEN

Chad

CHAD SAT THERE, FINGERS ON KEYS.

'What do you think you are doing?' the Supervisor hissed before springing into motion with lightning speed. Before Chad could even contemplate what to do, the man was on top of him. Without any forethought, Chad knew he had two options: One, let the guy slap him around, or two – fight back. As the Supervisor slapped Chad hard in the ear, the decision was made.

Option Two it was.

He flung his arms up with no target in mind. One of his hands hit the Supervisor on the nose, the force of the blow startling him, but it was the worst thing Chad could have done. The Supervisor grabbed him with both hands and threw him across the desk and Chad came face to face with the world's biggest ashtray. His body collided with it as he was flung across the desk. As Chad hit the ground, the man that inhabited Dipankar's body recoiled in pain, before hundreds of cigarette butts came raining down on top of him. If this wasn't bad enough, the hubcap itself teetered on the edge, before the heavy metal object fell and made direct contact with Dipankar's head.

He blacked out.

For the second time in a matter of days, Chad found himself opening his eyes to the realisation he was someone else. But this time, he hadn't woken up in the ramshackle hut. He was outside at the rear of the DOSTME factory.

The pain in his head was insane. It throbbed so hard that he threw up after taking his first breath. Workers in the loading bay nearby watched him for a few moments, talking in hushed tones. Dipankar's actions would end up being talked about inside by now. Sewing machine to sewing machine. A worker trying to access the Supervisor's computer? What sort of idiot would try to do this? Chad sat nursing his head for a few seconds and tried to get his thoughts in order. He ached everywhere, but the strongest pain came from his head. Without painkillers, he knew it was going to be a long day until the mother of all migraines would fade. His throat was the driest he'd ever felt. Once again, he knew that he'd give his right arm for a drink of water. A sudden movement to his left startled him. The Supervisor had returned.

No.

Wait.

It was his father.

Dipankar's father kicked him hard in the shin, before slapping him hard across the top of his head. The pain had Chad seeing stars again. He flung an arm up as he saw the next blow coming, cutting off Dipankar's father's next slap. The move caught the man off guard and he stepped back in shock. Chad could see the resemblance in the guy's butt-ugly face to his brother, the Supervisor. But Dipankar's father appeared to have seen the much uglier side of life, in the slums of Dhaka. He was older and appeared weaker, however what he lacked in physical strength, he made up for with an air of arrogance.

'You out of a job,' Dipankar's father said, 'what am I to do for money now?'

He kicked the dirt near Chad's feet, spraying it all over him.

Chad had never felt more helpless.

'Why is this happening to me, huh?'

Before Dipankar's father could speak another word, Chad jumped to his feet, startling the man again. Chad stood there and wiped the dirt from his face.

'The day I return to myself, I am going to hunt you

and your brother down, you sack of shit and you will understand what pain —'

It happened in a flash. With Chad's anger blurring his senses, he hadn't heard the Supervisor walk up behind him, or seen his clenched right fist.

How many damn times is this going to happen to me? Chad thought, as he passed out yet again.

But when he eventually came to, he was no longer out the back of the factory.

He was back in the meditation room.

CHAPTER THIRTY-EIGHT

Angela

THE NURSES WERE STARING, OPEN-MOUTHED.

'What the fuck did you just say to me?' the shade of Dr Smith's face had turned blood-red as she made her way to the side of Mary's bed.

'—Benedict is dead – because you lied to him,' Mary's eyes bore down on the Doctor as she wiped spittle from her chin.

Dr Smith smarted, and Angela's body winced in pain.

'What are you going to do when Jack finds out that you killed his father….Angela?'

The nurses would concur later that Mary already had her arms up protecting her head well before the Doctor got to her.

'How dare you!' the oncologist said, slapping her repeatedly.

From the other end of the ward, Rachel appeared and, shuffling as fast as she could go, she moved to defend Mary.

'You don't know what you are talking about!' the Doctor was shouting at Mary while the slaps continued.

'Stop it, you maniac!' Rachel cried.

She grabbed the Doctor. However, being so weak, she was unable to grasp at her properly.

Dr Angela Smith felt the tug on her coat and seconds before the two nurses arrived and pulled her away from Mary, she flung her left arm back in the direction of the person.

This time, her hand was in a fist shape, and not an open palm. The doctor's left fist connected with the tender spot below Rachel's right eye and she screamed in agony as she felt the intense pain explode on the right side of her face. On instinct, her body pushed herself backwards, trying to get away from the threat. With slippers on her feet, she lost her footing before falling to the hospital floor.

The other patients gasped as they heard the crack of Rachel's skull hitting the linoleum.

Ten minutes later, she was transferred to the ICU.

Thirty minutes later, she was placed in a medically induced coma.

Angela watched the shadows of the night meander across the wall of the hospital ward. The last time she'd checked the time, it was midnight, or one o'clock in the morning, she wasn't sure. Cold-arse's bed remained unoccupied.

Angela wondered how long it would be before she returned. Little did she know she wouldn't. It had been hours since she'd said those words to the 'other' Dr Smith. Angela wondered if she would be able to get through this incident if she made it back to being her normal self, and groaned when she remembered what she had said about Benedict. It would spread throughout the hospital, the damning accusations she'd made public.

What was I thinking?

Angela felt her eyelids starting to get heavy, hoping to all the gods combined that when she woke up in the morning, this would all have been a nightmare.

Angela felt as if she'd been dozing for a few minutes when something close by stirred her.

A man stood at the end of the bed. His face was impassive, which made it all the more frightening.

'How could you?' he said.

Benedict.

There was no way that he could be standing there, so she closed her eyes tightly, and did not open them again for some time. As she did, she let out a sigh of relief.

The ghost of her deceased husband was gone.

'Do you think you are done yet?' came the voice from nowhere. She wondered if she'd imagined it. But in the corner of her eye, she saw something and a gasp came from her dry throat. He sat on the edge of Cold Arse's empty bed, in a Doctor's coat, with a stethoscope hanging around his shoulders, his hair combed to one side.

'I'm sorry, what?' Angela asked.

'I said, do you think you are done yet?' the man replied.

'Am I done what yet?'

Henry the meditation teacher stared at Angela for a moment, before rising to his feet and coming closer. Angela felt as if she were going to vomit, and closed her eyes to steady herself.

'I beg you. How do I make it stop?' her words left her lips before she opened her eyes.

Henry stood with his back to her, walked around the corner and was gone.

CHAPTER THIRTY-NINE

Logan

LOGAN SAT ON COURTNEY'S BALCONY STARING OFF into the fading light. The night air was mild, though he wouldn't have cared if it were the middle of January. Sipping on a glass of Canadian Club and smoking his fourth Peter Jackson cigarette in under ten minutes, he wondered why he'd bothered buying a pizza on the way home in addition to the booze and cigarettes. He wasn't hungry. Today had been a head-fuck of biblical proportions. He didn't care if Courtney had a full day's bookings tomorrow, he intended to call in sick. Because he was sick. Sick of being trapped in Courtney's body. But there was one appointment in the diary tomorrow he didn't want to miss.

The ten minutes he'd spent with Filomena Springhare alone had been awkward. Filomena had repeated her concerns about her husband's affair in their private session, but truth be told, Logan didn't care. At first, Logan was sure Filomena knew it was Courtney who was getting it on with Jerry. But after a few minutes, it was obvious that she didn't know the woman's identity at all. Logan nodded and grunted from time to time, but his mind was miles away.

Beth was having an affair.

With a woman.

No.

Way.

As the appointment wrapped up right on 5.00 pm and Logan could see Jerry about to come back into Courtney's office, the last words from his wife did make Logan feel on edge.

'When I find out who this woman is, she'd better hope she books a one-way ticket to the moon,' Filomena said in a tacit tone. It wasn't just the way she said it, but rather the look in her eyes when she did.

'Well,' Logan emptied the tumbler, downing the liquid in his throat before reaching for the bottle and pouring himself another generous glass.

'—she needn't worry about Courtney bumping uglies with her husband tonight,' Logan said to the empty balcony.

He lit yet another cigarette, knowing that if at some point he didn't eat some pizza, he'd wake up with one serious hangover in the morning.

He took another drag from his cigarette and

watched a couple of boats on Lake Ontario dawdle off into the haze of dusk. His thoughts returned to the one person he wished were sitting by his side.

He'd even share his pizza with her. And his bottle of fast emptying Club.

Beth Jackman.

Where was she now? he wondered. What was she doing?

A sick feeling stabbed his chest.

Who was she with?

'Come in,' Logan said, his throat felt as if it had turned to concrete and his Adam's apple a block of steel three sizes too big.

Logan, the other one, walked in and gave Courtney a dispassionate look. Logan checked his body double over. Nothing out of place. Same clothes, same hair, same expression on his face that clearly said that he wanted to be anywhere but there.

Beth came into full view and he did a double take.

Dressed in her favourite black jeans, with a matching black cashmere sweater and knee-high boots, her hair was pulled tight into a ponytail.

Damn, he thought, *how did I never notice how beautiful my wife was?*

'Thank you for coming in today,' he said, as he

knew Courtney always did at the commencement of the session. 'How are you both going?'

His heart was beating against his chest so hard he felt the need to take a deep breath and hope to hell he survived the next fifty-nine minutes without doing something he couldn't undo.

'Good,' Logan's one word response said it all.

'As expected,' Beth countered her husband's lame response.

It was all he could do to not stare at her, but he cleared his throat. He had a plan.

'I want to do something different today,'

The other Logan blinked in disinterest.

Christ, he thought. *Is this the one expression I always have on my face?*

Beth sat forward, appearing interested.

'I would like to spend a little time with you both, one on one,' he said.

Logan noted the scowl on his other self's face. Clearly he didn't like the sound of that idea.

'What the hell for?'

Beth turned and gave her husband a sideways glare before returning her face to the counsellor's.

'If you think it will help,' she said.

Courtney smiled.

'Logan,' he smiled in Beth's direction, 'you first. Beth, go have a short break in the waiting room. Tindwer will make you a coffee if you like.'

Beth rose from the couch, giving her husband a

bemused look, which he didn't reciprocate, before reaching the office door and closing it behind her.

'Well,' the other Logan said, sitting back on the couch with an annoyed look on his face, 'what do you want to talk about, Courtney?'

Logan bristled but then smiled warmly.

'Logan, how long have you been coming to see me?'

The car salesman shrugged his shoulders and pursed his lips.

'About 4800 dollars long at least.'

Could the shmuck be more sarcastic? Jesus.

'Can I be honest with you then?' Logan asked.

His doppelgänger leaned forward and rested his elbows on his knees. His avoidance was starting to grate on Logan.

'You need to decide.' His tone became serious.

Before the other Logan could respond, he sat forward and shook his head.

'On what?'

'Whether you should stop wasting your time, Beth's time and quite frankly, my bloody time.'

Logan was stunned by the counsellor's forwardness.

As he began to speak, she cut him off and gestured to the waiting room.

'-I don't care about the money. I have more than I need and more clients than I have time for. So, your choice is this—' Logan glanced at the time on Courtney's watch, '—spend the next fifteen minutes telling me in glorious detail, how you intend to fight for your wife, and your marriage, or you stop wasting everyone's time and fuck off.'

Beth sat down on the couch and Logan could not help but see something in his wife's demeanour. She was upbeat and perky. *Glowing.* After ushering the other Logan out, he had found Beth leaning against the reception desk, whispering in hushed tones to Tindwer.

'Beth,' Logan said, 'I've had what I believe to be a positive conversation with your husband.'

Beth nodded, adjusting herself on the couch to make herself more comfortable, but she appeared distracted. Logan gathered his thoughts for a few moments, trying to remain in control. He had waited seven long days for this moment.

'Can I ask you—,' Logan took a quick breath, '—as I have asked your husband today, do you want this marriage to continue, or do you want it to end?'

The expression on Beth's face was one of surprise. Courtney had never been this direct in any of their previous appointments. Beth sat forward and as she did, Logan could see that her eyes had misted over.

'I appreciate your candour,' Beth said softly.

'-right now, if you want me to be one hundred per cent honest with you Court-ten-ay ,'

Beth turned to check that Logan was well out of earshot.

He was doing what he often did. Staring at the screen of his smartphone.

Beth stared at her hands.

'—I've met someone else. So, to answer your question, I think my marriage to Logan Jackman – is over,' she said.

The moment was upon him faster than he could think about it.

'Beth!' he reached for her hand. Don't—' He swallowed hard. He felt as if he was falling out of the chair.

'—don't leave me!'

CHAPTER FORTY

Amelia

THIS WAS A LIVING NIGHTMARE.

Over breakfast, Amelia found out Margarita's father had a gambling problem. He was stone-cold broke. It was the tense, whispered words she heard Margarita's mother fire at Francisco when they thought Amelia wasn't paying attention. *Horse Racing, that'll do it,* Amelia thought.

But it didn't stop there. The last thing Amelia heard before she gladly left the kitchen was some snide remark from Margarita's mother aimed straight at her husband, though this time pulling Margarita in to the ring. Something along the lines of *'Your father would bet on two flies to see who found the dung heap first,'* or words to that effect.

Then on the way to the bus stop, Amelia was set

upon as she was getting off the bus by Big Blonde and her gang of bitches. Amelia couldn't take them all on at once. One at a time, perhaps, but against five of them, punching, scratching and kicking, she had no chance at all. And if that wasn't enough, someone poured a large cup of cola over her as she lay on the ground.

Amelia lost it.

Another fucking cup of Cola being poured over me. She cried more than she'd ever cried before.

As the next bus pulled up and ran over her cell phone, which had been thrown in its path by Big Blonde, she hit rock-bottom. Amelia heard the metallic crunch, as the bus's front wheel made contact with the phone. She'd never been without a phone before.

No one came to her aid straight away. Some walked past her within a few feet, sneering and grinning at the sight of the teenager lying on the sidewalk in a pool of cola, nursing a blood lip and a black eye.

Finally, an old lady came to her aid, shuffling over and helping Margarita to her feet, before guiding her to a nearby bench.

'Are you okay?' she said, kindly.

'Why is this happening to me?' Amelia cried.

The woman smiled at her, not knowing what to say.

Amelia put her hands to her face as the tears flowed. The old woman sat next to her and patted her on the back.

'It's going to be alright, dear,' she said.

Amelia turned to her and managed the weakest of smiles.

'You think?' she managed to say.

Even her mouth hurt to say those two words.

Without warning, a flash of white startled both Amelia and the older woman as the Los Angeles Police Patrol Car rolled to within a few feet of the curb in front of them. As the police officer in the passenger seat rolled down his window, Amelia did her best to adjust her dishevelled appearance. She straightened her top and ran her hands through Margarita's wild mane of frizzy hair.

'Everything okay here?' the officer said, pushing down his mirrored sunglasses to reveal his brown eyes.

Amelia nodded.

The shock of being set upon by a group of school girls was so profound, it overwhelmed her. But the feeling of embarrassment was even more painful. Amelia had never felt so raw.

'I'm okay, thanks,' she struggled to say, knowing it was a lie.

The police officer nodded, before murmuring some words Amelia couldn't hear to his fellow police officer. The older woman patted Amelia on the back once again before rising to leave.

'Will you be okay dear?'

Amelia turned to her and said, 'I will be okay. Thank you for stopping.'

As the woman rose to her feet, Amelia heard words spoken from the Patrol Car.

'Sorry, what did you say?' she asked the police officer.

'Young lady, you look like you need to go home and get cleaned up,' he said.

Before Amelia could refuse, the cop had already stepped out onto the road, before opening the back door of the patrol car for her.

'It's fine, I will head off to school now,' Amelia said, trying everything she could to avoid feeling embarrassed.

The cop shook his head.

'Come on,' he smiled, 'someone needs to cut you some slack. Get in, we'll take you home.'

A few stray students watched Margarita get into the back seat of the car and Amelia could not hide her shame, bowing her head down in the hope she would be hidden from view.

'Everything alright back there?' came the driver's voice.

'Sure, tying my shoes,' Amelia lied.

The two cops shared a quick glance before the driver started the car and drove off.

Amelia felt light-headed. Leaning forward and resting her head on her knees with her hands over her face made the pain bearable. She wondered if they drove for long enough, if she would drift off to sleep.

Closing her eyes felt good. The swaying of the car as it drove down Sunset Boulevard put sleep within her grasp and for a moment nothing mattered.

The car rolled to a stop and Amelia woke with a start.

'Time to go inside and get yourself cleaned up,' the driver said, looking into the rear view mirror.

Amelia felt as if she'd been drugged.

She mumbled words of thanks, but as she put one foot on the ground, she looked at her surroundings.

'What the—' Amelia said.

She rubbed her eyes and stared at the home, wondering what the hell was going on. She stepped onto the lush, Holmby Hills lawn. Like many lawns in the mega-rich suburb, it could have doubled for the eighteenth green at Augusta.

'What am I doing here?' she asked.

The driver had put his window down and was staring at her.

'You said you wanted to go home, right?' The hairs on the back of her neck stand upright.

'But I live—,' Amelia was confused but managed to finish the sentence, 'in Melrose Hill.'

She checked herself to make sure she was still Margarita.

She still was.

The cop stared at her for a beat.

'You'd better get walking, I guess,' he said.

The patrol car's motor roared to life and she stared at him curiously, taking one last look at those eyes. She'd seen those eyes before.

The meditation teacher.

CHAPTER FORTY-ONE

Chad

THE FIRST THING CHAD SAW WAS THE CEILING FAN and wondered if it was the most joyful thing he'd ever seen. He lay there for a moment, feeling a huge wave of relief pass over him. He was back. A thousand thoughts sprang to mind. So many that he didn't know where to start. He recalled his last thought in that room—the hooker and the spa at St Barts—before feeling an immediate pang of guilt. But as he watched the ceiling fan, the scene began to change around him again. A strong gust of humid wind passed over him, followed by a putrid odour, and as he opened his eyes fully, a stab of heartache punched him in the chest.

Bits of dirt and dust blew up around him and as he rubbed his eyes, he realised this whole time that he hadn't been looking at the ceiling fan in the meditation room at all.

High above him in the dusk sky, was a black helicopter hovering in mid-air.

As he sat up, the pain in his head exploded. He threw up.

The helicopter moved away, relieving Chad of the suffocating dust storm, and Chad realised immediately where he was.

'You are shitting me,' he said to himself.

He was sitting right in the middle of the gargantuan garbage dump he'd seen for the first time this morning, when he had done the breakfast run for the brothers and sisters. He ventured a glance upwards, and the helicopter was now hovering much further away. Who they were looking for was anyone's guess, Chad thought.

He wished they were looking for him.

As a black crow landed no more than a foot away, picking at the ground, Chad glanced over to the bird and wished *he* had wings.

'Where's a can of Red Bull when you need one?' he said to the crow.

Thanks to the Dipankar's father's big mouth, Abhoy found him sometime later. His old man had apparently gone back to the hut to tell the family about the shame

Dipankar had brought on the family whilst he was at work earlier that day. He made out that Dipankar was stealing state secrets from his brother's computer. As dusk began to envelope the slums, the man gloated to Dipankar's siblings about where his eldest son had been taken and dumped. *'He's a piece of garbage and will be treated as such,'* he had said to them.

Horrified, they waited until their father disappeared before scurrying over to Abhoy's hut, and by the time he had arrived at the garbage dump, the sun had set. The biggest tip in central Dhaka was now shrouded in a cloak of darkness.

Abhoy had told him earlier that people didn't dare go near the dump at night. Darkness robbed you of the ability to avoid dangerous things such as medical waste, human faeces, dead and decomposing animals. Chad felt his chances of being found growing weaker, until he heard his name, faintly at first, and then growing closer. Chad could see a blurry figure scurry up the uneven pile of waste. To his utter relief, he spotted Abhoy at the top.

'What are you doing?' Abhoy peered down at his friend, 'why didn't you come back?'

Chad sat on the ground, with his legs crossed, his elbows resting on his knees.

'I can't do this anymore,' he said flatly.

'What are you talking about Dipankar, not do what anymore?'

Chad shook his head, wiping his forehead, before

resting his head on his crossed arms. He could feel his emotions getting the better of him.

Chad wiped the tears from his eyes, before he said, 'I can't live like this anymore.'

Abhoy made his way down to his friend, crouched and met his eyes.

'Hey,' he put a firm hand on his shoulder, '-now listen to me. I know you've not been yourself lately, but you need to get it together,' Abhoy said.

Chad laughed, 'what does it matter, huh?' he said.

For the first time since Chad had awoken as Dipankar, Abhoy gave him a dirty look.

'Get up,' Abhoy said in a clipped tone, grabbing Dipankar by the arm and dragging him to his feet.

By the time Chad was standing up, he noticed the throbbing in his head had subsided, but still his stomach ached from hunger and his throat felt so dry that it hurt.

Abhoy stepped forward and pointed his index finger in his friend's face.

'Have you forgotten the plan and who is depending on you Dipankar?' he said.

Chad screwed up his face, before a shake of the head.

'Sorry, I've been busy getting the shit kicked out of me for no reason at all,' he spat back.

'You were at his computer!' Abhoy shouted.

Chad didn't know what to say in response. Abhoy was right.

From Abhoy's and everyone else's perspective, this was what he was doing. He cursed himself for being so stupid. Still, a small voice inside him reminded him about how desperate he was. Very desperate. He was trapped in another human being's body.

And it wasn't Ryan Gosling's.

That may have made things a little different.

'One day I will explain to you,' Chad said, realising they were now standing in complete darkness.

'—but you'd better show me the way back,' Chad managed a weak smile.

They walked a little while without talking, before Chad remembered something.

'Abhoy can I ask you a question without upsetting you?' he said.

He knew playing the part of Dipankar and not himself was a smarter option where possible.

'What is it Dip?' Abhoy said.

'What did you mean by the "plan" before. What is it about?' Chad said.

Although Chad couldn't make out Abhoy's face in the darkness, he wouldn't have seen anything confronting. Abhoy had sensed something was amiss with his friend and did consider Dipankar had suffered some sort of amnesia. So, he was obviously getting used to it, in a way.

'Dipankar,' he stopped and grabbed his friend by the arm.

'We've been planning it for some time. We are going to run away.' he said.

Chad wondered how long this had been on the cards.

'Why are we running away Abhoy?' he said.

Abhoy walked on for some time without answering. Only when they had crossed back into the slums did he pull Chad to one side of the path and turned to face him.

He stepped closer and his words were a mere whisper.

'Your sisters, Dip.'

Chad felt a prickle of apprehension pass over his exposed skin as he saw the look on Abhoy's face, more than what he had just said.

'What about them, Abhoy?' he said. Chad wasn't sure he wanted to know.

He sensed hesitation from Abhoy, as if he didn't want to continue this conversation.

'What about them?' Chad repeated.

Abhoy swallowed before he said to Dipankar, 'you have seriously lost your memory, haven't you?'

Chad nodded.

Abhoy bit his bottom lip, staring at his feet.

When he met his friend's eyes, Chad could see the fear inside of them.

'Your father,' Abhoy mumbled, 'does things to them.'

Chad walked on in silence. He'd never felt so angry towards another human being as he did towards Dipankar's father at that moment. Abhoy didn't elaborate, but Chad knew whatever it was had disturbed his friend.

'Another question,' Chad pulled him aside from the busy thoroughfare. 'where does he go at night?'

Abhoy stared at a couple of rickshaws which scurried past within inches.

'He and one of his brothers,' Abhoy nodded, 'yes, the Supervisor. They meet and,' Abhoy hesitated, as if the idea of what they were doing was appalling, 'they go to a place where they can gamble and drink alcohol.'

'But—' Chad was blown away, 'how can he afford to do—' the look on Abhoy's face answered his question.

'Why do you think you work Dip?' he said, his eyes burned with anger.

Chad pictured the hut they lived in. The squalid conditions. And Dipankar's father was spending the money on gambling and drinking. Jesus. *Father of the fucking year,* Chad thought.

'Does my mother know about this?' he added.

Abhoy looked at Chad long enough for him to answer the question.

'But why do—' Chad's question was cut off,

Abhoy stepped closer. 'Because he has threatened

her time and time again. If she has a problem with it, he will marry off their daughters and she will never see them again,' he said.

'Fuck me—,' Chad words came and he didn't care anymore if Abhoy thought it was unusual for his friend to speak like this.

'—how much of an evil bastard is my father?' he said.

Abhoy took a deep breath, checking the world around them for a few moments, whilst gathering his thoughts.

'He's a very bad man Dipankar. I'm surprised he has not sold all of you for money. He and his brother, very bad men. Not all people are this bad, right?'

Chad stood there. His anger was stifling, but a movement behind Abhoy caught Chad's eye, momentarily distracting him. Glancing over Abhoy's shoulder, he watched an old woman in a hut attempting to get comfortable on a piece of cardboard on the ground. She used her hands beneath her head as a pillow, pulling a flimsy, threadbare blanket of sorts over her tiny body. As if she had sensed that he was looking at him, she opened her eyes. In the low light from a single candle close to her, she found it in herself to smile, as if she were at peace with her destiny.

Chad considered his $39,000 mattress.

Thirty-nine fucking thousand dollars, he thought.

Chad wished for the love of God that he could wave

a magic wand and the old woman could now be lying on it instead of that piece of cardboard.

The epiphany hit him hard. Like a sledgehammer.

All the money he could ever wish for or spend in his lifetime. The possessions, the cars, boats, Penthouse apartments, holiday homes, the collection of Breitling and Rolex watches or more Armani suits that he could possibly wear…what did it even matter?

What was the point of it all?

All this woman had was a piece of cardboard to sleep on and a thin blanket to drape over her. And yet, she still could manage a smile.

What he did at that moment just happened, out of the blue.

Chad removed his tracksuit top, and folding it into a small square, walked around Abhoy and stopped at the entrance to the old lady's hut. He held it out to her, gesturing that he meant no harm. The woman's eyes grew large for a moment, but then softened. Nodding, she beckoned him in. Chad bent down and placed his tracksuit top under her head.

'Sleep well tonight,' he said.

She reached up and took Chad's hand, squeezing it. As she smiled, Chad noticed that the woman possessed just two teeth. But her smile, he noticed, was sincere. Tears formed in the corners of her eyes. He looked back at Abhoy, who stood there shaking his head, but his smile was as warm as the old woman's. Chad left the hut, looking back as he watched her snuggle into her new makeshift pillow.

'Why did you do that?' Abhoy asked.

Chad shrugged his shoulders and grinned.

'The knock on my head is changing me, Abhoy.'

CHAPTER FORTY-TWO

Angela

THE MORNING SUN PENETRATED THE PASSING clouds over central London and Angela watched as the rays of light dance across the walls. The morning light reminded her of Bali. She'd lost track of how long it had been. Although it had probably only been a few weeks, it felt like years. She felt herself begin to bargain with someone…God? The universe? Whatever. She'd hand over her luxurious apartment which was located on top of the redeveloped Battersea Power Station. It cost more than most people would earn in a lifetime. Anything. She had to find a way back to the retreat, so she could sort this out. There had to be a way. Then she could fly back to London and deal with this problem at work. Simple.

'Come on!' she cursed to herself, 'think!'

Angela took a few deep breaths, and slowly felt herself grow calmer. She knew if she was going to get herself out of this pickle, she needed to take control of her anger. Starting now. Ever since the incident, nurses had been avoiding her, short of coming in to check her vitals every now and then, which they did silently.

Even though it was the 'other' Dr Smith who had been the real star of the show, it was obvious the nursing staff were growing cautious around 'Mary' too. She noticed that she hadn't seen the doctor since Rachel had been taken away, and she wondered if she'd even have a job to return to.

Angela's focus returned to the nurses, as she shook her head. *'They'd be losing their shit too if they'd woken up in someone else's body,'* she thought. After a pallid breakfast and a dribble of lukewarm tea, Angela put her head down and closed her eyes.

Sometime later Angela woke and for the first time since this nightmare had begun, she didn't freak out when she realised that she was still Mary. Angela sat up in bed and stretched her arms, forcing a smile to her face as a nurse walked past. But when she saw what the nurse was carrying, in a flash, she had an idea.

'Excuse me, nurse,' Angela had never met this nurse before, so she wasn't fibbing when she didn't know her name.

The nurse stopped and turned to Mary.

'What is it?' the nurse replied, curtly.

Angela grimaced at the woman's face, but she pulled

her lips apart and was sure it appeared as if she was smiling.

'I was wondering,' Angela sat up knowing there was no harm in asking, 'would there be any chance I could borrow that iPad?'

The nurse paused in reflection for a moment.

'Please,' Angela said. 'I've been here for so long, with no way of contacting my family.'

'Even if I wanted to, I couldn't,' the nurse said. 'Hospital policy. I'm sorry.'

Angela put her head back down on her pillow. She knew that her chances were nil, but it was worth a shot.

As the nurse walked off, Angela realised there was another way she could get online. It would be risky but what did she have to lose? *Nothing.* She would wait until the middle of the night. There was a computer in one of the consulting rooms, a few doors up from the ward. A few minutes on the computer would be all she needed. All she had to do was get in and out, undetected.

Angela opened her eyes and waited. It was 1.20 am. There was no movement around the ward but she waited for about ten minutes just in case. She knew the night shift nurses had a break around 1.30 am and she calculated that fifteen minutes should be enough to get there, use the computer and get safely back. She rose from her bed and made her way quietly along the darkened hallway, stopping to catch her breath every few steps. Finally, she reached the office door. To her overwhelming relief, it was unlocked. As Angela moved quickly to the other side of the computer screen, she sat down and held her breath.

She waited until the screen asked for the usual login and passwords. Once she entered her details Angela sat back and hoped to hell her info was correct.

A few seconds later, she was in.

As the Google home page appeared, she couldn't believe she was about to pull it off. She typed "The Samsarana Retreat. Ubud, Bali."

If I could find a contact email address, maybe I could email them.

She hit enter and took a deep breath while the page exploded to life. Links to a dizzying array of retreats, photos and maps appeared.

Ubud must be the epicentre of anything with the word 'retreat,' thought Angela, rolling her eyes. But as the oncologist scrolled through three, four then five pages, she realised that there was no place with the name The Samsarana Retreat.

She typed in the words again. The second time produced the same overbearing amount of information, and none of it relevant to her.

She had five minutes left.

An idea sprang to mind.

As annoying as her son's girlfriend was, Sophie was

efficient. She remembered Sophie had emailed her the link showing her The Samsarana Retreat, a week before they flew to Bali together. Angela pulled up a remote login to her email, punching in her details with stealth, a wave of anticipation giving her hope. She scrolled through hundreds of emails that she never bothered to archive. With every passing minute Angela's panic rose.

Where was the email from Sophie? She took a deep breath and could feel herself teetering on the edge of control. She moved the cursor to the search box and, fingers shaking, typed S-O-P-H-I-E and hit enter. Angela gasped.

Nothing was coming up. It was as if Sophie didn't exist – or at the least had never emailed her. She tried again, her breaths getting shorter by the second. S-O-P-H-I-E.

Nothing.

'Impossible!' she cried, realising immediately that she had said the words out loud.

She never deleted emails. Okay, she thought. She'd try Jack.

No email from Jack.

'What the hell!' she hissed.

Not a single email from her son.

'What next,' she grumbled, 'my flat doesn't exist I suppose!'

She ached for something tangible connected to her real life. Bringing up Google Images she typed in 'Battersea Power Station.' Angela felt the air in her lungs go ice cold. She couldn't believe what she was seeing.

The Battersea Power Station looked exactly how it did before the renovation. A run down relic of a bygone era, on the shores of the Thames River, and not the redeveloped residential, commercial and retail hub hundreds of people now called home. Including Doctor Angela Smith. She checked the date of the image. It was taken recently.

With a sudden nagging feeling in her stomach, she entered Jack's name into the search bar, but "Jack Smith" was too common, and yielded too many results. Undeterred, she replaced his name with Sophie's, but actually had left his name there as well.

'Jack Smith Sophie Heathmont.'

Enter.

Her hands flew to her mouth in shock.

'No, no, no!' she cried.

Hands shaking, she clicked on the news story and a headline filled the page.

'Jack Smith and his girlfriend, Sophie Heathmont, both 28, of London – killed in a terrorist attack at Denpasar Airport, Bali, five days ago.'

CHAPTER FORTY-THREE

Logan

LOGAN WAS A BROKEN MAN INSIDE A WOMAN'S body. Suffice to say he regretted his behaviour two weeks ago, when he fell to his wife's feet, begging her not to leave him. Beth's reaction had been swift.

'I don't know what has got into you Court-ten-ay,' Beth hissed from the doorway of her office. '—but whatever it is, you need to sort it out.' He knew that tone. And what it meant was that it was not negotiable.

He'd heard it when he told her he wanted to buy a Harley-Davidson Motorbike.

'No, Logan.'

He'd heard it when he told her he wanted to convert the garage into a luxurious man cave.

'No way, Logan.'

He'd heard it when he asked her what the chances were of her slipping a Batgirl costume on late one night.

He sighed.

Since then, he'd spent most of his time wallowing in the borehole of his own self-pity, which felt as deep as the Mariana Trench.

Logan-as-Courtney had taken leave on the spot, citing to Tindwer that she had been going through some personal issues and were on the verge of a break-down. It was the first time, he noted, that Tindwer's overenthusiastic demeanour disappeared. And it hadn't been replaced with sympathy. Something else had struck him recently. Courtney, herself, was deeply lonely. Pretty ironic for someone who helps couples find their way back into happiness, he thought. But he shifted his attention back to his own problems.

Jerry Springhare had stopped messaging Courtney a week and a half ago and Logan was relieved he was rid of the two-faced imbecile. He felt sorry for Filomena, though; she deserved better.

'What about you?' Logan mumbled. He'd been talking to himself more in the last week.

On the one hand it made him feel mildly concerned about his own sanity. On the other, he had no one else to turn to. He glanced over to the table and studied the one inch of liquid sitting in the bottle of Canadian Club. Next to the bottle was a packet of cigarettes and an overflowing ashtray. The bench was brimming with pizza boxes.

'What about you, dumbass?' he answered.

He stared off into the distance, wondering if this was the sum of his life now.

'Are you going to move onto the next thing, Logan, or are you going to fight to get Beth back?' he said in a low murmur. Logan shook his head, as if considering the question that he had posed to himself.

Music, he thought. He needed music.

He picked up Courtney's phone, curious as to what sort of music the marriage counsellor liked listening to.

When he hit play, his face erupted into a grin. Probably the first smile that had crossed his face for weeks, while the outdoor Bluetooth speakers pumped out unbridled irony.

'I want to break free,' Freddie Mercury in all his glory, Logan laughed. *Jeez, it felt good to laugh.*

'—I want to break free from your lies, you're so self-satisfied I don't need you. I got to break free.'

Logan remembered the famous video clip to the song: the four members of the band all dressed as women, parading around doing housework, or so he recalled. He laughed, thinking about the body that he himself had been trapped in for far too long. As the song wound its way to a close, Logan picked up Courtney's phone and did something that he had done too many times in the last few weeks.

He brought up Beth's Facebook profile.

A friend of his once called it 'Stalkerbook' and for the first time, Logan had to agree. Her profile photo was the same as it had been, the last time he had checked. Yesterday. She hadn't changed it for some time now. Beth at a friend's wedding, standing outside the reception venue in a stunning Samba cocktail dress, its light blue silk hugging her slender body, her Jimmy Choo high heels, elongating her calves. She looked gorgeous, he thought. He longed to hug her like the Samba cocktail dress did in the photo.

The background photo was unchanged as well. It was a shot of the Capilano Suspension Bridge Park in North Vancouver. A perfect Summer's day. Beth was standing right in the middle of the famous structure. It was a proud day for her, he recalled. The first day she'd overcome her fear of heights.

It was then that Logan spotted a post that Beth had put up, obviously late last night. He hadn't seen it until now. She had been out at BarChef – one of their favourite haunts, standing at the bar with a Sailor's Mojito, her favourite cocktail, in her hand. His heart ached to be there with her. Beth was gorgeous. An effortless white tank top, tight in all the right places. Her skin-tight army-green Mavi jeans with silver stud buttons…her hair up in a bun…the diamond earrings she loved, glistening from the flash of the camera…

A sound nearby snapped Logan out of his reverie. He looked up to the adjacent window to see a man descending the side of the building with well-practiced dexterity. He relaxed. It was just a window-washer. Dressed in black overalls, the man's baseball cap was tipped down shielding his face. Logan thought he'd heard a noise, but shrugged it off and went back to peering at the photo on the screen.

The song ended, and the apartment was filled with the same unnerving silence as before.

'I said —' Logan heard the voice again, much clearer now.

The window washer was staring inside. Creep.

He'd pulled his baseball cap up and was looking right at him now.

It took Logan a second to register who it was.

'—are you done yet, Logan?'

Logan stared at him, stunned, just as the cage began to descend at a steady pace, its thick black cords holding its weight.

He knew those eyes. It was the meditation teacher.

The question echoed in Logan's mind. *Are you done yet?*

He needed a drink. He took his next swig straight out of the bottle. Charming.

He returned to Beth and her cocktail. Flicking through the other photos in the album, he stopped dead.

What the hell?

Beth was toasting a glass with what looked like a Vanilla Hickory Smoked Manhattan – the bar's specialty. But it wasn't the drink that caught his eye. It was who was holding it.

Are you done yet?

Logan glanced again at the window, but the cables were gone. He ran to the edge of the balcony and peered over the edge, but there was no sign of the cage, or the man who was the spitting image of the meditation teacher.

He swayed a little from vertigo and wondered if he'd imagined the whole thing. Stumbling back to the table, he returned to the photo on Courtney's phone before slowly sinking into a chair.

Holding the other glass was Tindwer, her arm hooked around Beth's waist.

CHAPTER FORTY-FOUR

Amelia

'*WHAT THE HELL DO I DO NOW?*' AMELIA THOUGHT, her feet still planted on her billionaire neighbour's lawn. The twelve-foot high rendered wall of her own property, which enveloped her 10,607 square foot home and grounds, stared back at her, offering no answers.

Amelia walked further up her street so she could afford a better view of the imposing wrought iron gates. Standing this close to her own home made her feel nauseous.

She knew that if she attempted to enter the estate, the police would be handcuffing her hands behind her back within no time.

A small bus crammed with tourists meandered past the teenager and off down the road. With the Playboy Mansion only three doors up, the buses were a regular site around here. None of the passengers paid her any heed. As Amelia watched it disappear down her street, she pondered how long it was going to take her to walk all the way back to Melrose Hill.

Without notice, the huge gates started to open.

Amelia stole a quick glance up and down the road, wondering if someone was about to enter her estate, but there were no cars visible in either direction. She snuck back across to get a better look.

Someone was leaving.

The 'Nardo' Gray Audi RS5-E Coupe with its dark tinted windows, sounded like a race-car ready to roar down a racetrack and Amelia held her breath when she heard the sound.

Pierre.

Amelia got a good look at him through the open sunroof. Dark sunglasses, black hair, and a crisp white shirt, looking as sharp as he did most days.

Amelia wasn't sure whether she wanted to tell him off for letting him talk her into going to Bali with Gemma, or hug him.

Pierre rolled down the driveway but stopped when he saw the Latino teenager standing on the edge of the driveway.

He stepped out of his car and removed his glasses.

'What the hell are you doing?' he said.

Amelia stared at him for a moment before bursting into tears and falling to her knees. She heard his car door slam shut. *He's leaving*, she thought. *My life is over.* She wrapped her arms tightly around her legs in defeat. She waited for the inevitable roar of the motor.

'Are you alright, young lady?'

Amelia opened her eyes to see Pierre crouching in front of her. He placed a hand on her shoulder and a sudden jolt of electricity took her breath away. Pierre snapped his hand back and Amelia shot him a hurt look. He softened his approach.

'Are you going to be okay? What's going on here?'

Amelia met Pierre's eyes. She had never felt such sadness, as well as frustration, but also a sense of joy – being in his presence. She felt as if she was home.

Amelia pulled herself to her feet.

'You will never believe me, Pierre,' Amelia said.

'Okay, honey, I don't know how the hell you know my name, but—' his voice trailed away, and he stepped back.

Amelia glanced behind her personal assistant, watching the gates close.

She wondered if she made a run for it, would she make it through the gates before it closed. For what purposes she didn't know.

'Do you believe in karma, Pierre?' she said, staring at him with a neutral, almost resigned expression.

Pierre glanced to his left and to his right. No cars. This girl was all alone.

'Look, I'm not sure who you are, or why you are here. But if you are okay, it may be best that you go on your way,' he said.

'My name is Margarita Serrano,' Amelia said.

A flicker of recognition in his eyes, if only for a second. But it was there.

'Look, I have to get going…I can't really be late,' he said.

'So, do you?' she said, her eyes fixed on his.

'Karma?' he asked.

Margarita nodded.

'Sometimes yes, sometimes no.'

'Do you think Amelia Langston deserves a good dose of karma?' she said.

Pierre's demeanour changed. His stood straighter and eyed her suspiciously.

'Look, not sure where this is heading, um, Margarita, but you should definitely not be creeping around out the front of other people's houses.'

Amelia stepped onto the edge of the kerb and took a deep breath. What if this was the last chance she ever got to speak to him?

'Pierre. It's me. Amelia. You must let me explain. I am—'

'A whack job, I get it,' he said, moving towards his car.

'Go home, Margarita Serrano.'

As Pierre got to his car, she knew this was her last chance,

'Five millimetre round mole. Ten millimetres from the base of your Percy Pecker,' she said.

Touchdown, Amelia thought.

She was the only person he'd ever told. Pierre was private about most things, that mole and the nickname for his penis included.

He got back inside his car and started the engine.

Amelia knew she had about two seconds before Pierre drove away for good.

Pierre turned into the street and their eyes met for literally one, maybe two seconds.

'Agastopia,' Amelia cried out.

Pierre had chosen it years ago as a code word in the event of stolen identity or password theft on social media and so on. This way they would both know it was one of them. Not some hacker in some foreign country posing as her or him. As a bit of a joke, Pierre had chosen the world *Agastopia*. It meant admiration of a particular part of the body. It was a word that no one would be able to guess, and he knew that Amelia, like himself, would get a kick out of it. Agastopia.

He hit the brakes and the car skidded to a stop.

Amelia stood there watching, holding her breath.

Pierre took one last curious glance at her, and drove away.

CHAPTER FORTY-FIVE

Chad

CHAD FOUND THE NOTION OF SLEEP IMPOSSIBLE, even in the dead of night. Dipankar's youngest sisters didn't have the same problem, although given what Abhoy had told him, he wondered how much that had to do with his presence. The youngest had asked him again as they lay down to sleep on the floor, if she could hold his hand. The other sister lay next to her, snoring.

He would do anything in his power to protect the two of them from that monster.

Chad realised he'd dozed off, only as he heard Dipankar's father arrive home sometime later and realised that it wasn't just anger he was feeling, it was fear, for them. It was only after he heard their father begin to snore that he exhaled.

Chad peered down at the little sister, watching her

face as she slept, before turning his face to the ceiling. Her face came into his mind a few seconds later.

Serena.

As Dipankar's little sister murmured in her sleep, and gripped Chad's hand a little tighter, he felt his chest heave.

'I'm sorry Serena,' he said in a whisper.

Chad felt tears well in his eyes.

He continued to hold on to the little girl, doing his best to wipe his eyes and nose with his free hand. Chad could hear Dipankar's father move, followed by what Chad would remember as the loudest fart he'd ever heard anyone do. It sounded like a foghorn. The hut was awash with the stench of rotting meat, and Chad pulled his t-shirt up to cover his mouth, almost gagging.

'Christ, what do you eat?' he whispered.

'Now that is gassy, Chad,' the voice cut through the darkness.

Chad's eyes went to the door. He saw a head pop through. Even before his eyes adjusted, he knew it wasn't Abhoy.

The expression on the meditation teacher's face was impassive.

'Are you done yet?' he said.

Dipankar's little sister gripped his hand tighter.

Chad shook his head.

'No. There is something I have to do,' he said.

Chad stole a glance down at Dipankar's little sister,

but when his eyes went back to the front door, he wondered if he had dreamed the whole thing up.

Henry, the meditation teacher, was gone.

The morning light was creeping in through all the nooks and crannies above and Chad could hear the slum rustling to life. Dogs barked. People outside his hut mingled, talking as they walked past. The distant sounds of city traffic, the backdrop. The humidity always increased as the morning light grew stronger and he peeled his shirt off his skin to let some air in.

Another day in Dhaka, he sighed.

Chad felt relief, Dipankar's father was nowhere in sight. He rose from the floor, moving slowly, his body stiff and sore from sleeping on the bare ground, and found Abhoy out the front smiling when his friend looked him over with a grin.

'Ready?' Abhoy said.

'Never more,' Chad replied.

The two of them headed off to do the breakfast run.

After walking in a comfortable silence for about ten minutes, Chad stopped and turned to Abhoy.

'We need to leave today.'

Abhoy frowned.

'Today?' he said, surprised.

'We can't go on like this. My sisters cannot take this

anymore. Enough is enough. If it happens one more time, I will not be able to live with myself.'

Abhoy walked on for a time. Chad could see he was deep in thought.

'Are you sure Dipankar?' he asked him, the look on his face concerned, 'you really want to leave today?'

Chad didn't respond. He walked on and watched the throng of people all around them. It was the same depressing scene. Same people. Same faces.

Same sadness.

Abhoy had told Chad the basics of the plan the day before. A friend of Abhoy's brother in another part of the city would let them stay with him for a few days.

Although Chad hadn't met Abhoy's brother before, he felt as if he knew him from his friend's description. Abhoy told Chad he worked about 17 hours a day, as a bicycle courier. It sounded like punishing work, especially in this traffic. And for little money.

A friend would then get the children out of Dhaka and from there Abhoy, his brother, Dipankar and his four siblings would head for Chattogram, another Bangladesh city located a few hours away. Abhoy had older cousins who lived there. He told Chad they were decent people, who had done the same thing for others.

The plan sounded ambitious to Chad, but he knew that they were out of options.

He had to get the sisters away from Dipankar's father, by night fall. Dipankar's two brothers already knew of the plan. Chad felt a pang for the children's mother. He wasn't sure whether she knew of her husband's behaviour, but given what Chad knew about their society—a place where women and girls had very few choices—deep down he knew she would be relieved that the girls would at least would be safe. Perhaps one day they would be reunited, although he doubted it.

'Alright,' Abhoy said, still not looking convinced.

'I will have to get hold of my brother Madhu and make sure he is okay to leave today. Once I can do this, we can figure out when,' Abhoy said.

The pair continued to walk.

'Why do we need to wait? Why can't we just go now?' asked Chad.

Abhoy shook his head, grinning.

'What's so funny Abhoy?' Chad said.

'What do you think you will be doing today, Dipankar?' he said.

Chad had no idea what he was referring to.

'Getting the hell out of this place?' Chad said, it was more of a question than a statement.

Abhoy started to laugh as he continued on towards the tip.

'Did I say something funny?' Chad said.

Abhoy shook his head as his laughter faded.

'Sort of, Dipankar. You've forgotten, we have to work today. We will at least need to finish our shift, so not to raise any suspicions.'

Chad stopped walking.

'Work? I was fired, wasn't I?'

Abhoy turned his head and stared at Dipankar.

'Fired? If you mean you were sacked from your job Dipankar, you may have thought you were, but you weren't,' he said.

'I've still got a job in that hell-hole?'

It was the last place on earth Chad wanted to be. Currently, the garbage dump was a more attractive location.

'No matter what you do wrong at work, or how badly your uncle treats you. You have no choice.'

'They make me work at the factory anyway?'

Chad couldn't believe what he was hearing.

'You have forgotten what the Supervisor once said to you Dipankar,' Abhoy said.

He walked on for about six feet before he turned to Chad.

'He said you will work there for the rest of your miserable life.'

CHAPTER FORTY-SIX

Angela

ANGELA COULDN'T RECALL THE LAST TIME SHE'D shed a tear.

At her parents' funerals?

Nope.

The moment the priest said, 'I now pronounce you husband and wife'?

Nope.

The birth of her son?

Nope.

The death of her Husband? *Come on.*

Nope.

But after making it back from the office, she cried as silently as she could in the darkened ward. In the morning, the nurses offered to draw the curtain around Mary's bed. Angela nodded between sobs.

She closed her eyes and knew there was nothing left to care about.

'I want to die,' she whispered to herself, 'I deserve to die.' She pictured the last time she saw Jack and Sophie. Their enthusiasm had annoyed her. They had been so excited about the retreat. As Angela wiped her nose, the vision of their smiling faces just before the start of the meditation class brought a fresh wave of emotions.

'They were always so happy together. Kindred spirits,' Angela whispered to herself, 'and now they are gone.'

Angela's mind drifted to the early days with Benedict, when she felt the same as he did about their relationship. Years later, during a heated argument, it came to Angela in retrospect as no surprise, that before Benedict stormed out the front door of their home, he spoke a line from his favourite film, Highlander.

'You're a *bloated warthog*!' he complained from the hallway before the front door slammed behind him.

Angela sobbed as she pictured Benedict's face.

'I am a bloated warthog Benedict, I will never forgive myself for losing you,' she cried.

Five minutes later, Angela accepted the offer of a sleeping tablet from a concerned nurse. She felt uncomfortable seeing the trepidation on the face of the nurse who was about to enter her curtained off cubical, but soon sleep came without delay.

❀

Angela opened her eyes. The curtain was still drawn all the way around her bed, but the ward was in complete darkness. She wondered how long she'd slept for. It must have been all day. The silence was so pronounced that it made her feel uncomfortable and a part of her wondered if they'd abandoned the ward and left her alone to fend for herself.

Angela felt a slight breeze to her left. She turned to see Benedict on the chair two feet away from her bed.

'Am I dreaming?' she asked under her breath.

'I'm afraid not,' he said, his words were calm and measured.

'Are you here to take me to Heaven?' Angela whimpered through fresh tears.

'Is that what you want, Angela?' Benedict said, leaning forward, his face impassive.

'I want to be wherever you are, Benedict,' she said, she leant over to him with an outstretched hand. Benedict took it. Angela shuddered as she could feel his warm fingers intertwined with her own, even though she didn't know how that could even be possible.

'No Angela,' Benedict frowned, 'you don't need to die, my love.'

Angela shook her head.

'I could have saved you,' she said.

Angela's husband stood up and sat on the edge of her bed. He placed both his hands over hers, she could feel warmth in them. It felt like home.

'I know.' Benedict paused. 'The reason I am here tonight is to tell you something.'

Angela wiped the tears from her eyes and nodded.

'You may think your actions resulted in my passing, but dear Angela, they did not.'

'What?' she sat up a little straighter.

'It wouldn't have mattered,' Benedict said, his eyes looking into hers with sincerity.

'But I checked, I know—,' her words were cut off as he lifted his hand and stroked her face, the feeling sending a shock-wave of electricity through her body.

'—my dear Angela, the cancer was going to take me regardless. It's time to forgive yourself.,' his words were slow and in a near whisper.

Angela shook her head, she didn't believe him.

'You, for the first time in your life, are going to admit you were wrong, Angela,' Benedict's eyes were teasing, but decisive.

Angela closed her eyes and nodded.

'I want to hear you say it,' he said.

'I was wrong, Benedict. I wish I could go back and tell a thousand people I was wrong. Go back and tell the world how much of a bloated warthog I was and still am,' she said.

Hearing the words from his favourite movie brought a smile to his face. Angela had forgotten how intoxicating her late husband's laughter sounded.

'That's my girl,' he eventually said, his smile remained.

They looked at each other for a few moments.

'Do you really mean that?' he said.

'Yes, Benedict, I do.' She sat fully upright now.

'There are so many people I need to say sorry to, Benedict. And the number one person is you. I am sorry for being such an egomaniac. I hope one day you forgive me.'

Benedict nodded and without another word, Angela sensed he was deep in thought. As he took his eyes away from hers, Benedict looked over to the other side of her bed and nodded again.

'Do you believe her, Benedict?' said a voice from the shadows. She was sure it sounded like the voice of the Mediation Teacher.

'I do, Henry,' Benedict said.

Angela couldn't seem to speak, she was scared, confused and still in shock from what was happening before her.

Benedict rose and kissed her on the forehead. She could feel his warm lips touch her skin. It sent a wave of calm into the core of her being. She closed her eyes. He put his arm around her back and with her eyes closed, helped her lie down again.

She felt his warm breath against her left ear.

'Promise me,' he whispered.

'I promise Benedict,' she said.

For a moment, she wondered where he'd gone. It was then that Angela began to feel a hard surface behind her head. Light started to filter through her eyelids, growing brighter by the second. She took a deep breath and realised that she no longer felt the weakness in her body.

Something flickered above and Angela opened her eyes. She sat up too fast and the room started spinning. Henry the meditation teacher sat on the floor, watching her, his nod so imperceptible that anyone else watching him would not have noticed. But Angela did.

'Alright?' she heard a voice from her left.

Jack sat on the meditation mat next to her, his grin beaming.

Sophie leaned forward next to him, so they were now in her full view. They both smiled with their usual bright faces.

'How amazing was this class!' she gushed to Angela.

CHAPTER FORTY-SEVEN

Logan

LOGAN PULLED OUT OF COURTNEY'S UNDERGROUND car park. The late afternoon sun still brought a squint to his eyes as he turned into Queens Quay. He fished for Courtney's Prada sunglasses. Slipping them on his face still gave him a 'Mrs Doubtfire' moment and he chuckled. As he drove on, he wondered what Jerry Springhare would think of him driving a Lexus. As Logan recalled his words however, his face darkened. He didn't think that he would be able to look at Jerry in the same way ever again.

He was tempted to post an anonymous letter to the dealership regarding his Jerry's application for Penis enlargement medication, just for the fun of it. *Maybe later.*

As Logan drove down Lake Shore Boulevard, he

realised that the final blow was seeing the photo of Beth and Tindwer earlier in the day on Stalkerbook. He'd bet Courtney's Lexus there was something going on between them. There had to be.

But what did it matter?' Logan thought. '*I am a grown man, held captive inside a woman's body for Christ's sake. This is a nightmare.'*

The decision to drive to Tindwer's home was made on a whim. Logan realised that the only way to bring everything to a head was to confront her. He couldn't go on much longer like this. After that, Logan would go back to Courtney's apartment for the last time.

He still had another bottle of whisky in the kitchen. And once the bottle was gone, Logan would end it.

Logan continued towards Tindwer's home. He'd located her address in Courtney's phone and had let the guys at Google tell him how to get there.

He didn't want to think anymore.

It only dawned on him as he cruised through the intersection that he would drive directly past Courtney's office on route to her receptionist's home. As Logan saw the corporate offices come into view across the road on his left, he wondered if it was the universe who had sent him this way and not Google Maps.

There's coincidence, and then there's coincidence, he murmured. His instincts were right on the money. Out the front of the office building was Beth's car. The only person he knew in Toronto who owned a small lime green SUV with the number plate 'MIDORI.' Her favourite drink of choice. It stuck out like a sore thumb. As Logan slowed down, he then spotted Tindwer's black Audi A1 Coupe sitting in the carpark right next to Beth's.

He recalled the first time he read the sticker on the back window of her car on the way home. "HAPPI-NESS is FREE!" it said.

Logan parked the Lexus and took one last glance at Tindwer's words of wisdom. He wondered if Tindwer would quote the stupid sticker if she ever woke up in a man's body.

Probably not.

'Let's do this,' he scowled.

Logan's heart was pounding as he reached the top floor of the office. The building was in darkness apart from the faint light emanating from the EXIT sign and he could see muted light coming from Courtney's office. His heart rate increased and his hands were getting clammy and he wondered if turning around and going straight back to Courtney's apartment was a better idea.

'No,' he breathed, 'you are here. This needs to be done.'

Although he had the keys in his hand, he checked to see if the door was unlocked.

It was. He swallowed.

He opened the door, and holding his breath, quietly entered the room. A whisper of music was the first thing he heard. Then giggles and laughter, followed by chinks of glasses. He swore under his breath. The light, Jesus. It flickered. A low, yellow glow.

Fuck me, Logan thought. *Candles.*

Logan wondered what the real Courtney would think if she dropped into her office unannounced to find this. He caught sight of his reflection in the darkened glass and Courtney Lushgrove stared back. The wealthy marriage counsellor with the apartment, the car and the money. He briefly wondered if she was as lonely as he felt right now, but another chink of glasses snapped him out of his thoughts.

'Good luck,' Courtney said in the reflection.

He took a few steps forward, dropping Courtney's handbag on the reception desk.

Another ten steps towards Courtney's office, and Logan knew there was no turning back.

He stepped into the open doorway and gasped in shock.

'What the fuck!' he swore.

Beth and Tindwer were not alone.

CHAPTER FORTY-EIGHT

Logan

'WHAT ARE YOU DOING HERE?' LOGAN GASPED.

Beth wore only high heel shoes, with a glass of champagne in her hand. His wife didn't appear to reciprocate his shock at seeing her. Tindwer, scantily dressed, appeared a little more embarrassed, avoided eye contact with her boss.

The two women were sitting on the plush rug of Courtney's office with Jerry Springhare. The coffee table told Logan their party was in full swing. A small mirror sitting with a credit card near a tiny packet of what was clearly cocaine. An open bottle of champagne sat alongside a few burning candles.

Logan had a moment of gut-wrenching déjà vu.

The hotel room in Las Vegas.

Two hookers.

Champagne.

When one of them offered him coke, he had shrugged. Why the fuck not.

They were hookers though, for Pete's sake, came the voice inside of him, clutching at straws.

'How could you!' Logan screamed at Beth, struggling to stay in character, 'he's your husband's boss!'

Beth rolled her eyes and shrugged.

'Mind your own business, bitch'.' She looked past him and Logan whirled around to see Filomena Springhare standing in shock in the window of the office. How she had gotten all the way into Courtney's office undedicated, Logan had no idea.

'You!' she cried at Logan, 'I knew it!'

'Okay hang on, it's not what you think!' Logan sidestepped away from the party to prove his point.

Filomena stood agape at the three on the rug, black mascara trailing onto her cheeks, before composing herself, reaching into her handbag and pulling out a handgun. Stumbling back, she pointed the weapon in Logan's direction and then shifted it in the direction of her husband.

'I'm going to kill every last one of you!' she screamed.

Logan lunged for Filomena without a moment's hesitation and the gun went off, shooting a hole in the ceiling above the couch. The two women fell back and without any delay were both scrambling for the handgun which had fallen by the side of Courtney's desk. Filomena got there first, grabbing the weapon in her right hand, but Logan had reached out and had clamped his hand around her wrist.

Tindwer and Beth, saw their opening.

So, did Two-Faced Jerry and all three of them scrambled to their feet and started running towards the door. Tindwer and Beth didn't bother grabbing their clothes, high-tailed it out of the office in a skin coloured blur.

Logan made the mistake of taking his eyes off Filomena for only a split second. He wanted to see if Two-Faced was gone, but that was all the opening that Filomena needed.

Breaking free of Logan's hold of her wrist, she swung the gun in her hand towards his face, and pistol-whipped him with surprising force. Logan thought he felt his nose break. The pain shot right through his brain and he felt blood trickle down his throat.

He fell backwards and hit the floor just as Filomena scrambled to her feet.

'You cheating fucking asshole!' she screamed at her husband before pulling the trigger, the bullet hitting him fair square in the back of the head.

He went down, hard, on something still err, hard.

Out of the corner of his eye, he watched Filomena run out of the office, presumably after Tindwer and his wife. She stepped over her dead husband and was out the front door of Courtney's office in record time.

'Beth!' Logan screamed.

He stumbled to his feet, the pain of his broken nose throbbing in his skull.

'I'm going to fucking kill you two whores!' Logan heard Filomena shout.

Logan almost fell down the spiral staircase, chasing the sound of Filomena's voice, his heart beating so fast he wondered if he was going to pass out.

He pushed through the glass doors and out into the night air. The two women were in Tindwer's Audi, which was hurtling out of the car park at a breakneck speed.

Filomena had just fired another two shots off, one of them splintering the rear window as they sped away.

'Jesus!' Logan thought, *'who is this woman, a fucking assassin?'*

She ran after the car, knowing that it would have to stop at the intersection at the end of the carpark.

She stopped running and levelled the hand gun. She fired another shot, but missed. Logan watched in horror as the Audi ran the red light. He could hear Beth's panicked screams as the car veered into oncoming traffic. The road tanker had no chance of stopping in time, hitting the car on an angle, before the small car wedged itself in the truck's front bumper and both truck and car careered into the path of a Ford pickup. Both the tanker and Audi T-boned the pickup with such velocity that the metallic crunching sound of the collision was as loud as it was horrifying.

'NO!' Logan screamed, dodging Filomena and

running towards the carnage without any thought of his own safety, just as the SUV, the A1 Audi and the truck exploded in a huge fireball. Logan slumped to his knees.

Filomena had stopped running. She watched the flames dancing high into the night sky, before turning slowly towards the marriage counsellor. Logan's body was frozen in a state of shock and fear.

She started walking towards him, with murder etched in her eyes.

'Now for you, you home-wrecking bitch,' she said and before Logan could do a thing, she was within six feet of him.

With the gun levelled at his head, Logan knew this was it.

Time to die.

At least this nightmare would be over.

'Last words, slut?' Filomena spat. She held the gun with such poise, Logan knew there wasn't a chance in hell this was going to end in any other way.

Logan didn't even have time to close his eyes.

Click.

'Fuck!' Filomena cursed.

Click.

'You fucking shit!' she hissed.

She sprang forward and before Logan could react, she swung the handgun at his head.

His world went black as he fell to the ground.

A warm breeze passed over Logan, followed by a strange sense of calm. A bright light flickered in his eyelids and gingerly he opened his eyes.

'No way,' was all he could manage to say.

The black ceiling fan, swirled in a lazy circle from the thatched roof.

Logan sat up in a panic, meeting eyes with the meditation teacher.

With a start, he turned to his left.

The yoga mat next to him.

Empty.

CHAPTER FORTY-NINE

Amelia

FOURTEEN DAYS HAD PASSED SINCE AMELIA HAD seen Pierre. The walk back to Melrose Hill had taken her over three hours and by the time she made it home, her chest was heaving, her thighs were chafing and her back was killing her. The whole time, she had spent fantasising about running away. Except where would she go?

Margarita's last week at Melrose Hill was another week she swore she would do her best to forget. She refused to catch the bus to school for fear of bumping into Big Blonde and her gang. They'd found her in the gym anyway and as usual, she was no match for the group. Big Blonde learned to not travel without her pack in case Amelia bested her again.

Moving to Oakland offered Amelia one, albeit

small, silver lining, she thought, lying on the locker room floor. Leaving this hell-hole of a school.

The move itself to Oakland presented Amelia with some unique challenges.

Firstly, Amelia had never physically moved her belongings to another house before. Wealthy people didn't move themselves; they paid others to do it seamlessly for them. The only thing she had ever picked up as an adult was either hand weights in her gym, a glass of champagne, or a statue at an awards night. Margarita's family appeared to have nominated her as the Head Moving person. After she'd packed Margarita's own room, they asked her to pack up the kitchen. And then the study. Then the shed. The backbreaking work went on for three days.

The moving van arrived at 8.00 o'clock on Sunday morning. Spotting it rumble down the street, Amelia wondered if it would actually make it to Oakland. It was a pile of junk, rusted and beat up. The van must have come from the corner of a deserted farm, where it should have stayed.

Then there was the removalist, Pablo.

'Christ,' Amelia said under her breath as he shook her hand, holding it for as long as her lungs could allow. She was tempted to ask him if he had showered anytime in the last twelve months but she thought better of it. Amelia instinctively stepped back until her nose found fresh air. She contemplated asking her father where he'd found this guy. Surely, Pablo had to be bottom of the barrel, but she wanted to go one day without an argument.

Only once Pablo's shit-heap was packed until nothing else would fit in the hold, was she told that she'd be riding up front with him all the way to Oakland. The family car, she was told, had no space for her. But it did for Antonio.

While she was packing the van, Amelia felt his eyes on her too often. It was as if he could see Amelia hidden inside Margarita, in her red bikini. Margarita's mother told her she was imagining it and Amelia was starting to doubt this woman's maternal instincts, despite her seemingly 'caring' exterior, when she felt like it.

He had flicked a tongue around his lips when she first hauled herself into the front seat, and Amelia wanted to unpack the kitchen box, pull out a knife and cut his ugly little fucking tongue out.

How this woman could think it was better for her daughter to travel with this stranger rather than her son confounded her. But then, she had also unknowingly been putting her daughter into danger every day by insisting that she went to that godawful school. Maybe it was a generational thing.

By road, the trip should have taken around six and a half hours, give or take. She knew that they weren't going to make that deadline as soon as Pablo made the suggestion of ducking in to the McDonald's at Bowerbank. It was just off the I-5, and en route, he assured her. Amelia suggested they drive on. Taking the exit, her words fell on deaf ears.

With the drive through backed up, Pablo opted to order inside. Amelia pushed her burger around while watching him stuff handfuls of fries into his mouth with his fat greasy fingers, wiping his mouth on the sleeve of his shirt. On the way back to the car, he belched and this time Amelia almost threw up. He grinned at her while she pulled on her seatbelt.

'Ready to go, sweet-cheeks?'

He chuckled and turned the key. But the pile of shit refused to start.

What made matters worse was when she called Margarita's parents to tell them of the predicament, they breezily suggested that they would drive on to Oakland and meet them there. There was no point in doubling back.

Amelia could not believe it.

Pablo spent close to two painful hours fucking around under the hood. Amelia grew anxious, but after what felt like an eternity, the pile of junk finally started. As they approached the city limits of San Francisco, Amelia had considered opening her door and jumping out no less than six times. Either that, or stab the guy in his fat gut.

Pablo had talked endlessly, about his ex-wife, his family, his favourite fishing spots and television shows. From time to time, he made lewd and suggestive comments, which he punctuated with wandering hands that would creep towards her thigh. Amelia had spent the trip feeling around on the floor with her foot for something sharp.

During the drive, Amelia had at least found out where Pablo had come into the picture. He was a cousin of one of Aunt Sofia's neighbours and by chance, lived a couple of streets away.

Great, Amelia thought.

She prayed to the lord above that once they had unpacked the van, it would be the last time she would ever lay eyes on him.

'Someone is fucking with me,' Amelia said to herself. The house that Pablo had pulled up outside of made her skin crawl with unease. She'd checked Aunt Sofie's house on Google Street View the night before. This was not it.

Was this Pablo's house? Or a friend's?
Oh, no.

Amelia had spotted a rusty screwdriver near her feet a couple of hours ago and had worked it up the seat until she could shove it in her pocket. If something was about to go down, she would not hesitate to use it in self-defence. It was then that she spotted her father's station wagon.

'Sofia moved in last week,' Pablo said, shrugging his shoulders, 'this house will fit all of you much better.'

Amelia turned pale as she looked at the house and shuddered. It was sad and run down, the ugliest thing she'd ever seen, next to Pablo's van. Every window was barred. They must have come from Alcatraz when they shut the island prison down in '63, she scoffed.

As if he could read her thoughts, Pablo began to laugh.

'Don't worry Margarita. Everyone who lives in the Iron Triangle has bars over their windows. It's okay,' he gave her a sleazy wink, 'keeps you safe from all the crazies who live around here.'

Amelia could feel the burger in her stomach lurch.

Pierre had once mentioned the Iron Triangle. Initially named because of the intersecting railway lines which formed a shape of a triangle in Central Richmond, it was now home to some of California's most violent residents. And now, she lived here.

Who in their right mind would paint a house that shade of pink? she asked herself.

'Hey,' he leaned over, disturbing her thoughts, 'if you ever feel in danger,' his body odour was so strong Amelia almost gagged again, 'just call Uncle Pablo.'

He slid his hand over, and placed it on her leg. It was rough and clammy.

'Don't touch me!' Amelia screamed. She flung the van door open, and as her feet hit the ground, Margarita's parents appeared.

Crisis, averted.

After an awkward greeting with her Aunt Sofia, and

some hurried unpacking, Amelia was finally allowed to retire to her room for the night. The time was 11.00 pm, and she had never felt this exhausted.

She had taken a small souvenir from the trip, though. She fingered the rusty screwdriver that she'd hid underneath her mattress. She planned to take it everywhere she went.

Amelia lay on her bed in the tiny bedroom barely big enough for it.

The curtains on the window were in tatters, the walls a depressing shade of yellow. Not one wall escaped scuff and scratch marks. The room was stuffy, and hot. It smelt like dirty socks, or worse, *'Uncle'* Pablo. She shuddered and stared up at the ceiling. A single light globe swayed on a flimsy cord from left to right.

She kept the bedroom door open a crack in an attempt to keep the heat down. With the window refusing to open, Amelia had no choice. She needed air. It didn't help.

She could hear her parents and Aunt Sofia talking. It sounded as if they would talk all night. She would never tiptoe past them at this rate. Would she try though? As she lay there, Amelia realised that she was approaching a crossroad. She would have to run away. It seemed like the only choice she had before her. Where, she had no idea.

Amelia couldn't stay here. She knew that Central Richmond was like one hundred steps back from Melrose Hill. But at least when they lived there, it was

Los Angeles. And Los Angeles felt closer to home than here.

A noise brought her thoughts back to the present moment.

Margarita's father's phone rang.

Amelia jumped to her feet and padded quickly to the bedroom door, so she could eavesdrop on the conversation. Albeit, her father's side of it.

'Yes, I remember you.' Francisco said flatly.

Whoever was on the other end spoke for some time.

'Look, I don't know what to tell you, Pierre? Yes, I did pronounce it right, good. Look, Pierre, I know I'm pissed off with your boss, but—'

Amelia's mouth went dry. A flush of heat passed over her.

Pierre had called Francisco.

Her father had gone silent.

'—what do you mean? Who was out the front of her house?' Margarita's father said impatiently.

Amelia felt light-headed.

Oh, shit.

She recalled the fleeting recognition in Pierre's eyes, when she'd introduced herself as Margarita Serrano out the front of her own home in Holmby Hills.

Pierre had obviously remembered the Cisco Kid. Francisco Serrano.

'—Yes, I know Pierre.'

More silence.

'—look Amelia has nothing to worry about,' pause

– then, 'give me a break Pierre. So, you saw Margarita out the front of Amelia's house, listen—'

Amelia wanted to run out of the house and not look back. Margarita's father was getting angrier. She then heard footsteps heading in her direction. He threw open the door and light flooded the room.

'Margarita! What the hell were you doing at Amelia Langston's house?'

Trying to go home, Amelia thought. 'Um I was—' her words were cut off.

'Stupid girl!' Francisco said. 'Do you know what you've done?'

Margarita's father's face was like thunder before he put his phone back against his ear.

'She won't do it again Pierre. Amelia needn't worry. Please give her my best. And, if the film ever resumes production—'

Amelia knew that Margarita's father's chances of being rehired on any of Amelia's films was non-existent. She also knew that it was a small industry and once that word travelled about the Cisco Kid's daughter stalking Amelia Langston, he'd never be hired again.

Francisco went silent and wiped his eyes with his spare hand.

Shit. She resolved to leave the next day, before she did any further damage.

Into a future, with no future. She sighed.

'Okay Pierre, okay, I understand,' Francisco said.

Amelia knew this was her last chance, that she would never get the opportunity to speak to Pierre ever again.

Seconds before Francisco ended the call, Amelia grabbed the phone from her father.

' Jentucular!!' she bellowed into its receiver, *'Jentucular!'*

CHAPTER FIFTY

Amelia

ANOTHER SLEEPLESS NIGHT, INSIDE SOMEONE ELSE'S body. Sure, she had heard the stories of places in Los Angeles where the sounds of gunfire were a regular occurrence at night, but hearing it with her own ears was a different story. First came the sounds of cars. Cars driven at high speed, burnouts. Then the shouting, talking, arguing. Some of it sounded so close it could have been next door or out the front of the house.

But this was nothing compared to what happened next.

A woman's scream woke her out of a fitful doze and she wondered if she'd dreamed it. When she heard it again, she knew that she hadn't. It sent her mind into a spiral of thoughts.

'If I ever get back to my old life,' she felt tears forming

in the corners of her eyes, *'I need to make a lifetime of amends.'*

She wrapped her arms around her body, putting her head down, doing her best to give herself the one thing she wanted more than anything else at that moment. A hug from someone who cared about her. She'd never been affectionate. She'd been self-absorbed and selfish. How things were changing now, she reflected.

She heard the woman's high pitched scream again. This time there was an urgency to it and it seemed to stretch out longer this time around.

A second later – the sound of a lone gunshot pierced the air, and immediately the woman's screaming stopped. Amelia's eyes filled with tears.

'If I ever return to myself, I will come back for you, Margarita,' she whispered, holding herself as tight as she could. 'I promise.'

Her first day in Richmond Central was surreal. Over lunch, Margarita's mother and Aunt Sofia discussed the shooting in the adjacent street. A husband had shot his wife. Murder, shrugged her aunt, was just part of ordinary life around there.

It made Amelia feel sick, but she also had other things to worry about. Margarita and Antonio were due to visit City Central High the next day. The notion of entering another school had Amelia physically shaking as she pictured what might be waiting for Margarita as she walked through the gates. Antonio had told her that the school was one of the roughest in the Oakland area, if not California. She didn't know if he was saying it to rattle her or not.

'At least it's walking distance,' he shrugged, as if that made things better.

To top it off, he suggested to Margarita that she take some sort of protection with her. Amelia felt the blood drain from her face. Antonio shrugged his shoulders.

'This ain't Hollywood no more, Rita.'

Antonio stepped closer and patted her on the shoulder.

'Relax little sister. I'm not talking about a piece or anything. But maybe a concealed knife of some kind may a good idea.'

As Antonio slammed her bedroom door, leaving his words hanging in the air, Amelia made a snap decision.

Today was the day.

She couldn't face this reality anymore. If her destiny was being Margarita, then she would have to do it somewhere far from here. By late afternoon, Amelia had put together some items in a small backpack. She found some cash Margarita had hidden in a hollowed out book. *Smart girl.* It wasn't much, but it was enough to get her on her way. The rusty screwdriver from Pablo's van would be her only weapon for the time being. She decided that she would slip out of her room at dusk and head to the nearest bus stop or train station. Whatever could get her to the Oakland Jack London Square.

Once there, Amelia would book a one-way ticket on the next available Amtrak train to the Big Apple. She'd been to New York many times on various shoots. She knew it well enough, and on top of that, she knew people there. She realised they knew her as Amelia Langston, not Margarita Serrano, but she didn't care. She just wanted to be as far away as she could get from here.

For dinner, the movie star had a choice between Pizza, Pizza, or fucking Pizza.

Shit, Amelia thought. *If I have pizza one more time for dinner, I will turn into one.*

Aunt Sofia must have bought a year's supply of frozen pizzas, Amelia thought as she opened the freezer, helping her Aunt prepare dinner. She knew however that she didn't know when the next free meal would come, so she ate until she was full, before helping Aunt Sofia clean up the dishes.

Just like the last few days, Margarita's father had not spoken to his daughter at all.

Just before dinner, she heard him talking to Margarita's mother in hushed tones, in their bedroom. The walls were paper thin and she heard everything. Francisco blamed Margarita for his woes. Her mother replied that his woes started well before with his own actions, not those of his daughter's, but he wouldn't hear it.

Her family's enormous flat screen television was clearly too big for the cramped lounge room, and the rest of the family were crowded onto the couch, staring mindlessly at some reality show.

'*It better not be the fucking Kardashians,*' Amelia thought, and then sighed. Her issue with them seemed so futile now compared to Margarita's problems.

Amelia informed whoever cared to listen, that she was going to go to her room to continue unpacking, then turn in for the night.

'See you all tomorrow,' she lied, the last thing she would ever say to the Serrano family.

No one, not even Margarita's mother, responded.

Amelia gave the family one last glance.

'Adiós,' she said under her breath, adding 'good riddance,' as she headed for Margarita's bedroom.

At 8.30 pm sharp, Amelia took one more good look at the bed. She had fashioned as much of Margarita's clothing that she could spare to make it appear that Margarita was sleeping under the covers. She then pulled the blanket up high enough in the hope that if anyone poked their head into her bedroom in the middle of the night, they wouldn't give it a second thought.

Not that anyone would.

Satisfied, she stepped over to the window.

Initially encountering some resistance, the window eventually gave in to Amelia's grunts and slid open. She had discovered in horror a few days ago that three of the bars on her window had been previously cut, but right now, she was grateful that it provided a means of escape. When her feet hit the ground outside the bedroom window, Amelia was relieved that she had so far managed to make little to no noise, and she slipped down the blind side of the house, intending to navigate her way through the overgrown bushes in the front yard, which would cover her escape until she made it to the pavement.

From there, she'd be home free.

But as she crept down the side of the house, the next door neighbour's dog detected her movements, and barked sharply at her.

Amelia froze in panic.

Breathless, she stood there waiting to be discovered.

But no one came.

The dog found something else to bark at on the other side of his owner's house, and counting to thirty, she crept forward, passing behind the bushes in the front yard, before stepping onto the pavement. Only then, did she finally exhale.

'You are on your way,' she whispered.

She looked around, before one last check of the front of the house. All clear.

Amelia slipped the backpack on and headed off down the street.

By the time Amelia had reached the city streets of Central Richmond, dusk had turned to darkness and she could feel it creeping into her confidence, questioning the plan a couple of times as she continued on down the quiet streets. Amelia heard the loud doof-doof music way before the two cars had come upon her. As they drove past, she could hear some guys talking, but she couldn't clearly make out their words over the music.

Thankfully, they didn't pull over.

Twenty minutes later, Amelia could feel a rising sense of panic starting to overwhelm her. She believed she knew the way to the train station, but was starting to second guess herself now. She cursed leaving her phone behind – worried that any calls she made would be location-tracked. Why didn't she just swap out the SIM later on? *Rookie mistake.*

The streets of Central Richmond were eerily quiet for once and Amelia felt as if she was being watched. With every step, her anxiety increased. Why didn't she just do this during the day? She could have just skipped school…she could have…

Amelia's thoughts were interrupted by a group of about ten or so men, milling about on the pavement less than fifty feet down from where she had just appeared, a sound system bellowing out rap music. The men were all talking loudly over the music. A party of sorts. Amelia cringed.

Some of them spotted Margarita, stopped talking and casually approached her.

She crossed the road as her pace quickened, walking as fast as she could, trying as best she could to deter them.

'Hey, Margarita!' his voice carried across the street even with the rap music still blaring.

Amelia flinched.

She remembered that voice. Eight hours of it from Los Angeles to Oakland. How could she forget.

Pablo.

'Where are you goin', darling?'

His question was followed by ruckus laughter from his friends.

'She's a hottie Pablo!' one of the other men laughed.

Walking on, almost about to break into a run, Amelia spotted the heap of shit that was Pablo's van parked across the street.

At the sight of the van, Amelia had wished she'd never left Margarita's room.

Pablo and a handful of his friends ran after her.

'Honey!,' Pablo had caught up to her in no time, 'where are you going at this time of the night, huh? Do your parents know you're out?'

Amelia ignored his question and kept walking, head down.

Pablo's friends cut her off and she screamed as he

grabbed her from behind, pulling her back towards him. He put his lips on her ear.

'You should have taken my offer back at the McDonald's,' he whispered.

Amelia tried to break free of his grip. The other two men stepped closer and she knew that even with her martial arts training, she was no match for them in Margarita's body.

'Lucky for you, I have a mattress in the back of my van,' Pablo said.

Amelia's blood ran cold.

The car appeared from out of nowhere and for a moment, Amelia thought she was back on a movie set. The car's headlights blinded her and she could hear the roar of the engine coming straight at her.

Pablo and his two friends panicked.

'What the fuck!' someone shouted.

The car was coming at such a speed, Amelia thought the driver was going to run them over. But the driver hit the brakes at the last possible second and the car came to a screeching halt one inch away from the three men who still, incredibly, held on to her, although not for long. She was then flung to the ground as Pablo and the other two men began stumbling back in the direction of the others.

Amelia rolled over. The bitumen of the road was

rough on her skin and her body ached. She rose to her feet and stepped back from the car. Feeling light-headed, she squinted at the headlights but recognised them immediately.

'What the fuck?' she said.

The driver jumped out but stood behind his door. When he pointed the handgun in the direction of the men, Amelia couldn't believe what she was seeing.

It had to be a dream.

The explosion of sounds startled her. Gun shots. Lots of gun shots. The windscreen of the car exploded in a hail of bullets, followed by the car's headlights and the driver's side window. The driver lurched backwards, his right shoulder now oozing red. Amelia watched on in horror as he dropped to the ground behind his door.

Amelia could feel herself going into shock.

Someone tried to grab her from behind. His body odour gave his identity away in a heartbeat. Amelia resisted, throwing her arms up and freeing herself from his grip.

'Leave her Pablo!' a man's voice shouted from a distance.

But Pablo had grabbed a handful of Margarita's hair. The pain was excruciating. She lifted her arms up again in a vain attempt to make it stop.

Pablo was panting. He was out of breath. Without warning, he gave her one last violent pull, before letting go. She lost her balance and fell backwards, her head hitting the asphalt.

Amelia blacked out in an instant.

Amelia felt nothing.

I must be dead, she thought. But bit by bit her memory came back to her.

Pierre.

He'd come to save me.

She had recognised his car. When he stepped out of the Audi, brandishing the pistol, they'd met eyes for a fleeting second.

Pierre.

Amelia felt a light breeze and she began to drift off again, before a flickering light beyond her eyelids made her open her eyes.

The ceiling fan spun in a perfect circle above her. And Amelia sat up, still deep in shock.

Everyone was lying on their backs, eyes closed.

All except one.

Henry sat on his mat, arms resting on his crossed legs. His face bore a neutral expression. When their eyes met, she didn't know what to think. Let alone feel. Amelia turned her attention to her best friend who had been lying next to her.

As if on cue, Gemma opened her eyes and sat up.

She smiled at Amelia.

'You okay?' she whispered.

CHAPTER FIFTY-ONE

Chad

CHAD STOOD AT THE SEWING MACHINE WITH Abhoy standing next to him. They met each other's eyes and Chad wondered if he and Abhoy shared the same thought: that today would be the last time they stood in this very room. Without a sound, they sat down and readied their machines. The bell sounded and the shift workers began their day's work.

Chad had been grateful that there had been no sign of the Supervisor but his relief was short-lived.

'Ah. The dynamic duo is here again,' the Supervisor said sarcastically.

The teenagers didn't bother taking their eyes off their respective sewing machines. Chad had promised Abhoy on the way to work, that he would not take the asshole's bait, or compromise their plan. He continued to sew in earnest.

The Supervisor moved down the aisle, pausing in front of Dipankar's sewing machine, before someone called him away to the other side of the factory. He grumbled under his breath before walking off, bumping his nephew's table and nudging Chad's perfect row of stitches. Chad bit his tongue.

Chad had long ago lost count of how many DOSTME T-shirts he had sewn. If he ever made it back to being his real self, at least now he knew how to use a sewing machine. The realisation made him smile.

Realising the time, Chad's nerves started to rise. Their shift would end very soon. Part one of the great escape would commence soon after. For what must have been the hundredth time that day, he wondered if Abhoy was sharing his nerves. If he had, he wasn't showing it.

He knew that if they were found out, that the punishment bestowed on Dipankar and Abhoy would be harsh. He was sure of it.

The bell sounded. End of shift.

Chad stifled a stomach full of butterflies. His nerves were on edge. He glanced over to Abhoy, who rolled his shoulders and head after a long shift in front of the machine.

'Dipankar and Abhoy. Come to my office,' the Supervisor said.

The boys looked at each other with panic on their faces. They had no choice but to move in the opposite direction of where they hoped.

The two teenagers stood in front of the Supervisor's disorganised desk. He kept his eyes on them both as he placed a cigarette in his mouth before lighting it. Blowing out a lung full of smoke, he said '—I think it's time you two make a decision.'

Abhoy and Dipankar didn't move an inch.

The Supervisor lent forward and tapped cigarette ash into the huge ashtray, his mouth forming a snarl.

'Well? Are you going to make a decision?' he snapped.

'What decision are you referring to?' Chad responded. *Careful now.*

The Supervisor was clearly getting agitated.

'You think you are smart,' he said, sitting back in his chair, frowning.

'—you think you and your boyfriend here,' he made eye contact with Abhoy, 'are superheroes or something. Don't you?'

Chad could feel the anger he had struggled to keep in check, rising. He swore in that moment, if he ever turned back to the real him that the very first thing he would do would be to pay this guy a personal visit, then knock this piece of shit out.

'I'm Superman and this here is Batman,' Chad suddenly said. He had no idea where it had come from. It just did. The Supervisor's face turned red, and for good measure Chad added, 'do you have a problem with that *poo-breath*?'

The Supervisor suddenly broke into a fit of laughter and for a moment, Chad thought he was laughing at his smart ass quip. The Supervisor's laughter abruptly ceased.

'Okay then. I guess you have answered my question,' he said, butting out his fortieth cigarette of the day so far.

'You have no idea how much shit you have both caused. You two stupid, fucking boys,' he said.

Chad met Abhoy's eyes. He looked frightened.

'Yes, yes. You thought you could run away with them huh,' he said, pulling out yet another fresh cigarette.

'Well I have bad news for you both,' he checked his watch and nodded, before lighting the new cigarette. 'I received a visit today from Abhoy's father. Apparently, one of his cousins had told him of your little plan. Right about now, Dipankar, your father is heading home. And as soon as he gets there, he is meeting a man who will be arranging marriages for your sisters. Your brothers, well he has plans for them too.'

Chad could feel Dipankar's face turn pale, his hands curled into tight balls of rage.

'You are lying!' Abhoy shouted.

The Supervisor clearly appeared to be enjoying this, leisurely taking another casual drag of his cigarette. It was then that Dipankar's best friend sprang into action. Realising what Abhoy was about to do, Chad joined him and together they lifted the corner of the heavy desk, tilting the Supervisor's chair until he lost balance.

'You fuck—' his words were cut off, as the desk came crashing down right on top of him. It pinned him to the floor.

Abhoy and Chad made a run for it.

They ran hard through the peak hour traffic of Dhaka, knowing that they had a slim margin to get there, grab the siblings and get out. They crashed through people. They stopped cars dead in their tracks. Rickshaws didn't even count. A Bus missed them by inches. They didn't care.

Chad was the first to spot something way out of place.

Smoke.

They both ran for another hundred or so feet before Abhoy saw what his friend had been looking at and they came to an abrupt halt. *This is not happening*, Chad panicked, his lungs burning.

Onlookers were staring in the same direction and Chad could feel a deep sense of dread overtaking his tiredness from running so hard for so long.

The slums were ablaze.

Their slums.

'Come on!' Abhoy said, as he grabbed Chad by the arm and started running directly towards the fire.

As they came closer, Chad could feel fear restricting his throat.

The slums were a tinderbox and the fire had no trouble sweeping through it quickly, its smoke black and toxic blanketed the entire area, almost blocking out the fading light. The two of them rounded a corner, ignoring the people running in the opposite direction.

The fire had engulfed a huge area of the slums, with Abhoy and Dipankar's huts right in the middle of the flames. There was no chance of stopping the out of control blaze.

Chad stood next to him. He was lost for words. He couldn't lose another sister, let alone two of them. He felt someone bump into him, in the smoky haze. Visibility was next to zero.

His eyes went wide as he realised who it was.

Dipankar's oldest sister.

'Dip! Dip!' she screamed, 'he started this! He started this!'

'Who are you talking about?' Chad said.

'Father!' she shouted. 'He said some man was coming to take us away, and he barricaded us all in the hut while he was smoking and his cigarette started a fire,' she added.

'What!' Chad said, 'where is he now?'

Dipankar's sister shook her head, but even through the thick smoke she spotted someone which made her scream.

'There!' she said.

Chad met Abhoy's eyes,

They both turned back to Dipankar's sister.

'What about the others?' Abhoy said.

Dipankar's sister shook her head.

'We got out but we were separated!' she burst into tears.

'No!' Abhoy said, 'I'm going to look for them.' With a fleeting glance to Chad, he nodded.

'Go get your father.' Without another word, Abhoy ran into the black smoke.

Chad felt a rage explode deep within. He turned and ran in the direction that Dipankar's sister had pointed.

Chad miraculously spotted him after two minutes of running.

'You!' Chad shouted.

Dipankar's father swung his head around and spotted his son. He tried to pick up the pace, but the old man wasn't as fast as he was, and his lungs were already giving out from the smoke and fumes.

Exhausted by all the running he'd already done, Chad pushed on with every last ounce of energy he could muster. Dodging rickshaws, and crowds through the Dhaka streets, Chad gained more ground, but before long, a major city street separated them both.

As if sensing he was getting the upper hand, and to Chad's utter disbelief, Dipankar's father took one final look behind him, leering at his son, before brazenly giving him the finger and ducking between the cars and scores of bodies crossing this way and that.

Chad spun his head to the left and spotted a small break in the traffic.

'I've got you, asshole,' he said.

As he reached the middle of the busy road, still running as fast as his legs could take him, Chad looked to his right.

In that split second, he knew it was too late.

The rickshaw was never going to be able to stop in time, or have any chance to swerve, and the last thing Chad saw was the rusted out handle-bars, and the bewildered, horrified face of the driver. He bounced off the front of the vehicle, violently hitting his head on the surface of the road.

Everything went pitch black. His last thought was of Dipankar's sisters.

I'm sorry, he thought as he drifted into oblivion. *I should have tried harder.*

He felt the breeze on his face.

Light.

Something was flickering in his eyes and he blinked to reorient himself.

When he opened them, the first thing he saw was the ceiling fan. Then the thatched roof.

Chad sat up, gasping at the overwhelming shock of his transition.

He glanced over to the meditation teacher.

Henry was looking straight at him. He did not move.

Eventually, he nodded.

CHAPTER FIFTY-TWO

Angela

JACK AND SOPHIE LOOKED AT EACH OTHER BEFORE turning back to Angela.

'You okay Mum?' Jack said, his left eyebrow slightly raised.

The oncologist's thoughts were racing – fast. She couldn't hide the bewildered expression on her face.

'Did I fall asleep?' she asked slowly.

Jack shook his head from side to side.

'I don't know. Why do you ask?' he said.

Angela made eye contact with the meditation teacher, staring at him with squinted, narrow eyes. Henry didn't flinch. It wasn't the first time someone had given him that look, and it wouldn't be the last. Relief began to fill Angela from deep within.

But it was so real, so powerful. I really believed that he was—

The oncologist lent over towards her son, placing her hand lightly on his.

'I can't recall the last time I told you,' she curled her lips at their edges, her facial muscles stiff and awkward.

'—I lo-ve you,' she said.

Jack frowned.

'—You…okay mother?' he responded gingerly.

Angela ignored the immense awkwardness in the air between Jack and herself.

'I'm fine. I just felt the need to say it,' she said.

Jack nodded with a puzzled expression on his face. Even hearing the words echo in her mind, had made her feel out of sorts.

The meditation room was warmer than what she recalled at the start of the class and it made Angela light-headed.

'I think I need to lie down for a bit,' she rose ever so slowly to her feet.

'See you both for dinner?' she said.

Jack and Sophie nodded.

Angela closed the door to her room, pulling across the latch to ensure complete privacy. She sat on the edge of her bed and rolled her head around her shoulders. She watched the foliage of the rainforest swaying in the light breeze, as if she was mesmerised.

'It was all a dream,' she said, shaking her head, 'it had to be.'

But what a dream. It had shaken her to the very core. No other dream had ever done that.

Mary Wilson was there. One of her patients. And Benedict. And the 'other' Angela. Dr Angela Smith. It all came flooding back, as if the memory was seconds old. Oh and 'Cold Arse,' A.K.A. Rachel Winterbottom? The woman in the bed next to Mary? What happened to her in the end? Deep inside, something gnawed at her. Guilt? She didn't know. Maybe it was time to change.

Angela stared out the window and wondered if she could.

Minutes passed.

It was then that she saw her smartphone on the bedside table, its battery indicator still full. She looked at the time on the lock screen. She'd only been gone an hour.

Curling up on the bed, she was overwhelmed by the powerful desire to go home.

Jack and Sophie would pretend to be upset, but she knew deep down they would be relieved. They could spend the rest of the holiday doing what they wanted without her acting like a third wheel.

With that revelation, Angela sat up, and immediately felt light-headed, but shook the feeling away. She would contact her travel agent without any further delay. Her only stipulation would be that it had to be a first class seat. She didn't care which airline.

Her eyes moved to the little red notification button

over her email app. There had been dozens of new emails since breakfast. Her finger hovered over the icon before pressing it.

After reading the subject of the most recent email in the box, Angela froze.

What the fuck?

It was an email from the General Manager of the hospital.

The emailing heading: 'Disciplinary meeting regarding incident with patient Mary Wilson.'

'What the hell?' Angela gasped. 'It was a dream!' she said out loud, her voice desperate.

She read the email and felt her body turn rigid. The incident the email was referring to, allegedly occurred 48 hours before Angela left for Bali. The tone of the email was serious. There was talk of pressing charges.

'Who the fuck is fucking with me!' she hissed, standing up, turning around, and throwing her phone hard onto the bed.

A knock on the door startled her.

'What?' Angela snapped.

'Cleaning service madam,' the small voice said nervously from the other side of the door.

'Fuck off!' Angela snapped.

She walked around to one side of her bed and picked up her phone. She dialled her travel agent's number.

Logan

Logan sat up on the yoga mat, his breaths short and panicked. The mat next to his was empty and his eyes darted around the room. Everyone else was getting to their feet. Some commented on how good the class had been, others chatted in hushed voices that Logan couldn't quite make out. Everyone seemed so relaxed, and it made Logan feel more uptight.

'Beth?' he said, looking around.

His eyes found their way to the meditation teacher.

Henry smiled back, but the gesture revealed nothing.

'Beth?' he repeated this time a little louder.

He rose to his feet and swayed a little. He felt as if he'd been asleep for weeks.

Silently, he shuffled towards the door. His mind was a whirl of thoughts that he found hard to control.

Beth was gone. Logan knew it. By the time he reached the hallway in the resort leading to their room, his anxiety had intensified. *I fucked up and now my wife is dead.*

He eventually got the door open after two failed attempts with the access card.

Logan's eye's went wide.

He ran over to his wife and wrapped his arms around her in a tight embrace.

'Hey, hey,' she said.

She let go of him and led him over to the bed.

'What's got into you?

'I think I fell asleep. When I woke up, you were gone!'

Beth smiled.

'I was, but—,' she blushed, 'I think I got a bit of what do they call it?' she tapped her fingers on her stomach, '—Bali belly,' she said.

Logan laughed, then cleared his throat, changing his look to one of concern.

'So, it was either stay in the class and give everyone else something to remember, or get out of there and avoid a very embarrassing situation.' She blushed again.

'So, what happened while I was gone? You look pale – are you sure you don't have a touch of it too?' She reached out and touched his forehead with her palm. 'Your temperature seems okay.'

'That class was intense,' Logan said '—and I had the mother of all dreams. Fuck.'

Beth nodded attentively. He looked into her eyes and knew in that moment that he was going to work his butt off to make this marriage survive.

Beth's phone tinged. She patted Logan on the leg and headed for her bedside table. Logan could not help but watch her fondly. She read her screen for only a few seconds before her hand shot to her mouth and she gasped.

'What the hell?' she whispered.

Logan stood up.

'What's wrong?' he said.

She held up her hand while she read on for a few more moments. When she was done, her wide eyes finally met his. She sat down heavily on the bed, her phone was still in her hand.

'There's been a shooting at Court-ten-ay's Office,' she said. 'Her receptionist Tindwer was killed in a car accident right out the front of the office as she tried to get away from someone. Court-ten-ay herself is in hospital but her condition isn't serious.'

'No way,' Logan found the words hard to speak. He sank to the bed. The room started spinning.

'But that's not all. A body was found in the office.' She paused, unsure of how to continue. 'It was Jerry Springhare.'

Logan felt as if he were about to faint again.

Amelia

Gemma was getting a bit embarrassed by all of this attention. Ever since they'd left the meditation room, Amelia had not let go of her.

'Honey, what's got into you?' Gemma said.

Amelia knew people were looking, but she didn't care in the slightest. She took a deep breath in and inhaled the humidity, the breeze that carried the slightest whiff of chlorine from the pool. God, it felt so good to be back in her own body.

Her body. Fuck.

Margarita. Did she even exist?

Why does it even matter? she wondered. *It was a dream.*

Unable to get the thought out of her head, Amelia pulled out her phone, opened Facebook and punched the letters 'M-A-R-G-A-R-I-T-A space S-E-R-R-A-N-O into the search box.

'What are you doing?' Gemma asked.

'Hold on,' Amelia said.

Amelia found her in the list, five names down. Her face and hair were unmistakable, exactly the way Amelia remembered. She clicked on her profile and looked closely at the photo. Although Margarita was smiling, Amelia could see it was forced.

She swallowed, suddenly feeling her throat turn dry.

Still in her hand, her phone began to ring. The number had a Californian prefix, but wasn't listed in her address book, although that didn't mean anything.

'This is Amelia,' she said as her phone touched her ear. She listened for a few seconds and then gasped.

Gemma stared at Amelia.

'What happ—' she began.

Amelia reached out for her and Gemma took hold of the movie star's hand.

'Okay, okay. I will be on the next flight.' She ended the call.

'What's wrong?' Gemma said. Amelia swayed a little. She felt nauseous.

'It's Pierre,' she replied at last.

'Pierre?'

Amelia stifled a sob.

'He's been shot. They don't know if he is going to make it,' Amelia said. 'I hope you don't mind Gem but I'm heading back home, I need to be with him.'

Gemma nodded.

'Of course. I'm coming with you,' she added.

Amelia looked deep into her friend's eyes, 'No, Gem, you wanted to come on this holiday for so long...'

Gemma wondered what had happened to her friend in the meditation room. Amelia had never put anyone's feelings before her own.

'Amelia, we have the rest of our lives to do this again.'

Amelia took a deep breath. She wondered how quickly they could leave.

'What about the Australian movie?' Gemma said to Amelia as they headed off towards their suite.

Amelia shrugged.

'Pierre comes before any movie,' she said.

Chad

Chad felt like he had had an out-of-body experience. He sat there in silence. He wasn't sure how to feel. Actually, yes, he did. Ironically, he wanted to click his fingers and go back to being Dipankar. He wanted to catch Dipankar's father more than he'd ever wanted to do anything else in his life. Chad looked down to his right hand. He turned it over and felt a sudden rush of emotions welling up in his throat. It was the hand that Dipankar's youngest sister held on to – so she could feel safe enough to sleep. He wiped his eyes.

His mind went back to the smart-ass grin on Dipankar's father's face, the second before he woke up back in this room. He struggled to keep down his intense, burning anger.

Another face came to his mind and Chad could feel his teeth clenching. The supervisor of the very factory his company owned in Dhaka.

But then, there was Crystal. Chad turned and met his wife's eyes.

She'd never looked more beautiful to him in that moment.

'Stand up,' he said.

She gave him an odd look, before rising to her feet. But before she could wonder what he was up to, he manoeuvred himself to one knee and reached for her hand.

Crystal looked down at him and wondered what the hell was going on. This was not her husband, surely.

He gazed at her for a time before he really surprised her.

Tears came from his eyes, and he felt them roll down his cheeks. He let them.

She couldn't recall the last time she had ever seen this happen.

'I have a lifetime of arrogant and downright egotistical behaviour I need to make up to you Crystal Garcia-Miller.'

Crystal could feel most of the other people in the room watching them, and she couldn't help but blush.

'—and once I've done that, I want us to renew our vows. Somewhere warm, tropical. No fanfare. Just the two of us.'

Crystal could feel her own eyes getting teary.

But Chad was not done.

'—and there is something else I need to tell you.'

'What is that?' she whispered, trying to hold back her own emotions.

'I love you more than you will ever know.'

Crystal bent down and hugged him, to a round of applause.

'Oh and there's one other thing,' Chad said, as he looked up and met her eyes.

'I need to go somewhere,' he said.

'When?' Crystal said.

Chad checked his watch and then looked back up to her.

'Now. You can come if you like, but I have to literally go right now,' the millionaire said.

'Where?'

Chad rose to his feet.

'Dhaka.'

CHAPTER FIFTY-THREE

Angela

ANGELA HOPPED INTO THE REAR OF THE BLUEBIRD Taxi after saying her awkward goodbyes to Jack and Sophie. They waved to her as the car rolled away.

Angela couldn't believe she had hugged them. She hadn't hugged her son since he was a child. She thought back to the night before when she had broken the news to them over dinner that she was booked on a Cathay Pacific flight and would be heading back to London the next morning. She had made it clear it wasn't them, but rather the 'invigorating,' meditation class, she felt as if she wanted to get home and sort some things out as soon as she could. Sophie and Jack seemed surprised to say the least, though she could tell that they were relieved. Now they could relax, for real. They could do what they wanted to do, when they wanted to do it.

Angela sat in silence as the cab drove through the streets of Denpasar, heading for the airport. She couldn't wait to sit down in the luxurious seat and take that first sip of champagne, which was always served before take off in first class.

Watching the sea of mopeds swarming around the cab, Angela thought long and hard.

It had to be a dream.

It had to be.

How could it have been anything else?

But why was she facing a disciplinary hearing over an incident with Mary Wilson?

She'd checked the email a dozen times. And then some. She called the hospital and spoke to Administration to ensure that the email was from a legitimate source. It was.

Was it all some sort of elaborate hoax? Angela wondered, and the second she had, the cab driver slammed on the brakes and her head snapped forward. Angela could see the taxi had been cut off by another car, but the words were already out of her mouth.

'What the fuck are you trying to do, kill me?' she said.

'Sorry, sorry,' the driver said, 'cut off. Cut off.'

Angela saw a flash of Benedict's face, there on the bed with her – when she was Mary – the night she had promised to do better. As she rubbed her neck, Angela felt her irritation return. *You're dead, Benedict, you want me to make a promise to a dead person?* To Angela's relief, she had now arrived at the Departure Terminal of Denpasar International airport. She took a deep breath, composed herself and tipped the driver.

Not that five dollars was a lot, but the fact that she did it was out of character.

Tight arse.

The process to get from the cab to her first class seat on the plane was, to Angela's delight, non-eventful. The queues at the airport were short, and the Customs officials were friendly. It all seemed as if it was meant to be. She even afforded herself some perfume at the duty-free plaza on her way to the gate. Angela couldn't remember the last time she'd purchased perfume.

It felt good. She felt good.

Whatever this issue was at work – she'd sort it out. She had pull. She had friends in high places. She would call on all her resources to get back in the good books. Life would go on and all would be as it was.

Angela settled into her first class seat, as other guests around her settled in to theirs, the flight attendants buzzing about, helping people stow their bags, pouring on the type of kindness reserved for those that could pay. It was First Class after all.

She gazed out the window, watching the ground staff finish their final preparations before the plane took off. She could feel the dryness of her throat and smiled at the thought of the first sip of the bubbly, ice-cold liquid touching her lips. *Ah.*

The captain started making his pre-flight announcements and she snapped out of her reverie, realising that the other passengers around her had glasses in their hands, but certainly not her.

'Excuse me,' she said to a flight attendant some distance away.

'—I didn't get my champagne,' she said in a levelled tone.

The flight attendant shook her head, 'I'm sorry madam, we are about to take off. We will have to organise one for you when we level out.'

Angela gritted her teeth.

After a smooth take-off and some subtle sways of the large aircraft, Angela was getting thirsty now. And impatient. After failing to attract the attention of any flight attendant she spotted one on the other side of the cabin.

'Excuse me,' Angela said, not caring to hit the call button like most passengers did.

The flight attendant smiled in her direction but continued to talk to another passenger who was wearing some kind of sand-coloured linen safari suit with a matching hat. Angela thought he looked ridiculous.

All I want is my fucking glass of champagne for fuck sake. Is that too much to ask?

The flight attendant was still busy with the other

passenger. You'd think they were old friends and they hadn't seen each other for years, Angela thought bitterly.

Angela held her gaze and tapped her fingernails on her side table.

Her anger was rising. This passenger was the one thing between the flight attendant and Angela's champagne. She was losing it now.

'Are you going to be long?' she said in a frustrated tone.

Nearby passengers gave her sidewards glances.

The flight attendant turned to her again.

'I will be with you in a moment!' she said, in a clipped tone.

Angela could feel her white-hot anger rising. No one treated Angela Smith like this. She waited another two minutes but then felt every last shred of diplomacy leave her body.

'All I want is my glass of champagne!' she said, a little louder, and Angela had to admit, it felt good to let off some steam.

The flight attendant patted the man on the shoulder. Glancing over in Angela's direction, she walked towards the galley. One minute later, she arrived at Angela's seat, with a glass of on a tray.

'My apologies for the delay, madam. Here's your champagne.' The flight attendant smiled.

Angela looked down at the glass and snarled under her breath. The bubbles were settling and she was pretty sure that it was only half full.

'You're fucking kidding,' she grunted. She raised the glass to her mouth and as the liquid touched her lips, Angela felt as if she was going to explode in a biblical rage. She rose from her seat and marched up the aisle towards the flight attendant on the other side of the cabin, attending to other passengers.

'Think you're smart don't you!' Angela said.

The flight attendant didn't batter an eyelid.

By now the passengers around Angela were whispering to each other and staring at her.

'I'm fucking talking to you!' Angela said in her harshest tone in the direction of the flight attendant.

The woman made eye contact with her, before walking over to her, taking her sweet time.

'Excuse me,' she said to Angela, 'what did you just say to me?'

Angela could feel fire in her chest. Her eyes were bulging and the veins in her neck were tight and pulsing.

'This champagne is lukewarm and you only half filled the glass!' Angela could feel her voice rising in volume. She could feel her chest getting tight and her heart beating too hard.

'Do you think that by speaking that way to me it will improve the situation and resolve it?' the flight attendant asked.

Angela lost her shit, throwing her glass at the flight attendant, before losing her footing and falling backwards into a vacant seat.

'I just wanted my glass of fucking champ—' Angela's words were cut off.

The pain inside her chest was hard to fathom. She had never felt anything like it before.

Both of her hands flew to her chest, as the excruciating pain shot through her. Her chest tightened and she was finding it hard to breathe.

Angela stumbled out of her seat and fell to the floor.

'She's having a heart attack!' someone said.

Angela lay there looking up to the cabin ceiling. Yes, she knew she was having a heart attack. *Idiot*. It couldn't have been anything else. Passengers came to her rescue as she gasped for air. The flight attendant she'd had words with, stood looking down at her impassively.

'Help me!' she gasped at the woman.

The attendant turned and nodded to the guy in the safari suit. He looked strangely familiar.

The guy in the safari suit.

It can't be. It was him.

Hands in his pockets, the meditation teacher made his way down the aisle, disappearing beyond the curtain.

'*No!*' Angela screamed.

Logan

Logan held Beth's hand for the entire flight home and she gazed at him as he dozed. They'd cut their trip short, flying out the day after the class.

They had two hours layover at LAX before their connecting flight to Toronto. When he wasn't sleeping, he spent most of the flight from Denpasar to Los Angeles trying to figure out if he could tell Beth what he had experienced.

Honey, I became Courtney. Oh sorry, Court-ten-ay. That's better. I spent hours counselling couples. This included you and me. I think Courtney was doing it with Jerry at some point. Bubbles and Lube. I put a stop to it. I think Filomena knew. Oh, and at one point I walked in on you with your hand around my boss's dick and you were high on coke, wearing only high heels. This was just before you and Tindwer, who, I think, were having an affair, were killed in a fiery car crash.'

The more times he ran the scenario through his head, the more insane it sounded.

But as far as he was concerned, it happened. And anyway, the news doesn't lie. Unless he was still inside some sort of dream.

Logan had pinched himself several times on the flight just to be sure.

Finding a bar at LAX and a quiet spot overlooking the busy tarmac, he and Beth ordered a few drinks and stared out of the window. They sat there in silence.

Beth turned to Logan and placed her hand on his leg.

'There is something I think I need to tell you,' she said.

Logan took a drink of his beer.

He turned to his wife and nodded.

She fixed her eyes on the tarmac, and without turning to him said,

'I kissed Tindwer.'

He stared at her, nodding in silence.

'—I bumped into her one night at BarChef, when I was catching up with Lucy and Kim,' a couple of Beth's girlfriends from school, Logan knew them well.

'You were wearing your white tank top and army-green Mavi jeans,' Logan said.

Beth's eyes widened.

'How'd you know that?' she said.

Logan patted her on the shoulder.

'I dreamt it when I fell asleep in the meditation class,' he said.

Beth looked perplexed.

'Are you mad at me?' she said, looking deep into his eyes.

'No,' he said.

She looked surprised. He had always been the jealous type and she knew it. He studied her face. She didn't just look relieved, she looked almost liberated.

'I know I deserved it, Beth,' he said, turning back to his view of the tarmac.

Logan watched a Pacific International Airlines plane

crawl past them through the window before disappearing from view.

'—I didn't treat you with the respect you deserved,' he said.

She held his hand.

Logan stared at her for a time.

'Do you mind if I ask you an awkward question?' he said.

'Shoot,' she said.

'Did anything ever happen between you and Jerry?' Logan said.

Beth burst into laughter. She placed Logan's left hand in hers.

She took a deep breath, still trying to maintain her giggles.

'Look into my eyes. I'm not sure where you got that from,' she eventually said.

'—but I can promise you anything. A Harley-Davidson Motorcycle. A luxury man cave in the garage. Me wearing the Batgirl costume every Friday and Saturday night – for the rest of my life. Nothing ever happened between me and that now dead boss of yours.'

Logan nodded.

The relief was overwhelming.

For now.

CHAPTER FIFTY-FOUR

Amelia

AMELIA HAD CHARTERED A PRIVATE JET FOR HER
and Gemma for the trip back home from Bali to California. She had slept on and off during the flight,
fraught with worry about Pierre.

Pierre. You can't die. You can't.

Amelia had already organised Pierre's transfer from
the Richmond Hospital to the UCSF Medical Centre
one hour into the flight, and while Gemma dozed,
Amelia did some digging on Margarita, and learned that
what she had experienced in her body, had, in fact,
really happened. Margarita was injured when Pierre had
been shot. Amelia was determined to find her.

Eventually, to her relief, she did.

The teenager was suffering from severe concussion,
plus a host of other injuries. She and Pierre had both

ended up in the hospital closest to Richmond, so she organised for her transfer also. Seventeen hours later, Amelia and Gemma touched down at Oakland International Airport. It felt good to be home and in her own body. The traffic on the Bay Bridge crawled at a snail's pace but it didn't bother her. Amelia gazed at the skyline of San Francisco. A clear morning: the sky was a picturesque, cobalt blue. Amelia felt invigorated and alive.

During the flight, she had watched Gemma from the corner of her eye. Now that she was back to being herself, she vowed to be a better friend to the one person, who had always been nothing other than loyal, genuine and there for her.

The car pulled up at the front door of the UCSF Hospital and Amelia was already halfway out of the car door before it pulled to a stop. It took Amelia ten minutes to find Pierre through the maze of corridors and endless wards and it was all Gemma could do to keep up. She hadn't admitted to Gemma that she had felt a flurry of butterflies swirling around her stomach. When she finally arrived at the right ward, the nurse sitting at the desk looked at her solemnly.

'It was touch and go for a while. Pierre was fighting for his life,' the nurse admitted. 'But he's doing much better today.'

'Can I see him?'

The nurse rose to her feet. 'This way.'

Halfway down the corridor, Amelia tapped the nurse on the arm.

'Can you do me one small favour?' she asked.

'Sure Ms Langston. What would that be?' the nurse said.

The movie star smiled at her and she noticed the nurse blush a little.

'You can call me Amelia,' she said, 'I need to find another patient here at the hospital.'

Amelia gave the nurse Margarita's full name.

The nurse jotted down the name.

'No problem, I will let you know,' she said.

When they arrived at his room, Pierre's eyes were glued shut. She knew he was alive, but it still made her heart skip a beat.

Sensing her, he gingerly opened one eye and grinned.

Amelia rushed to his bedside and hugged him awkwardly.

'Easy, easy there.' he whispered, hugging her back.

'I missed you girlfriend,' he said.

Amelia stood back and squeezed his right hand.

'Please tell me you are going to live,' Amelia said.

'You had her worried, like I've never seen before,' Gemma said to Pierre.

Amelia's personal assistant nodded. He was relieved to see them too.

'Excuse me,' Gemma said, 'I'll be back in a minute.'

Amelia watched Gemma leave, before turning back to Pierre, fighting back tears.

'We need to talk,' he said.

Amelia wiped the tears from her eyes.

'You've got that right honey,' she said.

Pierre watched her for a time before leaning in closer to her.

'—Rita,' he whispered.

CHAPTER FIFTY-FIVE

Chad

CRYSTAL TRAVELLED TO DHAKA WITH CHAD, telling him that the notion of staying in Bali by herself felt odd. As the plane touched down at the Hazrat Shahjalal International Airport in Dhaka, Chad could feel his anger clawing at him from within.

Attempting to study the landscape from the window as the plane came in for the final approach, Chad didn't want to admit to Crystal that he was hoping to catch a glimpse of the slums. He found himself looking for any signs of smoke.

His efforts proved fruitless on both counts. Besides, the air around Dhaka was so polluted, smoke from a slum fire would not have stood out anyway.

He'd had plenty of time during the flight to compartmentalise his thoughts. At some point, he would tell Crystal everything. He was grateful that she hadn't asked, although he knew she had wanted to. He played a potential opening line in his mind:

Crystal, I became another human being for a while.

He knew she wouldn't believe him.

It didn't matter anymore.

Chad's first port of call would be the DOSTME factory, where the Supervisor would get what was coming to him. He was going to make sure that the guy would later regret ever setting foot in that factory.

His second port of call would be the slums. He would just have to find someone to help him find the exact place he wanted to locate.

Chad needed to see it for himself. He wanted to make sure.

Did they survive the fire?

What about the mother?

Chad's mind then went to Dipankar's father. *What about him?*

What he would give to find him.

Chad and Crystal checked into the Le Méridien Hotel. After settling into their suite, Chad asked Crystal to come and sit with him on the sofa.

'I need to go out. I don't know how long I am going to be, but when I get back, I promise I will explain everything,' he said.

Crystal nodded, before she reached over and rested her hand on his lap, 'just promise me you will stay safe,' she said.

Chad rose to his feet, pulling her into an embrace. He held her for a long time in silence.

'I will Cheech,' he whispered, before kissing her forehead.

She smiled back at him.

He hadn't called her that for years. She loved that nickname.

Chad jumped into the cab a few minutes later.

By the time they had left the compound of the hotel, Chad had negotiated with the young driver to be his driver for the duration of his stay. Chad asked the guy what he earned for a month's pay, then promised to double it, for a few days' work. The drive between the hotel and the factory was as chaotic as he had predicted. Despite feeling as if he had only been here two days ago, he was still surprised by the sheer number of vehicles and people around them.

Chad instinctively started scanning all the random faces. He didn't want to miss out on the slim chance he would spot Dipankar's father. Or Abhoy. The cab turned the corner of yet another grid-locked street. Rickshaws, buses and cars seemed to jostle each other for a slither of space on road.

It was then that Chad then saw the building in the distance.

DOSTME INT.

Don't

Stop

Me.

Chad swore to himself.

He'd distanced himself from the cringey slogan for some time but he knew that when the cab pulled up at the front door in a few moments, that one thing was for certain.

Nothing was going to stop him.

The stifling heat of the day welcomed Chad as he stepped out of the cab.

'This is it,' he breathed.

He strode into the entrance of the factory, and people milling about at the front door stepped out of his way. Chad looked around, watching face after face look up at him from their sewing machines. Many of them stopped working, faces watching this strange white man standing there out of curiosity. He looked so out of place.

The noise in the room evaporated.

Chad walked through the aisles, looking for the row of machines that Abhoy and Dipankar called home, sewing for hours, upon hours. He felt sad watching the other workers sitting in the same spots. They looked as tired and overworked as they had.

As if on cue, a voice came from behind him.

'Why has everyone stopped sewing!' he shouted.

'Get back to work or else you will lose—'

The Supervisor noticed Chad and his voice trailed away and the two men stared at each other. The room now fell into a complete and eerie silence as every sewing machine on the floor ground to a halt.

'Mr Miller?' the Supervisor said.

He looked at Chad with a mixture of surprise and shock.

'—to what do we owe the pleasure sir?' he said.

Chad walked towards him., and as he got closer to the man, he slowed. He pictured the vision of the man through Dipankar's eyes. But standing there, eye to eye, he was nothing but a bully.

'Can I have a word with you?' Chad asked.

'Of course, Mr Miller. Come to my office,' the Supervisor said.

The sewing and noises of the room began to return to normal.

'Mr Miller. You should have given us some notice and we would have prepared a welcoming party for you,' the Supervisor said, waving for Chad to come in and sit.

Chad sat down.

He stared at the man long enough for it to become awkward. Chad didn't care.

'You no longer work here,' Chad said firmly.

The Supervisor baulked at this news.

'What do you mean?' he said.

Chad took a deep breath, but right before his very eyes, the man on the other side of the desk then pulled out a cigarette and lit it. Chad couldn't believe the nerve of the guy and it only served to make him angrier. As the Supervisor tapped the ash from his cigarette into the world's biggest ashtray, Chad snapped. In a lightning move, he reached over to the hubcap and pushed it upwards, sending all the butts falling right into the Supervisor's lap.

'What are you doing!' the Supervisor cried.

Chad leapt to his feet. He yanked the Supervisor up and out of his chair, pulling him towards the entrance to his office. For the first time, he saw fear in the asshole's eyes.

'This,' Chad said, 'is for all the people you treated like a dog. He punched him in the jaw with such force, the Supervisor went sprawling backwards.

'Things are going to change around here,' he said to the room.

He grabbed the Supervisor by the scruff of his neck, pulling him to his feet.

The Supervisor squirmed, believing he was going to get punched in the face again.

'No, no!' he pleaded.

'Don't worry,' Chad said, 'I've got other plans for you.'

He dragged the Supervisor through the factory before pulling him out the front door and onto the street.

Chad spotted the four policemen standing near his taxi.

He dragged the Supervisor over to them.

The senior policeman nodded.

'Mr Miller,' he said. 'Thank you. We've long suspected the things you told us about this man. It will be our pleasure to take him off your hands now,' he said.

During the long flight, and whilst Crystal slept, Chad spent hours on the phone talking to various people between Boston and Dhaka.

By the time he'd touched down in Bangladesh, he knew the police would be on hand ready to arrest the Supervisor.

But he made sure that he had a few moments with him first.

Chad watched the Supervisor getting pushed into the back of the police car. Dozens of factory workers stood outside the factory. They could not believe what they were seeing.

The car pulled out into the busy traffic. Chad smiled faintly. His work here was far from over.

CHAPTER FIFTY-SIX

Chad

THE YOUNG DRIVER HAD AN IDEA OF WHERE CHAD wanted to go. During the drive to the factory, Chad had told him about the slums he was looking for, and the garbage dump. Chad was surprised to learn that the driver had grown up in the same slums as Dipankar and Abhoy.

Thirty minutes of ridiculous city traffic later, the cab pulled over. Chad recognised the slums in an instant. The driver asked if Chad wanted him to tag along. Figuring that it was good idea to have someone local along just in case he ran into trouble, Chad agreed.

People crammed the narrow streets and Chad could feel all eyes upon him, which he found a little disconcerting. He almost wished that he was a Bangladeshi boy again, so he could slip through the crowds unnoticed.

After about twenty minutes, Chad rounded a corner and stopped. He felt his body go rigid, as a sick feeling formed in the pit of his stomach. It was just as he remembered it, except now the shacks were in smouldering ruins, the air thick with the rank smell of burning rubber. The fire had taken out a significant portion of the slums and the area looked like some kind of post-apocalyptic wasteland.

Chad could see figures scouring through the black dirt, attempting to salvage anything they could from the rubble. He walked further until he came upon where he believed Dipankar and Abhoy's shacks once stood. There was nothing left. He closed his eyes and pictured Dipankar's brothers and sisters. Their faces, their smiles, their innocence. He wondered if they'd survived. If not, then what sad, short lives they had lived. He rubbed the palm of his right hand anxiously. Tears filled Chad's eyes as he crouched down to the ground, his emotions overwhelming him. He thought about the little sister he'd had for a short time.

He'd failed Serena. And now he'd failed her too.

A dog appeared at his side, sniffing and nuzzling him. Even though the animal smelled like sewerage, Chad patted him, and the two sat side by side.

'I've had better days too,' he said to the stray, before rising to his feet and wiping his eyes.

Behind him, he heard the driver speak, engaged in a

conversation with a local man. Chad recognised a word and spun around to face them.

'What did you just say?' Did I just hear you say the name "Abhoy"?'

The men gave him a strange look.

'Yes,' he said.

'Do you know him?'

'Yes,' he said.

Chad's face brightened.

'You know Abhoy?' he said, a smile breaking out across his face.

'I am his brother,' he said.

For a moment, Chad forgot himself and hugged him.

'Is he okay? Did he survive the fire?'

Abhoy's brother nodded slowly.

Chad felt his knees weaken.

'He's okay?' Chad asked.

Abhoy's brother shook his head and looked at his feet.

'He is in the hospital. Quite sick from the smoke.'

Two hours later, Chad entered the hospital ward and shuddered at its surroundings. It was in a terrible state of disrepair. The place was so old, he wondered how the building had not been condemned decades ago.

But the ward was something else.

The long room was packed to the brim with patients with two tired nurses attending to them in turn. The air was thick with despair and humidity, both of which Chad was almost becoming accustomed to.

There was no sign of Abhoy.

Abhoy's brother had told him back at the slums that he knew nothing of the fate of Dipankar and the rest of his family, and Chad hoped Abhoy himself could provide some answers. The DOSTME CEO walked all the way through the ward until he spotted a boy covered in bandages, who looked like he was in pretty bad shape right at the very end. Chad realized it was him.

On the opposite side of the ward to Abhoy was a bed with the curtains drawn all the way around. He shuddered at the thought as to who was behind the curtain and what injuries or sickness they had. Or worse, maybe they had just passed away.

Abhoy's eyes were closed and Chad stood at the end of his bed, breathless with nerves, not sure of what he would even say to him once he woke up.

He stood for a moment and looked up at the ceiling. He wasn't religious, but then he had never denied the existence of God either.

'Please God, let this kid survive,' Chad said. He sat down on a tired plastic chair next to Abhoy's bed and wondered what to do next.

After a few moments he started humming the David

Bowie song "Space Oddity," and his favourite lines from the song: 'for here am I sitting on a tin can far above the world.'

Chad hummed the lines a second time as he stared off into the corner of the hospital ward, but when he finished, something really strange happened.

A voice nearby sang the next line, 'planet earth is blue and there's nothing I can do,' in a bare whisper.

Chad turned his attention to the young guy in the bed.

'How do you know that song?' Abhoy rasped.

Chad smiled. Relief at seeing Abhoy with his eyes opened overcame him.

'A friend sang that same song not long ago. How unusual,' Abhoy said before coughing.

'You have no idea how glad I am to see you alive,' Chad said.

Abhoy gave him a quizzical look.

'You have no idea how much I have no idea who you are and why you are here,' he said.

The two of them broke into laughter at the very same time.

Chad's voice then turned sombre.

'I'm too afraid to ask you something,' he said, rising from the chair and standing next to Abhoy's bed.

Chad took a deep breath. This was going to be hard and he almost didn't want to know the answer. But he knew he needed to ask.

'Abhoy, you are going to wonder why I am asking you this, but I'm just going to ask it. I see that you have thankfully survived the fire, but what about your friend Dipankar and his family?'

Abhoy closed his eyes. He took a deep breath and seemed to be lost in thought. Chad could feel his anxiety reach fever pitch.

This does not look good.

Dipankar and his family are gone. Chad felt the sadness rising.

Finally, Abhoy opened his eyes and fixed them just past Chad.

'DIP!' he said loudly.

The DOSTME CEO had no idea what was going on. Chad wondered if Abhoy had not lost his mind from the trauma. Maybe he was grieving for his friend and this was part of it. *Shouting out his name?*

A sound behind him brought his attention back to the present. It was the curtain being pulled aside from the bed behind him.

Chad spun around.

Dipankar.

Staring at him with a huge bandage wrapped around his head, he leant to one side so he could make eye contact with Abhoy around a speechless Chad.

'What?' he said.

Standing shyly next to him was a little girl. Her hand was holding her brother's but she looked up and smiled at Chad with a cheeky grin.

The little sister.

She's alive.

Chad's tears came and didn't stop.

CHAPTER FIFTY-SEVEN

Angela

ANGELA OPENED HER EYES, AND GROANED IN horror.

No!

She was back in the hospital ward. Her eyes darted to her arms. They were skinny, white and pale. She reached up and touched her head.

'Jesus!,' she screamed out loud.

She was bald.

Angela stumbled out of bed and raced to the toilets. When she reached the basin she looked into the mirror and saw a face. The reaction was swift. She lost control of her bladder before sliding to the floor and passing out. Ten minutes later, she came to, back in the hospital bed, hoping that it was all a dream. She opened her eyes and gasped.

'Angela, you fainted in the toilets, are you okay?'

She took a second look at the Doctor's name tag and stifled another helpless groan.

The doctor's name tag read 'Dr Mary Wilson, Oncologist.'

Unlike during the 'meditation,' Angela had looked into the mirror and this time had seen herself, looking as sick as Mary did when she was stuck inside her body.

Angela just stared at her, dumbfounded, and lost for words.

Doctor Wilson called out to a nearby nurse.

'Nurse, get Angela here something to calm her down please,' she said.

Angela was so numb with shock she could not move.

'NO!' she shouted. 'I didn't mean it!' Her eyes stared pleadingly at the Doctor.

Dr Wilson watched Angela, her face expressionless.

'Doctor Wilson?' another nurse said. 'Your husband and son are here to see you.'

Angela turned her head and this time she found out what she saw so overwhelming that she threw up in her lap. Mary Wilson had walked away from Angela and to one end of the ward. There she greeted two well-dressed men. One appeared to be her husband. She gave them both a kiss on the cheek.

'Hi darling,' the man said.

'Hi mum,' the younger one added.

The younger man then stepped aside to reveal a woman of similar age. She embraced Mary warmly.

'How are you honey?' Doctor Smith said to the young woman.

Angela looked at the group helplessly.

Benedict.

Jack.

Sophie.

Logan

It was Logan's idea, which surprised Beth to say the least. He wanted to visit Courtney in hospital the day after arriving home from Bali. She could still feel the lingering effects of jet-lag and wanted to sleep it off. But he had insisted.

When they arrived at the door to Courtney's private room, no one was more surprised than her to see them.

'What are you guys doing here?' Courtney said.

Logan followed Beth into the room all smiles.

'What about your holiday?' she said.

Logan held an impressive bunch of roses in one hand.

'We felt with everything that had happened back home, we would cut it short. We have the rest of our lives to go back to Bali, right Logan?' Beth said.

Logan nodded, stepping to one side of the bed and smiling awkwardly at Courtney.

It felt so good to be looking at the marriage counsellor this way.

'I'm sorry about Tindwer,' Logan said.

'She was a beautiful girl,' Courtney said, sadly.

'Jerry,' Logan said without even thinking about it.

Courtney blushed, her eyes darting to the corner of the room.

'I fucked up big time,' Courtney said. '—a marriage counsellor having a fling with a married man.' She didn't bother to make eye contact with either of them.

'They'll probably pull my license after all this anyway,' Courtney said.

'We all make mistakes,' said Logan, 'it's part of being human.'

Even in the short time since they'd found out what had happened back home, Logan was remaining stoic and he knew it. It was as if he stood straighter now. His confidence had returned, but with it something else. Calmness, maturity, maybe.

'Well it doesn't matter,' Courtney said, wiping a tear from her eye.

'—even if I get through this, I don't think I want to do it anymore.'

Beth and Logan didn't know what to say – so they said nothing.

'What happened to Filomena?' Logan said.

'You haven't heard?' Courtney said.

Logan met Beth's eyes.

'They say she did it on purpose, but the cops wouldn't elaborate on the details,' Courtney said.

'What?' Logan asked.

Courtney stared down at her hands again.

She could feel the weight of the guilt pushing down on her.

'She was cornered, not far from my office. The police had her surrounded.'

Courtney fell silent as Logan could feel his apprehension rising.

'They say she fired a shot at them, but a witness claims it didn't happen. Either way, they shot her dead, Logan.'

Logan tried to remember the scene as it happened. The last thing he remembered when he was Courtney. Filomena had pointed the gun at him – but she'd absolutely run out of bullets. Either way, Filomena Springhare was now dead, along with her husband and Logan felt a bit awkward when he returned to the memory of Jerry standing there before Courtney at the front door to her apartment.

He also felt conflicted. Head office offered his job to Logan and he had accepted.

Courtney sat in silence for a time staring at the roses.

'Jerry, what a loss,' Courtney said. She had a strange expression on her face.

Logan looked over to Beth, and froze.

Her cheeks were blushing a bright red.

Amelia

'How did you know?' Amelia asked Pierre.

Pierre stared at her, before his eyes drifted.

'I knew the only person I'd ever spoken to about my mole was you. And then there was our code word,' he said, adding, 'the new one, and the old one too. Agastopia and Jentucular. Well done.'

Amelia smiled. Pierre lent closer to her.

'And when I touched Margarita. I can't explain it. It was if the universe was trying to tell me. I know I sound as if I've been doing cocaine, but it's all true honey,' he laughed.

He checked the doorway and lowered his voice

'But there's something I never told you Amelia,' he whispered.

Amelia suddenly felt her nerves tingle. 'You've got me as nervous as hell Pierre.'

He smiled before taking her hand and holding it.

'Before I worked for you,' Pierre whispered, 'I once was a guest at the Samsarana Retreat, myself.'

Amelia couldn't believe what she was hearing.

'It happened to you?' she whispered.

Pierre smiled, as Gemma appeared in the doorway, 'a story for another time,' he said.

Jennifer the nurse knocked at the door.

'Ms Langston, sorry, Amelia,' she said, 'I have located her.'

Amelia looked at Pierre and then to Gemma.

'You guys catch up for a while,' she said, rising to her feet, 'I need to take care of something.'

Five minutes later, the nurse nodded in the direction of the doorway to the ward.

'First bed on the left,' she said.

'Thank you,' Amelia said to the nurse, adding under her breath, 'show time.'

Spotting Margarita, she felt as if the world was about to stop spinning.

'Hello,' Amelia said, walking up to Margarita's bed.

The teenager had a bandage on her left arm, bruises and scratches covering her neck and one half of her face. Her eyes had bags under them. She appeared to have not slept for days.

Amelia was used to people falling over backwards when she entered a room, but Margarita didn't react in any excitable way.

'Hello,' she said back to Amelia.

'How are you holding up?' she said.

Her eyes began to well with tears, before Margarita's bottom lip began to quiver.

'I was miserable when I lived in Los Angeles,' she

wiped the tears from her eyes, 'but after you fired my dad, we were forced to move up here to Central Richmond.'

Margarita burst into tears.

'—I tried to run away, but then was set upon by a group of men. But to be honest, I can't remember a thing about what happened.'

Amelia stepped closer, but Margarita held up her hand.

'—listen, I don't know why you are here. But you'd better be gone before my father gets—'

Amelia heard the door open behind her. Francisco Serrano stood there, with a blank expression. Margarita's mother stood beside him, the expression on her face as impassive as her husband.

'Amelia Langston,' Margarita's father said, 'what a surprise.'

EPILOGUE – PART ONE

Twelve months later.
Double Six Resort, Seminyak, Bali.

'You okay?' Benedict asked his wife. The couple sat on their sun lounge overlooking the resort pool. Mary's son Jack and his fiancé Sophie frolicked in the water, waving to Mary and Benedict. The lovebirds looked happy and relaxed.

The couple waved back.

'I was just thinking,' Mary said, staring into her Mojito, before looking over to her husband.

'—something one of my patients said to me last year,' she said.

Benedict lent closer.

'It was quite profound, that's all. Watching Jack and Sophie in the pool, made me think of it—' she said. Benedict took a sip of his Old-Fashioned, watching Jack and Sophie in the pool before turning back to Mary. '—she said to me, just before I finished for the day, to never, ever take you, Jack or Sophie for granted.'

Benedict raised his eyebrows, 'that seems quite specific,' he said, before adding, 'did you ever ask her why she had said it?'

Mary took another sip of her cocktail, before finding herself staring across the pool in deep thought, before turning back to her husband. She felt a tinge of sadness.

'No, I never got the chance.

The nurses recalled her crying for hours long after I left work that day. Something had broken her heart. She passed away that night.'

Amelia stood against the railing of her balcony and watched the goings-on below with happiness. Gemma came barrelling out of the sliding door holding two espresso martinis. She handed one over to her friend and took a sip from the other.

'That tastes amazing,' Gemma said.

Amelia smiled back.

She looked out across the resort pool once again and then to the waves rolling in to the nearby beach. Amelia had promised Gemma that they would return to Bali within twelve months. She was happy to be back.

Amelia was about to say something but her phone pinged. She checked the screen and squealed.

'Look at her will you!' she said.

She showed Gemma the phone.

Margarita stood there in her karate uniform. Wrapped around her waist was a blue belt.

'The girl's really something,' Gemma smiled, looking at Chuck Norris standing right next to Margarita. He had one arm around Margarita, and his other hand was giving the camera a big thumbs up. Amelia smiled and felt her eyes water. Chuck Norris had posted the photo on his very own social media page.

What a guy. Amelia loved that man.

She was starting to feel the same way about Margarita. All she had needed was a bit of positive reinforcement. Amelia was also surprised at how physically strong Margarita actually was. *Both inside and out*, she thought. *Never, ever, judge a book by its cover.*

Amelia looked into Margarita's beautiful eyes in the photo. She looked happy and confident. Margarita's eyes reminded Amelia of her father and her mind drifted to the Cisco Kid and all that had happened a year ago.

A couple of days after first seeing Francisco at the UCSF Hospital, she sat down with him and talked for a long time. She told him she knew of his gambling problems and she offered him a deal he couldn't refuse. She would offer him a full-time job working in her production company as a set designer but all he had to do was agree to go and see a counsellor for his gambling addiction. Amelia made no qualms about it. The only stipulation was that as long as he worked for her, Francisco was to never gamble again. If he was caught, the deal was dead.

Amelia also offered to help him and his family move back to Los Angeles. She wanted Margarita out of Oakland.

They became good friends. And in the end, it was Margarita who convinced Amelia to do something bold, and although initially hesitant, Amelia finally agreed.

Amelia Langston closed down her Twitter account a couple of months ago.

It was Amelia that had talked Margarita into starting martial arts. She made the conscious decision not to buy Margarita any gifts, or give her any money. She wanted the two of them to have a friendship based on nothing but shared values.

Amelia agreed to do a talk at Margarita's school about the positivity of Martial Arts for the body, mind and soul. And after the one-hour talk at Sunset Boulevard High, Amelia Langston told the surprised crowd she would pick out one lucky student, who would get to have some photos taken with her backstage.

The girl smiled widely as Amelia pointed to her.

Big Blonde.

She waved and smiled excitedly at her friends as she followed Amelia backstage and into one of the empty dressing rooms. Amelia closed the door of the dressing room quietly.

She then smiled at the schoolgirl and said, 'where's your phone?'

Big Blonde pulled it out of her pocket, logged in and switched on the camera app. She handed it over to Amelia, who walked over to the dressing room door, and opened it, and handed the schoolgirl's phone over to Gemma before closing the door.

Big Blonde stood there, confused.

'My phone?' she said.

Amelia walked up to her and put her index finger so close to Big Blonde's face, it almost went up her right nostril.

'Your phone is about to go where you left Margarita's phone that morning you and the other bitches bashed her at the bus stop.'

The girl stumbled backwards.

'You know what I do to bullies?' Amelia said angrily.

'No' the girl flinched.

'I remind them what twenty years of karate can do! And then what I do is post a photo of that girl to my Twitter followers, telling them this is what a gutless bully looks like.'

Big Blonde burst into tears.

'I didn't know you knew Margarita!' she sobbed.

'This is not about me,' Amelia said. 'Think of what

psychological affect your bullying has on girls like her,' she hissed.

'Okay, okay,' Big Blonde replied.

Amelia stepped back and took a deep breath.

She straightened her clothes and opened the door to the dressing room.

'I will not put your photo on Twitter,' she said to the schoolgirl, 'but if I hear of you even considering bullying another person...ever...you are going to be famous for all the wrong reasons.'

She nodded for Big Blonde to get out with a flick of her head.

The school girl didn't look back.

Amelia looked over to Gemma sipping her cocktail. She made sure that every morning when she woke, she would remind herself of everything that she was grateful for. And Gemma and Pierre were always top of the list.

Gemma had quit her job at Netflix, after Amelia gave her an executive position with her company, and invited her to move in to her sprawling Holmby Hills home.

It came as no surprise to Gemma after she moved in, that someone else also moved into the guest house.

Pierre.

Her former P.A. had refused the offer of a job at Stonelang Productions no matter how much Amelia begged him. Although she pleaded with him to come and work with Gemma, he shook his head and said that it wasn't where he felt like he belonged. He loved PR. He said it was in his blood.

Thanks to a favour returned to Amelia from an old friend who ran the company, Pierre took up a position in a top PR firm in LA and even Amelia had to admit that she had never seen him happier.

'Hey, I know you,' the voice was close by and it startled Amelia quickly out of her daydream.

She turned to her right and realised the person speaking to her was on the balcony to the room next door.

'Excuse me?' Amelia said.

The woman stood there smiling.

'You were at the Samsarana Retreat last year and-' when Gemma stood alongside Amelia, the woman gasped, '-and you were there too! Wow, this is such a coincidence.'

Amelia and Gemma met each other's eyes, before they turned back to the woman. They remembered her.

She was there with her husband.

'I was there with—' she turned and called out, '— Logan, come here.'

The man arrived next to her and Amelia now remembered the couple from the meditation class.

'Hi, I'm Logan and this here is my wife Beth,' he said.

'You guys were at the Samsarana Retreat last year, right?'

Amelia and Gemma nodded at the same time.

Logan shook his head, letting out a huff.

'Hell of a class, huh?' he said.

Amelia felt a tingle move up her spine.

'You could say that' she said.

The four of them stared down at the pool for a time.

'That couple-' Gemma pointed down to the pool.

'- I heard they are renewing their vows tomorrow night at sunset, over there on the beach.'

They all watched the couple with interest.

'Hold on,' Amelia turned to Gemma, 'they look familiar.'

Amelia smiled when the couple looked up at the four people on the adjoining hotel room balconies. They waved before turning to each other and reaching for each other's hand.

Their fingers interlocked.

They turned in the other direction and stared out across the water. He kissed her lightly on the head and she laid her head on his shoulder.

EPILOGUE – PART TWO

Chad

Chad wondered if the universe was at it again. At breakfast the next day, he bumped into the other couples who'd been in the same meditation class that they had attended at the Samsarana Retreat, one year earlier. He realized they were the same people he saw on the balconies the afternoon before looking down at them. Chad thought he had recognized them. By the time Crystal and Chad had finished eating, the group had come together and were chatting like old friends.

When Crystal suggested the idea to Chad, he smiled.

'You read my mind,' he whispered.

Crystal cleared her throat.

'I know this is short notice, but if you are free, we

would love you to attend our ceremony at sunset tonight.'

When Crystal had suggested they go back to Bali to renew their vows, Chad knew there was other business he would like to attend to whilst they were there.

As the car wound its way up into the hills of Ubud, he stared out the window and remembered the last time they travelled along this road.

So much had happened.

Chad had stepped down as CEO of DOSTME International ten months ago. He had many more fulfilling things to focus on. He handed over the reins to his right-hand man. The guy had been worthy of the role for a long time and so far the guy's tenure had worked out perfectly for them both.

The last thing Chad did before he stepped down was shut down the two factories in Dhaka.

But that was only half of it.

Knowing what affect this closure would have on the employees of the two older facilities, Chad found a much more modern factory on the outskirts of Dhaka and reopened operations there within six months. When the new factory was open for business, Chad ensured the workers received a fair pay rate.

Chad knew that the financial reporters back in the

States baulked at his sudden transformation from a bottom-line vulture, to a do-good millionaire-going-through-some-sort-of mid-life-fortune crisis. Some analysts didn't mince their words, reporting that an increase of the worker's wages would make DOSTME International unprofitable and send the company to the wall. However, following the publication of a magazine article interviewing Crystal about her husband's over-haul of his business, sales in DOSTME clothing hit an all-time high and the increased profit was shared by all the employees of the DOSTME manufacturing plant in Dhaka.

After Chad located Dipankar and his sisters, following the fire, he helped to create a foundation in Bangladesh to help those in need. He and Crystal donated $100 million dollars towards it. It would help those in need with education, and other services in the hope to break the cycle of poverty. Chad and Crystal were intelligent people. They knew the insurmountable level of poverty in Bangladesh and the fact that they couldn't help everyone. But at least they would make a difference to many.

Chad learned that Dipankar's mother and two brothers sadly perished in the fire which ravaged the slums that fateful day. The blaze, started by Dipankar's father, also took the innocent lives of nineteen others. Although he could have easily stopped the fire at its infancy, he chose to flee instead.

Dipankar's father, Achintya was located twenty four hours after fleeing the slums and Chad had heard that upon arriving at the crowded jail, Dipankar's father had a reunion of his own. In the packed holding cell, his brother, Arup, better known as the Supervisor, was huddled in the corner, smoking his way through his packet of Benson and Hedges as if his life depended on it. As news filtered through the holding cell of what Dipankar's father had done, things got out of hand quickly.

The other men in the large holding cell found out that the two brothers were also going to be charged with offences related to the sexual abuse of children. The fact that they were related to the children added fuel to an already explosive situation.

The other inmates decided to take justice into their own hands.

The two men probably wished they could have ducked into the Samsarana meditation room and switched identities themselves.

Achintya did not make it out of the cell alive, his injuries consistent with a blunt force trauma to the skull, which authorities could not rule out as an accident, though it couldn't be proven. Arup, once the big man at the DOSTME factory, had apparently found that he was no match for men his own size. Although he did his best to fight back, his time in the holding cell ended on a stretcher. He remained in a vegetative state until he died four months later.

And then there was Aparajita.

Chad thought of her all the time now.

The name meaning 'one who cannot be destroyed,' was Dipankar's little sister's name.

Along with her older sister Pratyusha, the two sisters were doing well. Under the umbrella of the foundation that Chad and Crystal had set up, the two sisters now lived with a relative, in a modest home in one of the nicer parts of Dhaka. The girls were now attending school and Chad and Crystal were in regular contact with them from Boston. Chad loved his video calls with the two sisters. They were cheeky, quite funny and they brought a smile to his face every time he called.

And then there was Dipankar and Abhoy.

Since the two of them had played an integral part in the Foundation's operations in Dhaka, Chad asked them what their thoughts were about undertaking a formal education. He was pleased to see that they couldn't have been more enthusiastic. He wondered if they would ever continue on to university. Maybe even Harvard one day. Perhaps the girls would join them. But he knew that whatever they chose to do, he would be proud of them regardless.

Chad felt the tap on his hand and turned to Crystal.

'Whatchya thinking about?' she said, reaching over and resting her hand on his.

'I was thinking about everything that's happened in the last twelve months,' Chad said.

'It's been quite the journey,' she smiled.

'That it has,' he said.

They both took a sharp breath in as they realised they had arrived.

The couple walked into the reception area, and were welcomed warmly by the receptionist. When Chad told her they were here to see Henry the meditation teacher, the woman wasted no time in responding, as if she had been expecting them.

'He's between classes. I will take you there now,' she said.

Chad could not help it. His nerves were firing on all cylinders. He held on to Crystal's hand tightly, feeling a rush of anxiety but also excitement at hopefully being able to get some well overdue answers. His expectations were low, but deep down he hoped he would walk out of here with the mystery solved.

As they arrived at the door to the meditation room, Chad felt a jarring sense of déjà vu. He literally felt as if he had stood at this doorway only five minutes ago.

It was surreal.

He would admit later to Crystal that he felt something else, standing there.

Fear.

A small part of him, wondered if by stepping foot in the meditation room, Henry would do it to him again.

Crystal nudged him and Chad gingerly stepped into the room with her by his side. Henry sat on his mat, dead still, with his eyes closed, Chad felt as if he were invading his space. His face conveyed complete calmness and Crystal wondered if he was in some sort of trance. Without warning Henry's eyes slowly opened. He stared straight ahead, and appeared to gather his thoughts.

'Come,' he said without turning in their direction.

Chad and Crystal took another step forward, before he finally turned his head in their direction.

'I've been expecting you,' he said.

Chad felt a shiver run up the length of his spine as he realised that Henry's eyes were fixed right on him. But his serious expression mellowed and he took them both in with a pleasant smile.

'Both of you come. Sit there,' he pointed to a mat close to him.

Chad and Crystal took their places and waited expectantly.

'Mediate with me,' he said.

Before either of them could respond, Henry began the slow process of closing his eyes.

But Chad's eyes remained very much open.

Henry's grin appeared before his eyes flicked open.

'Chad you have nothing to fear, my friend. This is not that kind of meditation today. Trust me,' he said calmly.

The meditation was like nothing they had ever experienced before. Chad could feel his breath moving in and out of his body as if his lungs were brand new. The only person he could ever explain it to was the woman sitting next to him holding his hand. No one else would get it, or probably believe him.

As the session drew to a close Henry whispered, 'Open your eyes.'

'Whoa,' Crystal whispered, 'that was incredible.'

Henry smiled. He nodded.

'Your husband wants to ask me a question.'

Crystal instinctively turned to her husband, but Chad remained focused on Henry.

Now it was Crystal's turn to wonder if he was in a trance. Chad started to speak, but Henry raised his hand.

'Before you ask me,' he said directly to Chad, 'can I ask you a question first?'

Chad nodded.

'Do you feel better for it?'

Chad's eyes fell to the floor, the space between himself, and the meditation teacher.

When he slowly raised his head and made eye contact with the man sitting across from him, his words felt strong, and self-assured.

'Yes, I do.'

Henry took a long and measured breath. His chest rose, and then fell in a slow and graceful movement.

'If there was one thing more you could change, Chad, enlighten me.'

There was no thought required. Chad knew the answer.

He could feel his chest tighten as pure emotion brought the words to his lips.

'I would tell Serena that I am sorry. That I love her. That I miss her more than anyone could ever miss someone.'

Crystal tightened the grip on his hand. Tears ran freely down her cheeks. Henry closed his eyes and Chad's eyes were filled with tears also.

'I am ready for your question now.'

The moment was finally upon him. Twelve months in the making.

'How?'

Henry slowly opened his eyes.

'How?' he said.

'How, does it happen?'

Henry's lips moved almost imperceptibly into a smile and his answer came after another pause.

'I thought you might want to ask me why?'

'Why?' Chad said, confused.

'Why – you,' the meditation teacher said.

Chad shook his head, a grin now crept on his face.

'No. I have a good idea as to why I was chosen. I am more curious as to how you did it.'

Henry turned to Crystal and said, 'Crystal, would

you allow me to spend a few minutes alone with your husband?'

Crystal nodded.

'I'll see you back at Reception,' she leant over and kissed Chad on the cheek.

'Thank you, Henry,' she whispered.

Henry smiled faintly and nodded before watching Crystal walk out of the room.

When she was out of sight, Henry surprised Chad by rising to his feet.

'Come, Chad. I have something to show you.'

The meditation teacher walked to the wall directly behind where he sat.

He opened a concealed door hidden in the wall, and nodded for Chad to follow.

Chad found himself in the small and tight space behind the door, which Henry closed behind them.

'Follow me,' he whispered.

He led Chad down a narrow hallway. It was dark and much cooler than in the meditation room. Low lights dotted every ten or so feet lit the hallway in a medieval glow. Chad felt like he was in a castle.

The hallway curved around a corner and stopped at the top of a tiny and cramped iron staircase. Chad wondered how Henry would fit down the narrow structure, let alone himself, but Henry moved down the staircase with ease. Chad followed. By now he was curious as to where Henry was taking him. They had to be directly beneath the resort, Chad was sure of it.

Another narrow hallway, almost identical to the first, eventually led to a lone door. It was small and ancient. A quick scan of his surroundings, and Chad surmised this had to be Henry's private quarters. The room was sparse, but comfortable. Chad smiled at the only modern thing in the room. Everyone deserves a good night's sleep, he chuckled.

Natural light filtered into the room. As he walked further in, Chad could see the source of the light. A floor to ceiling window afforded Chad an astonishing view of the Ayung River, with the lush tropical rainforest enveloping the view from every side. He felt as if he were looking through a window to the lost city of El Dorado.

It was breathtaking.

Henry waited for Chad's attention. He nodded for him to follow him through an archway to the other side of the room. There, against the wall was an elaborate place of worship. Chad had seen these everywhere in Bali. They were as ubiquitous as scooters on the road. A stick of incense burned, nestled in one of the many jars found on the display.

Henry slowly dropped to his knees, and as he did, instructed Chad to do the same.

Without turning to his guest, he said, 'you asked me how it works. Are you sure you are ready to find out?'

Chad looked at him but Henry didn't move an inch.

'Do you share this secret with many people?' Chad said.

Henry shook his head.

'No.'

'Why am I so special then, Henry?'

Henry didn't respond.

He focused his attention on the shrine and reached over to touch something. He placed his hands around a palm-sized decorative crystal ball. He stared at it for a short time, before holding it out for Chad to take.

Chad took the crystal ball in his hand.

It was cold to touch but was the clearest crystal ball he had ever laid eyes on.

After a few moments, Chad said, 'is this it? Are you telling me this is what decides?'

Henry stared at him long enough for Chad to start wondering what on earth was going on.

Henry did something Chad had never seen him do before.

He broke into a fit of spontaneous laughter.

'Alright, I am just messing with you,' he said.

He reached over and took the crystal ball out of Chad's hands.

'The answer you are looking for is through that doorway,' he said.

Chad followed Henry's gaze. The door located at the other side of the room was partly concealed with a curtain draped halfway across it.

Chad rose to his feet, and took one final glance at the meditation teacher who directed his eyes to the door, which Chad opened and stepped into the hallway. This one was similar to the last two, but seemed to stretch on for much further.

The lights were more spread out and it made the hallway quite dark. Chad could feel the hairs on the back of his neck prickle. He had no idea where he was going but had faith.

He walked on.

Finally, he could see his destination. A bright light bled into the dark hallway and Chad's senses assured him that it had to be daylight. It brought him a sense of relief.

He reached for the handle and carefully pulled the door open. The door opened to, what Chad would later describe to Crystal, as a hidden cave with an entrance leading to the rainforest. Stepping through, his eyes took a moment to focus as the bright light streamed through the foliage. The vegetation was thick here. Lush and dense, the ground was soft under his feet. Chad felt intoxicated by the beauty, but was confused.

'What am I doing here?'

He turned back and could see that the cave was almost completely concealed by the rainforest.

A familiar sound snapped Chad out of his many thoughts.

'Where the hell am -'

His question was cut off by the sound of a car, driving nearby. Chad pushed through the dense foliage.

Now he was really confused. He was at the driveway leading up to the retreat.

What the hell?

He fought his way through yet more jungle before he was able to finally, step out onto the road. He was starting to wonder if Henry had literally led him down the garden path.

It was then that Chad heard a sound.

'Woof.'

He stopped dead and listened again before realising that he was just on high alert, and it was probably just the sounds coming from the rainforest.

God knows what animals were in there, he thought.

'Woof.'

There it was again.

This time it was louder.

'Woof.'

'Woof.'

Chad swung around, looking in all directions, before his eyes rested on a figure. The beggar that he had shunned a year ago, sat in silence, watching his every move.

How had he missed her before?

The woman wore a large flimsy hat. Her head was down as if she was staring at the ground, and Chad immediately felt a little ashamed of the way that he had treated her back then. He swallowed.

Chad heard the sound again. And this time, he stood frozen in shock.

'Woof.'

'Woof.'

'Did you just, err, say something?' he said nervously.

The beggar did not move.

'Can you hear me?' Chad said.

The woman ignored his question.

But without warning, she reached out her hand.

It was full of string bracelets.

Chad stared at her hand, before reaching for his back pocket and his wallet.

He looked inside and realised he had forgotten to grab some extra cash at the airport. He had about $1000 US in cash in Indonesian currency and he pulled half of it out. It wouldn't make up for his rudeness, but perhaps it would be a step towards making amends.

He reached down to place the money in her hand, but just as he did, a field of energy passed through them both, startling him.

The woman remained motionless.

'Woof, woof,' she said.

Chad stood back, aghast.

'Why do keep making that sound? Why do you keep saying those words?' he said.

The woman said nothing and Chad wondered if she understood English. She put the bracelets and cash in a small bag and as Chad started to walk away, he turned to take one curious glance at her. She took off her hat and looked at him.

Chad froze.

She looked older.

A scar ran down the left side of her face and her skin had weathered.

But her eyes…

The millionaire stared in astonished silence.

'Serena,' he eventually whispered.

EPILOGUE – PART THREE

Beth

The sunset that formed the backdrop for the ceremony on Seminyak Beach was breathtaking.

The dusk was awash with patches of dark blue, straddling a thick band of the most incredible shades of purple and pink. The setting sun, a large circle of gold, lay on the horizon, ready to fall out of view and welcome the morning in the Northern Hemisphere. Dozens of tourists were capturing the moment with their mobile phones.

Crystal wore a white, flowing summer dress, with flecks of light blue shimmering against the sunset, and Beth noticed that Chad could not take his eyes off her. With her long hair effortlessly twisted into a casual low chignon, her diamond earrings danced lightly every time she moved. She radiated pure joy. Chad wore mustard coloured chinos, and a white linen shirt, with light brown leather boats. Standing a few feet away from the couple were two young Bangladeshi girls, in matching dresses in the same colour as Crystal's. Beth would eventually meet the two sisters and learn that their names were Aparajita and Pratyusha.

Behind Chad, in line with the sisters, stood two dark skinned young men. Beth wondered who they were. They were dressed in almost the same attire as Chad. Chad glanced at them and grinned, and they grinned back. Logan would later solve this curiosity for his wife, when he was introduced to them. Abhoy and his best friend Dipankar. If Beth didn't know better, the children were the unofficial wedding party for the American couple. She thought it was the sweetest thing she had ever seen.

The small crowd sat in rows. The hotel had set up a beautifully decorated gazebo just a stone's throw from the water. Amelia and Gemma sat together in the front row. Dressed in beautiful evening wear, they didn't seem to care that they were slightly overdressed for the occasion. The movie star looked confident and relaxed, and Beth could not help but eye off Amelia and Gemma several times, with a touch of envy. They seemed so glamorous and so…free.

Logan sat in the seat next to her, eyes focused on the screen of his phone. Beth looked at the beautiful sunset unfolding before her, then back to her husband and sighed. The decision to leave him had been on the cards for some time. Things settled after they got home from their last trip to Bali. For a while, he was a changed man, but as he settled into his new role as Jerry Springhare's replacement, she found that he was exhibiting the same egotistical behaviours as his boss did, and it wasn't long before he'd fallen back into the same habits. The only reason they had returned to Bali, was that Logan had badgered her. Their first night there, she caught Logan getting the phone number of some girl by the bar, while she had been in the bathroom. She'd rounded the corner and stopped mid-step, and in that moment she knew that he was never going to change.

By the next morning, Beth had a plan. The day after the ceremony, she would book Logan in for a three-hour spa package, knowing that he'd have to surrender his phone for at least that long. She pictured the note that she would leave him in the room welcoming him into the next era of his life, as a born-again bachelor and smiled. While Logan's body was being slathered in oil, Beth would have her bag packed and be in the next available Bluebird Taxi on route to the airport. There was always half a dozen of them lined up out the front of the hotel.

She had already checked flights. There was one to LA that she could make just in time.

As Logan read the message, the plane would be on the runway waiting for clearance to take off.

The next day Beth had literally just found her seat, and as a habit, strapped her seatbelt in as soon as she sat down. She was so caught up in the excitement of her sneaky exit plan that she was oblivious to the person who had just walked up the aisle and had stopped right beside her.

'Hi, I'm in the seat right next to you.'

Beth snapped out of her thoughts and looked up at the woman looking down at her, with a smile which hijacked Beth's ability to form words.

Hannah, the woman with the incredible smile, she learned, was French-Canadian. A freelance journalist who lived in Montreal, she had recently moved to Toronto for work. Visiting her brother and wife who had recently moved to Bali, she was heading home after two weeks hard-earned relaxation.

Hannah and Beth talked almost non-stop all the way back to LA, exchanging phone numbers when the plane landed, plus most delightful and tantalizing goodbye kiss Beth had ever experienced.

For the first time in a long time, she felt truly alive. As she waited for a cab out the front of the airport, she wondered how things would turn out for her soon to be ex-husband, and her very much ex-marriage counsellor.

Logan

Six months after Beth walked away from their marriage, Logan decided he needed a fresh start. The company was opening a brand-new dealership and Logan decided to apply for a transfer. He'd never been to Saskatoon, in the Saskatchewan Province, but word had it that it was a town on the up and up.

The reason behind his decision was two-fold.

Firstly, he didn't want to deal with bumping into his ex-wife and her now live-in girlfriend around Toronto. His friends told him the city was big enough for the two of them to live their lives without ever crossing paths.

But Logan was still struggling to let her go. He couldn't bear the thought of even seeing her.

Second, Logan hoped that he could start over.

Saskatoon was just over one thousand seven hundred miles away. Surely that was enough distance for him to completely reinvent himself.

But as the old saying goes, a leopard can't change its spots.

No matter how far he moved.

And neither could Logan Jackman.

Courtney

Courtney was struggling to deal with the shame she felt following the drama in her workplace. Not surprisingly, she'd lost all her clients.

People stared at her in Cafes and Restaurants. She could see the disapproving judgement in their eyes followed by conversations in hushed tones. It was soul-destroying.

Courtney knew the only way to alleviate the problem was to get out of Toronto.

One loyal friend suggested her home town. It was far enough away but was breathtakingly beautiful. Not a bad place to start again.

By the end of that year, Courtney had made the move. She sold her expensive apartment in downtown Toronto and was able to purchase a sprawling house in the town of Saskatoon.

The house was large enough for Courtney to set up a dedicated space for her Marriage Counselling business.

Not surprisingly, under a new name.

And as fate would have it, four weeks after moving to her new town, Courtney bumped into an old client from Toronto at a local bar.

Suffice to say, after a few drinks, their conversation became quite interesting.

Bubbles.

And Lube.

Crystal

Chad and Crystal realised they were both standing in the right place at the scheduled time. But there was something missing. Or rather someone. *The Celebrant.*

'Well at least we are on time.' Crystal said.

Chad shrugged his shoulders, obviously unfussed. Something caught her gaze out of the corner of her eye: a couple walking along the water's edge, heading in their direction.

As they moved closer, Crystal's face broke into a smile of joy.

Henry and Serena walked along the sand, Serena leaning on his arm for support as she navigated the terrain. As they arrived at the Gazebo, Henry helped her find a seat, before strolling up the middle of the aisle and stepping between Chad and Crystal.

'Not sure if I ever mentioned,' he grinned at the couple, 'but I'm also a celebrant.'

Crystal smiled at Chad.

'Perfect!' they laughed.

After the short ceremony came to an end, the guests rose to their feet and congratulated the couple, before mingling as the sun met the horizon and the colours of the incredible sky became an inky grey.

Crystal had been trying to find her husband for a few minutes, before she spotted him out by the water line with Serena. Her heart warmed for them.

Together after all these years, she smiled.

Chad

Chad and Serena walked along the beach together. She hadn't said much since the day he had found her and he hadn't wanted to force her. He knew she would talk to him when she was ready to.

'I was in Patty's Bar when the first bomb went off,' Serena said. 'Later, when I opened my eyes, I couldn't remember a thing. And I mean a thing. My physical injuries were pretty serious, but nothing could replace my total memory loss. My face was a mess from the burns, and it took weeks for the swelling to go down. The scar never went away.'

Chad nodded, but didn't say anything. He let her continue.

'A few of us were taken away by some locals who told us the hospital was so overwhelmed with casualties from the bombings, that we'd be lucky to get treated anytime soon. And they were right. We could have died. They took such good care of us, in the end I felt as if I belonged there, with them.'

Chad listened to Serena, who told him that the people who took care of her lived around Ubud, quite close to the Samsarana Retreat. It had taken her ten years to regain just snippets of her life before the bombings. She had no memory of the bombing itself.

Serena told him that one of the spiritual elders told

her that she would remember her older brother, and that he would one day come to the Samsarana Retreat and pass through the veil. Serena didn't know what that meant, and was hesitant to ask. She asked the elder when this would occur. His response was short. He either didn't know, or didn't want to tell her.

Serena admitted it all sounded quite ridiculous, until she asked Chad what it was like to experience it for himself. She agreed that there would be many that would never believe him. After her near-death experience, and years of recuperation in the hills of Ubud, she was invited by the spiritual elders to become involved in the project, as part of a small group who would help the elders confirm that the chosen were deserving of the 'experience.'

Serena wasn't given any further details, and Chad knew better than to ask.

'Perhaps the 'Samsarana Resort' is the wrong name for that place' Chad chuckled. Maybe they should have called it 'the Karma Retreat.'

'You mean you didn't know?' she laughed. 'Samsarana,' was believed to be the origins of ancient text connected to the belief of Samsara. It's kind of a fundamental part of Indian religions linked to karma theory which as you have kind of already experienced, is the belief that all living beings go through births and rebirths.'

Chad shook his head. It was in front of him the whole time.

They walked for a while in silence.

'Are you coming home?' he asked at last. Serena shook her head. Her current life, she said, was her destiny and she had made peace with that long ago. Aside from the memory loss, her physical injuries were significant. Most had healed, but the bombing had permanently damaged her legs. Although able to move, she found it too painful to walk long distances.

Chad stood with Serena on the water's edge, and brother and sister took in the fading hues of the late afternoon sky.

'How am I supposed to go back to the States knowing that you're here?' said Chad.

Serena gazed up at the faint pinprick of stars that had appeared, as a faint smile appeared on her face.

'You have a wonderful life now, brother,' she turned and faced him, 'and you have done more good in the last twelve months than you could have ever imagined.'

She bowed her head in contemplation, before raising her eyes to his.

'I have to stay here. I have found what I believe to be my life's calling. And I've also found my own version of true happiness. Even more so since someone special found me,' she said.

Serena's eyes were glistening in the faint light of the nearby torches and Chad embraced his sister tightly. After some time, he stood back and laughed, tears in the corner of his eyes.

'Looks like Bali is going to be a regular destination for me now,' he said.

Serena nodded, 'I hope so. We have some catching up to do.'

Chad nodded over to Crystal, indicating that they were heading back to the Gazebo.

'One last question,' Chad said as they reached the entrance.

'Where did he come from?' Chad smiled, nodding over in Henry's direction.

Serena smiled, watching Henry talk to the children. They were laughing at what he was saying. *That guy is a natural with everyone*, Chad thought.

'He survived the bombings too,' she said, waving to Henry, who gave her a wink.

'Jesus. Henry was there too?' Chad looked shocked.

'Yes,' Serena said, 'but he'd managed to get through with only a few cuts and bruises. Henry was taken into the care of the spiritual leaders, at the same time as I was. And it was in the hills of Ubud that he met his wife." Wait, he's married?' Chad raised his eyebrows for a second before the penny dropped.

He couldn't believe it. He started to laugh and Serena laughed with him. He looked over to Henry who bowed his head slightly, smiling warmly at them both. Chad smiled back at his brother-in-law, before Henry cleared his throat, quickly hushing the group.

'On my count everyone,' he said with an authoritative voice, before continuing, 'One, two, three!'

Everyone's eyes turned and fixed on Chad.

'WOOF, 'WOOF!' they said in perfect unison.

Chad shook his head and grinned.

'Serena,' he turned to his sister, 'you cheeky little shit.'

THE END

COMING IN 2023

Detective Megevand is back.

If the detective thought the case of the haunted house in
The Luxury Orphanage was confronting, nothing will
prepare him for this new and mind-blowing case.
London may never be the same again.

KEEP IN TOUCH

Feel free to drop me a line at my website,
grantfinnegan.com, or on Facebook at
facebook.com/grantfinneganaus

Sign up for my newsletter at
grantfinnegan.com/subscribe-to-grants-newsletter/

ACKNOWLEDGMENTS

Erica Wheadon for your thorough editing. Ben "Yoda" Hourigan for all the formatting and back-end work required to bring this novel to the world, plus all the other various things you do for me. The crew at Damonza (Damonza.com) who designed the front and back cover for this novel. I love it, as I have done with all the previous covers. David and Christine Windebank for your never-ending support for my writing. Andrew Parsons for being the perfect sounding board for rational ideas and also the crazy ones.

I'd like to also make a special mention to all those people spread across the globe who I've met through writing and who keep in regular touch and continue to support my work – thank you. It is never, pardon the pun, taken for granted.

As with previous novels in this acknowledgement section, some other points you may find interesting (or for some it may send you to sleep rather quickly). The supervisor in Dhaka at the DOSTME factory, and his hubcap ashtray in particular, come from my real life, at a previous job. I used to deal with a supplier where my contact had an old hubcap on his desk, which he used as an ashtray. The walls of his office were a sickly yellow and the ashtray was always full, yep. Unfortunately, his habit eventually took his life.

Although I had the idea for this novel a few years ago, I couldn't think of how to 'bring it to life,' as far as how these people would end up going from their lives and into the body and life of someone else.

Then it happened.

It may come as no surprise to some that this event occurred on a dark and lonely street in Legian, Bali, 2019.

My wife and I were walking back to our accommodation after having dinner. Although it wasn't terribly late, the street alongside the beach was eerily quiet. Like Stephen King spooky.

We came upon an old lady sitting on the curb, selling string bracelets. My wife purchased two bracelets and gave her some extra money. After we'd walked on further for a few moments I had the light-bulb moment. It was the missing link I needed. This is where the character Serena was born (although she was not originally related to Chad). From there, the idea of the people coming to Bali to a retreat where it would all happen in the meditation room was an easy progression and one I thought that was pretty cool.

If you want to go to a place where the locals are really kind and simply beautiful humans, go to Bali and spend time there. Tourism is their livelihood.

If you do go to this wonderful place, don't look too

hard for the Samsarana Retreat in Ubud (or anywhere else on the island for that matter) – it doesn't exist. Or does it? (*Just kidding.*) I also loved the fact the word 'Samsarana' is directly connected to the ancient belief of karma.

The character Logan Jackman's name is a homage to one of my favourite movie characters and stars: Wolverine/Hugh Jackman. What an Australian legend.

I realized after writing this novel I have a bit of OCD when it comes to the band Queen, and the movie *Highlander*, having mentioned them both (again) in this novel. What can I say other than this: my favourite band and an awesome movie. I may have to mention them both again in the next novel, or every novel, until someone begs me to stop.

Last time I was in London, I could not help but be in awe of what they had done with the Battersea Power Station, so I had to mention it in this novel too. Very cool. I think I am sometimes an architecture nerd.

As I wrap up my long-winded acknowledgements section of *The Karma Retreat*, I will get slightly serious for a moment.

I'm running out of adjectives to describe what your support means to me. I thank the lucky stars above every day for you being the backbone for this thing I love to do (and also being in my life): Sharon, my amazing wife, thank you for all you have done to contribute to this novel. I love you.

ABOUT THE AUTHOR

Grant Finnegan is an avid reader of many genres, from action-thriller to supernatural mysteries and many others.

Some of his favorite authors and strongest writing influences are names familiar to most: Stephen King, the late Clive Cussler, Janet Evanovich, Lee Child, and Douglas Kennedy, to name a few.

Grant resides in the bayside suburbs of Melbourne, Australia. Most days he can be found walking along the beach discussing the world we live in with his wife. If he's not there, he's in the kitchen cooking up a storm, at his desk writing, or staying active through various physical activities.

Grant's other pastimes include snowboarding, windsurfing, and traveling the world. He has a soft spot for London and the United Kingdom, Queenstown on the South Island of New Zealand, and the island of Bali, Indonesia.

Bubbles.
And Lube.